MARKED BY AN ASSASSIN
ETERNAL MATES BOOK 8

FELICITY HEATON

Copyright © 2015 Felicity Heaton

All rights reserved. No part of this publication may be reproduced, stored in a retrieval system, or transmitted, in any form or by any means mechanical, electronic, photocopying, recording or otherwise without the prior written consent of the publisher, nor be otherwise circulated in any form of binding or cover other than that in which it is published and without a similar condition being imposed on the subsequent purchaser.

The right of Felicity Heaton to be identified as the Author of the Work has been asserted by her in accordance with the Copyright, Designs and Patents Act 1988.

First printed October 2015

First Edition

Layout and design by Felicity Heaton

All characters in this publication are purely fictitious and any resemblance to real persons, living or dead, is purely coincidental.

THE ETERNAL MATES SERIES

Book 1: Kissed by a Dark Prince
Book 2: Claimed by a Demon King
Book 3: Tempted by a Rogue Prince
Book 4: Hunted by a Jaguar
Book 5: Craved by an Alpha
Book 6: Bitten by a Hellcat
Book 7: Taken by a Dragon
Book 8: Marked by an Assassin
Book 9: Possessed by a Dark Warrior
Book 10: Awakened by a Demoness
Book 11: Haunted by the King of Death
Book 12: Turned by a Tiger
Book 13: Tamed by a Tiger
Book 14: Treasured by a Tiger
Book 15: Unchained by a Forbidden Love
Book 16: Avenged by an Angel
Book 17: Seduced by a Demon King
Book 18: Scorched by Darkness
Book 19: Inflamed by an Incubus (2022)

CHAPTER 1

His leather boots were loud on the polished black stone floor that reflected warm torchlight up at him, a clunk and a scrape as he trudged along the broad arched corridor of the main entrance of the guild, heading towards the first reception room. He adjusted his grip on the black pack slung over his good shoulder and stifled another grimace as he dragged his injured left leg in line with his right and braved another step. Fiery pain bolted up the limb from a point just above his ankle, shooting through his entire body.

Harbin growled under his breath, grinding his teeth together as he bore the pain and forced himself to keep moving. He could rest soon. He could sleep for days and forget his injuries and the fight that had brought him dancing too close to death.

Again.

But, fuck, it had been a good fight. It had been worth it. The pain. The taste of blood on his tongue. The sharp crack of bones breaking beneath his fists and the metallic tang flooding the air as his claws rendered flesh. A judder went through him, a brief flare of pleasure that wracked his tired and battered body. It had been worth it, for that momentary and elusive sense of calm and belonging, of retribution and release, and the one thing he craved above all others. The one thing that fuelled him, drove him to keep striding forwards, stopping him from looking back, and that he did his best to pretend didn't exist inside him like an eternal bloody flame.

Penance.

Penitence.

Harbin pushed away from those two words. They had no place inside him. They were impossible for him to achieve, the one thing beyond his grasp, forever just out of reach. His sins were too great. Atonement was nothing more than a dream.

Or maybe a nightmare.

One that haunted him despite his best efforts to escape it.

Voices rang along the black walled corridor towards him and he ignored them, not interested in the idle banter of the rest of the guild males as they took a welcomed breather from their profession in the safety of their home. He was only interested in taking a breather himself. A long one. Maybe those days might roll into a week of sleep.

He sighed at the thought.

His broken body probably needed that much rest in order to recuperate swiftly, and gods knew his mind needed that amount of time to pull itself back together. Unlike some members of the guild, he didn't have the advantage of being able to accelerate his healing process. The elves were lucky sons of bitches.

Although, you couldn't pay Harbin enough to make him switch places with Fuery. The male's eyes were verging on black now, only a sliver of violet remaining around his pupils like a dying corona of the light in him. How long before Fuery lost himself to the darkness?

Hartt, the chief and founder of their guild, often wore a look when he was watching Fuery, one that told Harbin that the elf knew their comrade was circling the drain and it was only a matter of time before the darkness consumed the last of him and transformed him into something straight out of a nightmare.

Harbin dragged his bad leg up and managed another step, quickly shifting his right before his fractured tibia gave out under his weight. It was times like these, when he was fresh from what had felt like more of a war than a fight, but had emerged the victor against all odds, that he couldn't help wondering just what colour his eyes would be if the darkness that lived within him could show in them just as it could with the elves.

Would they be darker than midnight?

Was he as close to falling into the abyss as Fuery was?

On days like today, he felt as if he was. Every inch of him hurt now as it sank in that he was home and his mission was done, but it wasn't a physical pain. He could no longer feel the hot burn of his wounds. He could only feel the cold burn of the hollow inside of him, the scraped out chasm where his heart used to be.

Harbin idly rubbed his chest with his free hand, not feeling the pain as his left shoulder blazed, his healing skin rupturing again beneath his tight black t-shirt. Warm wetness bloomed there, soaking into the cloth before trickling down his biceps.

"You look like hell," someone muttered as they passed him, heading towards the doors.

Harbin ignored them and kept moving forwards, determined to reach the sanctuary of his quarters and lock himself away for a week of uninterrupted sleep.

He finally stepped into the first reception room, an equally black affair that had always looked as cold and imposing to him as he supposed it was meant to be. Hartt had done a good job of creating the perfect image for their guild, building a black fortress in the middle of what had once been little more than a wasteland in the free realm of Hell. An entire town had sprung up around the guild, catering to those who were drawn to it, either as a client.

Or an assassin.

Harbin had visited other assassin guilds in Hell and none had the nightmarish quality of their home. He put half of their business down to pure aesthetics. People saw the guild and it matched the image in their head of what an assassin's home should look like—cold, dark and dangerous—and they gave it their business. Hartt had been a clever son of a bitch when he had started the guild all those centuries ago. The elf certainly had a head for business.

One that matched his head for killing.

"Hartt's seeing people about it now."

Harbin glanced across at two young males where they lounged in the horseshoe of black velvet couches near the unlit monstrosity of a marble fireplace to his left. They were both new recruits as far as the other guild members were concerned, having only completed a few easy jobs for little pay.

The blond raked his fingers through his short hair and cracked a wide grin. "I might go for it."

Harbin snorted at that at the same time as the young wolf male reclining near the blond.

"I'd pay double to see you go up against a shifter... and a cat no less. At least that Harbin guy isn't around to hear about it."

That stopped Harbin in his tracks and he frowned across at the two males, studying the brunet wolf to see if he was speaking the truth. A cat shifter?

He had turned towards them before he had even contemplated moving and was at the back of the couch where the wolf shifter lounged before he had even realised he had moved. He stared down at the pup and the male slowly lifted golden eyes to him, his expression falling slack and lips parting as he took him in.

Harbin couldn't blame the kid for looking shocked at the sight of him. He rarely interacted with the other assassins, definitely never with the rookies, and he probably looked as if he had been dragged through the darkest reaches of Hell.

Which he had.

"Cat shifter?" he said and the male nodded dumbly. "Hartt has a job requiring the elimination of a cat shifter?"

The wolf gathered his wits and shot him a cocky smile, one that irritated Harbin because it said what the wolf wouldn't. It asked whether he was hard of hearing or just plain crazy. He hadn't lost his mind. Not yet anyway. He just wanted to be sure that he had heard things right, because in the close to twenty years that he had worked with Hartt as an assassin, there had never been a job involving a cat shifter.

The blond kid got off the other couch and quickly crossed to his friend, hunkering down beside him and bringing his mouth close to the wolf's ear.

"What the hell are you doing? That's Harbin… Hartt said not to mention it around him," the blond whispered so low he practically mouthed the words, but Harbin's sensitive ears picked them up.

Harbin narrowed his silver eyes on both males, his lips compressing into a thin line as he contemplated the only reason why Hartt would want to hand out the job before Harbin could hear about it.

The cat shifter was a snow leopard.

He growled, flashing short fangs at the males, and shoved away from the couches, limping quickly across the black floor towards the door in the corner of the room to his left that would lead him to Hartt's office. He shoved it open, the slam of it hitting the black wall on the other side echoing around the room at his back and the corridor in front of him, and snarled as he picked up his pace. His left leg trembled under the strain but he gritted his teeth and pushed onwards, the fire burning up his blood keeping him going.

Someone had put a contract on a snow leopard shifter, one of his kind, and he wanted the details.

He wanted to know why Hartt wouldn't give the job to him.

Silvery fur rippled over his forearms before he could stop it, a brief flash of his other form brought out by his agitation. He sucked down a breath and controlled it, his skin cooling as the fur disappeared.

It wasn't as if he held any allegiance to his kin anymore. He had burned that bridge twenty years ago and there was no way in Hell of reconstructing the charred remains of it. The thought that Hartt believed he was incapable of dealing with a snow leopard shifter mark was insulting. He could be as methodical and removed from the situation as he always was. The rage that had consumed him in the aftermath of the event that had driven him from his pride had made sure of that. It had killed all of his softer emotions and only a hunger for bloodshed and death remained.

He passed several doors to other offices, his own included, his gaze locked on the black door at the end of the corridor ahead of him. If Hartt was in an interview, the assassin in question was about to get a rude interruption and shown the door in a not too friendly fashion.

Harbin slammed the flat of his left palm into the door and it flew open.

Hartt was instantly on his feet behind the broad ebony desk directly in front of Harbin, an obsidian blade clutched in his left hand and his skin-tight black armour sweeping over his body as his clothes evaporated. His violet eyes pinned on Harbin and his pointed ears flared back as he bared his fangs on a hiss.

The second recognition dawned in his gaze, he huffed and the blade disappeared, leaving his hand free so he could plough his fingers through his blue-black hair, pulling the longer lengths back from his face.

"It isn't wise to barge in uninvited where elves are concerned." Hartt slumped into his tall-backed black leather chair and blew out his breath as he dragged his hand over his face.

Harbin knew that, but he also didn't care. His blood was burning too hot, running too fast. He wanted answers and he was going to get them.

"A snow leopard?" He grabbed the door and slammed it shut behind him.

Hartt slowly lifted his violet gaze to him and raised an eyebrow.

He also didn't care that his chief didn't approve of his aggressive behaviour. If they came to blows, it wouldn't be the first time. Hell, it wouldn't be the hundredth time. He had lost count of how many times he and Hartt had fought over something. Hartt was as hot-headed and hot-blooded as Harbin. Sometimes they just needed to blow off steam and the most trivial thing became something to fight over.

Nothing like a good brawl to release some tension.

"I'm not giving you the job." Hartt held his gaze and then slowly raked his eyes down the length of him. "Have you looked in the mirror? You're in no state to take on another mission right now."

Harbin knew that, and he also didn't give a damn.

A hot twinge rocketed up his left leg from his fractured tibia, as if his body was trying to emphasise Hartt's point. Son of a bitch. He gritted his teeth and schooled his features, trying to hide the pain from Hartt. The elf merely sighed again.

"You need to rest and recuperate. Sit this one out." Hartt straightened in his chair and began shifting papers around on his desk, a clear 'you can leave now' that Harbin chose to ignore.

This conversation wasn't done.

It didn't matter that he had just rolled back into the guild after tracking and eliminating multiple targets in a mission that had been demanding to say the least. There wasn't another assassin in the guild who had the patience or balls to tackle such a job, one where they had to take out an entire party of demon mercenaries without alerting the others to the deaths of their comrades.

He had spent three weeks orchestrating it, slowly intervening to adjust the movements of each member of the group to his favour so he could separate them and deal with them individually but swiftly.

None in the guild had the strength to take down five demons of the Fourth Realm in one battle. Attempting to take them down one by one had been dangerous enough and difficult to say the very least. If they had grouped together, they would have easily overpowered him and sent him back to the guild in a box with their regards.

"You know you need your best tracker on this." Harbin dropped his pack on the floor and eased down into the chair opposite Hartt, making it clear he wasn't going to just leave quietly and forget this mission as his boss wanted.

Hartt's violet eyes remained locked on what had to be a particularly interesting paper based on how much attention he was giving it.

"You don't have an assassin here who can track like I can… and I know snow leopards. I'll get the scent of the mark long before one of the others could find them without using their nose."

"I don't want you on this job. You have your orders, Harbin. Rest and recuperate." Hartt deigned him with a quick glance, his sharp gaze pinning Harbin with a look that warned him to let it go.

It wasn't going to happen.

"I'm taking this job." Harbin settled both hands behind his head, masking his grimace as his left shoulder blazed in protest, and cupped his neck as he stared at Hartt. "And if you try to give it to someone else, I'll hear about it and I'll track them down and kill them."

Hartt's black eyebrows pinched in a frown. Harbin knew he was pushing his luck by threatening other members of the guild, but he needed to be back out there. He *needed* it.

Why?

He hadn't crossed paths with a snow leopard in a long time. He had avoided them as best he could, spending most of his time in Hell and sticking to cities when he had to visit the mortal realm. He even avoided fae towns because they often had a small population of shifters residing in them.

Why was he so eager to place himself on a collision course with one now?

Hartt's questioning look asked him the same thing, and he didn't have an answer for the elf. It was just a need that burned inside him, a quiet voice that urged him to take the mission and discover why a snow leopard, one from a normally peaceful species, was the target.

That same quiet voice supplied that it was because he feared.

Harbin snorted at that.

He feared nothing.

No one.

Not anymore.

It was curiosity driving him. Plain and simple. He was curious to see what a snow leopard had done to make themselves the target of an assassination.

"Fine," Hartt said, jolting Harbin back to the room. Before he could open his mouth to speak or move a muscle to leave the chair, Hartt's expression turned flat and cold, silencing him and freezing him to the spot. "You get the job on the basis that it will be done as a team."

Harbin growled. "I don't need a fucking babysitter."

Hartt flashed fangs at him. "You have one or you don't get the job. Fuery is due to return. You'll track the mark and we'll meet you in five days, tracking you via your implant."

Harbin stared across the black desk at the elf male. He had been on the verge of refusing to work with Fuery, a psychotic son of a bitch on the best of days, when Hartt had mentioned the royal 'we'. Hartt was taking the job with him.

The bastard was coddling him.

He wanted to growl again at that but held it locked inside where his animal form shifted violently in response to his aggravation, wanting to tear into the male opposite him for daring to doubt him.

He drew in a deep breath to settle himself and blew it out slowly, finding a sliver of calm that he could cling to and that allowed him to see the reason for Hartt's coddling in his purple eyes.

He was concerned and reluctant, and Harbin could understand that.

It had nothing to do with his current condition. Hartt knew his history. The elf had crossed paths with him at the darkest point in his life and Harbin owed him more than he had ever been able to put into words to tell him. Hartt had been the one to pick him up, give him a new place to call home, and a new purpose.

He had given him a new life when his old one had crumbled around him.

Harbin had spent two decades as an assassin, but he had also spent two decades devoted to tracking down and killing the people who had attacked his pride.

Archangel.

During those twenty years, he had slowly shifted from spending most of his time hunting Archangel members to spending most of his time carrying out assassination contracts on other targets. Hartt had been the one to guide him on that path, helping him track Archangel at first and then helping him let go of his past as best he could and move forward with his life.

Now, Harbin no longer lived to make Archangel pay. He lived to kill and he didn't care who was a victim of his blades. He only cared about feeding his hunger. He craved the emotionless state that came before a kill. He had embraced the cold and methodical part of himself that allowed him to do his job without feeling a damned thing.

Without remembering the horrors of his past and that it was all his fault.

Harbin closed his eyes and ground his teeth, shunning the memories that tried to surface by focusing on his next mission. Forever looking forwards and never looking back at the ghosts that chased on his heels, the spectres of a time he didn't want to remember. All that mattered was chasing the high of feeling nothing. Feeding the beast inside him. There was always a next mission. Another mark to put to the blade.

He slowly opened his silver eyes and fixed them on Hartt, the cold filling him as he shut down all of his feelings in preparation for the mission ahead.

The snow leopard was a mark and nothing more.

He would track them as Hartt requested, using his knowledge of his kind to his advantage.

And then he would kill them.

CHAPTER 2

Aya's back hit the wall with enough force to shake snow from the roof. It fell in a waterfall behind the male in front of her, a brief shield that gave them a flash of privacy as his mouth descended on hers. She shuddered from the fumbling clash of their lips and his taste as it flooded her senses, drawing all of her focus to him and bringing every nerve to life within her. She moaned into his mouth as he found his stride and his kiss turned passionate and demanding.

Possessive.

Her body heated, fire sweeping through her as she desperately tangled her fingers in his hair and clung to him, riding the storm of the new feelings and sensations as they bombarded her.

He groaned, the sound a sweet hit of pleasure that her body responded to against her will, arching into his. A solid wall of muscle and power greeted her, pressed against her and made her only quake for more.

His hands clamped down on her, one grasping her right hip and the other burrowing beneath her fall of silvery hair to grip the nape of her neck, holding her in place against him. She shuddered again, a fierce hot shiver that he responded to by angling his head and deepening the kiss, leaving no part of her untouched.

The voice of reason surfaced at the back of her mind, telling her that she shouldn't be doing this, but she shoved it aside, ignoring it as she began to kiss him back, attempting to match his fervent passion.

She bravely met his tongue with hers and fought back, earning a husky growl as her reward. His grip on her tightened and she flinched as his fingertips pressed in with bruising force.

Desire instantly turned to panic. The heat of passion became a cold prickling down her spine. Her chest tightened, lungs seizing as she fought his hold but he refused to let her go.

No.

Screams rose around her, the terrified shrieks of young and old alike, and she shoved at the male's chest, battering him and trying to break free of his hold. The man said something and only gripped her harder, his voice no longer matching the deep one that had teased her ears just moments before. She opened her eyes and stared into his cold dark eyes, seeing a different male before her. A mortal male. Fear crashed over her as the scent of blood assaulted her and the white world she loved so dearly was painted red beyond him.

No.

Aya twisted her hands free and shoved hard at his chest, sending him stumbling backwards and slipping on the icy ground. She broke right, skidding herself as her boots fought for purchase. Ahead of her, two more men in black fatigues dragged an unconscious male member of her pride across the snowy square in the centre of her village. A woman with blonde hair spilling from underneath her black skullcap followed them.

Her green eyes swung towards Aya and narrowed.

She said something and pointed towards her.

Aya's heart leaped into her throat as she heard the man behind her getting to his feet and dodged right again, heading between the two small wooden framed buildings, clutching the pale grey stone bases that supported the black beams and plaster walls, keeping the delicate structure off the permanent snow, for support as she did her best to run. The scent of blood grew stronger and hot tears spilled down her cheeks as she ran towards the source of the smell. She had to help them.

A male twisted into her path when she reached the wider street at the end of the alley, his agonised wail cutting short as he fell to the snow. He landed face down in the white powder and she skidded to a halt beside him.

"We have to move." She grabbed his arm and tried to pull him up, determined to help him flee the battle that had erupted in their peaceful home.

Her eyes darted around, heart pounding as she scoured her mountain village for more mortals, fearing they would catch her and the male if they didn't move quickly. They had to escape. Her gaze shot right, towards the edge of the village and a path that would take them up the dangerous rocky peaks in the distance there. If she could gather as many of her kin as she could and guide them there, they could shift and escape the mortals.

"Come on." She tugged at the male.

He didn't respond so she manoeuvred him onto his back so she could grasp him by his arms and drag him to safety.

Her blood chilled and she snatched her hands back.

Dull lifeless eyes stared up at her, his pale skin splashed with crimson that soaked the ground where he had been laying.

Aya stared back at him, her skin prickling and her mind going blank.

She slowly shook her head, refusing to believe what she was seeing. It wasn't possible.

She lifted her chin and looked in the opposite direction to the mountain path, her gaze sweeping over the madness unfolding there, struggling to make sense of what was happening. Black shadows moved everywhere, attacking her kin.

Killing her kin.

Aya's lips flattened and then peeled back off her short fangs, all thoughts of running leaving her as she took in the pandemonium that had erupted in her peaceful home. She growled and shoved off, leaping over the dead male and heading for the second square ahead of her, where several females were attempting to fend off another group of shadowy figures. She tore at her clothes, stripping off the layers as she sprinted hard. One of the females went down as she attempted to protect a young boy. Aya snarled and her claws grew at the same time as her fangs.

She roared as she reached the end of the alley between the small houses and leaped high into the air. Pain shot through her bones as they transformed and silvery thick fur swept over her body. She came free of her clothes at the apex of her jump and growled through her teeth as she began to descend, heading straight for two males.

The click and slide of metal on metal stole her focus and she snapped her head up, her eyes settling on the third man in the clearing.

He raised his rifle and took aim.

Fired.

Aya shot up in bed, her rapid breathing and the frantic beat of her heart the only sound in the dark room. Sweat trickled down her spine and between her bare breasts as she fought for air, her wide eyes locked across the room on the wooden chest of drawers and wardrobe that lined the pale blue wall. A cool breeze caressed her left side, washing in from the small gap at the bottom of the sash window there, carrying the calming scent of the night. She breathed deep of it, struggling to settle her pounding pulse and her emotions. Her fingers tightened in the cream covers pooled in her lap, twisting them into her grip as everything crashed over her, a thousand memories she would rather not possess.

Ones she had buried deep and finally forgotten as she moved on with her life.

Until that male had walked into the club last night.

The return of her nightmares was his fault.

She hadn't seen another snow leopard in over a decade and she had never wanted to see one again.

She had been happy living without the reminder of what she was, because now it was only a cold and dark reminder of what had happened to her. It took her back to that day when her life had been turned into a waking nightmare, everyone she had loved stripped from her as she had fought to save them all.

Aya bent forwards and ploughed her fingers through her damp black hair, pulling the jaw-length strands back. She clutched the sides of her head and tried to focus on her breathing as memories surged to the surface again. Her throat closed and her heart thundered against her ribs, a sickening rhythm that echoed in her ears together with distant screams and pleas for mercy.

She shook her head in an attempt to dislodge those memories and growled.

She wanted to forget again.

She needed to immerse herself in the tangled fae and mortal world, losing herself in it and surrounding herself with people, or she would only sink deeper into her memories, her instincts forcing her to seek out the familiar faces of her past so she would no longer feel alone. She needed to escape that past, and that meant returning to the club. It had become her sanctuary over the past few years, a place she returned to nightly to talk with the people she knew there, fulfilling the deep need to be part of a group that had been formed in her decades at the bustling pride village where she had grown up. Now, she sought crowds whenever she woke, escaping the emptiness of her apartment, hurling herself into the fray and dancing or drinking the night away.

It was a risk, because she knew the male might be there too.

A flash of silver shot across the darkness of her closed eyes. It drifted back and split, forming into two piercing orbs and a messy tuft atop them. The male. She had felt the intensity of his gaze the moment he had entered. It had sent an electric shiver through her, a bolt of awareness that had shattered everything around her, leaving only him behind. She shivered again beneath the covers, her heart beating harder for a different reason as heat swept through her as it had last night when his gaze had drifted over her, taking her in from head to toe.

He shimmered into being in her mind and she snapped her eyes open, breaking the illusion.

Aya shoved the covers off her bare legs, shifted them over the right edge of the double mattress and rose from the bed. She stretched, moaning as she arched her back. There was nothing quite as enjoyable as a good stretch when she woke up.

She lowered her arms and checked the clock on her bedside table. The numbers cast a green hue across her small bedroom, providing the only light. It was already growing late. She had managed to sleep through the day before her nightmare had begun.

Hopefully tomorrow she could do the same again without the nightmare.

She padded across the narrow span of wooden floor to the bathroom opposite her and flicked on the light, flinching as the white tiles reflected the brightness and seemingly magnified it, hurting her sensitive eyes.

Aya gave them a moment to adjust before opening them again. Her reflection in the mirror above the grey vanity greeted her. Or possibly mocked. She looked awful. Her silver-gold eyes were bloodshot, last night's make-up smeared like black ash all around them, emphasising how tired they looked. She tugged her fingers through her messy black hair, trying to smooth the wild short strands that stuck out in all directions at jaw level. Silver threaded her hair, turning her stomach. She would need to dye it again soon. She hadn't been able to face herself with her natural hair colour since starting her new life. It was a reminder of her past, another thorn that only tore at her and left her bleeding inside.

She had loved her silver hair once, back when life had been carefree and simple, and she had lived at the pride village.

Back when she'd had a pride.

She turned her cheek to the gaunt female in the mirror and headed towards the double shower cubicle that took up the entire right side of the room. A shower would help clear her head and set her back on track.

Aya slid the door open and stepped into the cubicle. The water was cold as she lifted the lever to start the flow, but soon warmed to her preferred temperature. She turned beneath the spray, closed her eyes and sighed as the hot water pounded down on her back. The effect was immediate, easing her muscles and washing away her bad memories. She focused on showering, using the routine to empty her mind. Once she had rinsed the conditioner out of her hair, she switched off the water, slid the door open again and grabbed a towel from the rack.

Her mind drifted as she dried off, thoughts of who would be at the club tonight keeping her occupied. She shut out any about the male and scrubbed the towel across her hair. Satisfied that she wouldn't leave a trail of water across the pale floor tiles, she stepped out of the shower and moved to the next step of her routine.

When her hair was tamed, the fine black strands styled to lay flat on top but flick outwards and upwards at the ends in a cute way, she applied her standard black make-up around her eyes, a dash of lip-gloss, and a quick spray of perfume.

Aya padded out into the bedroom, grabbed her white strapless bra from the floor where she had tossed it last night before falling into bed, and put it on. She followed it with a matching pair of knickers from her chest of drawers at the foot of the bed and then sidestepped to her wardrobe and pulled the doors open.

Jeans.

She grabbed a pair of black ones from the pile at the bottom of the wardrobe and tugged them on. They were tighter than she remembered. She growled as she wriggled into them, muttering beneath her breath about cutting back on the sweet treats whenever she visited a coffee shop or hit the grocery store.

She had always been average, not a woman blessed with a stick-thin figure and never one to want to look that way either, but she was holding a little more winter padding than normal. Back at the pride, she had gotten away with indulging in her love of food, needing the fuel to keep her warm. Old habits died the hardest. She never had managed to shake her constant craving for food, even in the warmer weather of London.

Her silvery gaze roamed over the hangers filled with a range of camisoles, t-shirts and long-sleeved tops. The weather was cooler now, but she found herself picking a silver halter-top with a plunging neckline, one she hadn't worn in months.

It had nothing to do with the male.

She just wanted to feel good about herself tonight and dressing to impress would certainly boost her mood. She wasn't planning to catch his eye if he was there again tonight, definitely wasn't interested in sending any signals to him. She planned to avoid him and catch the eye of another male.

Any other male.

Hell, maybe she would flirt with a few of them.

The attention from them would definitely make her feel fabulous.

She might even do more than flirt.

It had been a long time since she had been with a male, and she needed a little physical contact, a little craziness to blow off some steam. It might even change her outlook for the better, making her forget her worries and see some good in the world again.

Aya pulled the silver top on, tugging the triangular cups beneath her breasts and smoothing the material over her stomach. It barely reached the belt of her jeans and it would flash her belly if she raised her arms above her head, but she didn't care.

Tonight was about feeling good and forgetting, not about worrying what others made of her figure. Their opinion didn't matter. She was happy as she was and she refused to change herself to suit anyone's tastes.

This was her life and she was going to live it.

She blew out her breath, closed the wardrobe doors and gave herself a quick once over in the mirror on the left door. She brushed her fingers through her hair, fixed a smile on her face to shove her nerves away, and turned away from her reflection. She found her favourite black ankle boots with their short square heels perfect for adding a little height but not making her ache as she danced, or compromising her balance, and put them on.

There. Ready to face the world.

Aya walked into the small living room adjoining her bedroom and grabbed her keys and small purse off the sideboard to her left near the main door. She resisted the temptation to check her reflection again in the oval mirror above the sideboard, heading straight to the door instead. She made fast work of the locks, opened it and stepped out into the brightly-lit cream corridor. The locks clicked back into place as she closed the door and she pocketed her keys and hurried along the corridor towards the stairs that would take her down to the main entrance hall several floor below. Her heels clicked on the steps, punctuating the silence, and the pace of them picked up as she crossed the entrance hall.

The night air was even cooler now as she pushed the glass double doors open and she breathed deep of it. The scents hit her hard, a myriad of smells that had her instincts sharpening as they awakened a desire to identify each one and map her neighbourhood. The nearby restaurants provided the strongest range of smells, tempting her into taking a detour. She resisted the call of food and hailed a taxi instead. The black cab slowed and pulled over, and she made her way between two parked cars to reach it.

The journey to the club passed in silence, her gaze fixed on the outside world as it whizzed by in a blur of coloured lights and black shadows, her animal side shifting restlessly beneath her skin. She wanted to be out in the darkness, prowling the parks in her snow leopard form and marking everything with her scent so all shifters in the area would know this was her patch. How long had it been since she had shifted?

Too long.

Years at best.

She put it off for as long as she could, but the need to shift steadily built inside her, growing stronger with each day that passed, until it grew impossible to ignore, even when she wanted to avoid the reminder of what she was.

The male had brought the need from a growl to a deafening roar in her blood.

Now, she itched with a hunger to let her snow leopard side out, her fingers twisting the silver material of her halter-top into her palms as she fought that urge. Maybe when she got back tomorrow morning, she would look into booking a short break up north. Over the years she had been away from the mountains of her homeland, the rugged valleys of Scotland had become her favourite place to get lost in the wilderness and spend days roaming in her animal form.

The cab ground to a halt, jerking her away from a fantasy about drifting through the heather with only nature for company and basking on the rocks. The bright neon sign of Switch blazed off to her right, the bouncer outside it nodding as he noticed her. He stepped away from the open doors of the back-street nightclub and she smiled as he pulled the cab door open for her.

Aya slipped the driver his money, plus a generous tip, and stepped out of the car.

"Rocky," she said as the big shaven-headed bouncer grinned down at her before giving the car door a gentle push.

It slammed shut with enough force to rock the cab.

Bear shifters didn't know their own strength, and Rocky was no exception. Aya had taken to calling him Rocky a few years ago when she had started frequenting the club and they had spent a quiet night talking. He came from a small pride of bear shifters in Canada, near the mountains she had named him for. His circumstances were similar to hers, so she understood why he had wanted to keep his name to himself, using the boring alias of Tom instead.

He had taken to the name she had given him and now everyone called him Rocky.

Aya glanced towards the dark entrance of the club, her heart beating a little quicker and her palms sweating as she struggled to keep her breathing even and convince herself to go inside.

Rocky clapped a meaty hand down on her bare shoulder. "He ain't here."

Relief swept through her, and she tried to hide it from Rocky, but realised she had failed when his grin stretched wider, tugging at a vicious scar that ran across his lips on the right side and down to his square jaw. He was as rugged as the mountains he hailed from too, but handsome nonetheless, especially when he wasn't playing his role of bouncer, scowling at customers and keeping watch over the club he called home.

His rich brown eyes sparkled with mischief.

Aya held her hand up to silence him before he could talk about the male shifter she wanted to avoid.

"Here's hoping he buggers off to Underworld," she muttered and amusement joined the mischief in Rocky's eyes.

They had bonded over a dislike of that nightclub too, and it wasn't only because it was a competitor for Switch, the club she favoured and he worked for. It was because that club employed two males from a species both of them wanted to keep their distance from—a bear and a snow leopard shifter.

Distant sirens made her lift her head and peer along the dark street in their direction. It wasn't the safest neighbourhood in London, but that didn't bother her. Life had taught her how to handle herself, how to fight and survive, and she wasn't afraid to deal with anyone who got too familiar with her when she didn't want their attention.

She wasn't afraid to kill someone.

The male snow leopard included.

He was stronger than her, but that wouldn't stop her from making him familiar with her claws if he tried anything.

Rocky trudged across the narrow strip of pavement to the door of the club and resumed his position beside it, pressing his back against the red brick wall and folding his arms across his broad chest. His muscles bulged beneath his tight black t-shirt and all humour fled from his face, the hardened expression he wore turning him into a daunting male with a dangerous edge.

Anyone roaming the street looking for a fight would think twice before bothering him or trying to gain entrance to the club.

Aya hoped that went for the male snow leopard too.

She flicked a glance at Rocky, toyed with the idea of asking him to stop the male from entering the club if he did show up, and then walked into the dark entrance without saying a word. This was her turf and she wasn't going to let anyone see her scared when she was on it.

If the male showed up, she would deal with him.

She wanted him to walk right through the doors at her back.

She wanted him to dare to set foot in her territory again.

Because she wasn't the sort of female who would let a male walk all over her.

Not anymore.

CHAPTER 3

Aya jerked her chin up, brushed her short black hair back from her face, and strolled into the club with just enough sway in her hips to have a few of the hungrier males in the expansive room looking her way. Colourful lights flashed in time with the pounding tempo of the rock music, a visible beat that spoke to her animal side and had her prowling through the half-filled club, heading towards the bar at the far end. The hazy glass panel at the front of it changed colours, fading through green, yellow, red and blue. Purple lights above the bar washed over the white metal top and the people lining it, telling her that Amanda was in charge tonight. The colour changed depending on who was the boss behind the bar. Her luck was in. Amanda made the best cocktails. Things were already looking up.

She skirted the edge of the dance floor, her eyes raking over every male on it, assessing them in turn, seeking out her first partner. Some of them glanced her way, taking their eyes off their females and giving her their attention instead. She smiled at them all, a range of shifters and fae, and some mortals mixed in. Any one of them would do.

She turned back towards the bar and a group of mortal males broke apart to allow her passage, creating a clear run between her and the bar.

A male there caught her eye.

A vampire.

It wasn't often she saw their kind around, but he was unmistakable as he lounged casually on a stool, his right arm propped up on the bar behind him. His deep crimson gaze locked on her, sending a thrill coursing through her blood, and she added a little extra sway to her hips and slowed her pace, capturing and holding his focus on her.

He was perfect.

It was little wonder many of the single females in the club were watching him closely.

With neatly styled dark hair, shorn close around the sides but left wild on top, and wicked full lips set in a classically handsome face, with a strong jaw, straight nose and sculpted cheekbones, he was the image of perfection.

The embodiment of masculinity.

The black shirt he wore was slightly open at the collar, revealing defined muscles that hinted at a body to match the perfection of his face.

His sensual lips tilted in a ghost of a smile.

He thought he had found a victim, a walking blood bag who would feed him, and she wasn't about to tell him how wrong he was about that. Biting was off the agenda. She never allowed fangs near her flesh. The way his gaze dipped, roaming down the line of her throat, and his lips curved further told her he had noticed that, and the way his eyes brightened, burning faintly in the low light, warned he liked it.

She was playing with fire, but she didn't care. Not tonight.

Tonight was about forgetting, and he was the perfect male to erase the past from her mind.

Aya halted at the bar and flagged the only female member of staff. Amanda. The brunette smiled, nodded and went to work on her drink, mixing her the same potent cocktail she always requested.

The vampire leaned closer, inhaled slowly and growled low in his throat. A shiver bolted through Aya, a flash fire following in its wake, and she slowly slid her gaze towards him. His eyes met and locked with hers, and her breathing came quicker. Vampires were alluring, but this male was something else.

Something more.

Crimson eyes held hers and the sensation of danger she had felt when approaching him increased, but rather than triggering a need to escape his presence, it drew her to him instead. Tonight, she was in the mood for danger and seduction, and this male would give that to her.

"It's on me," the male said as the bartender dropped her drink off.

Amanda nodded and moved away to the till.

The vampire pressed two fingers against the base of the martini glass and pushed it across the white bar top to Aya, his charming smile holding.

"You look like you need this," he murmured and her sensitive hearing picked up his words over the loud thumping music.

Aya held his gaze as she took the drink, swallowed it down in one go and set the glass back down on the bar.

"I need more than this," she whispered and inched closer to him, so her hip brushed his thigh.

His gaze lowered to where they touched, narrowed and then darted back up to hers. He growled, flashing short fangs, grabbed her right wrist and spun her towards him. Hunger filled his eyes, need that she felt echoing inside her. She had been alone too long too. She needed to lose herself in someone, had to purge the bad memories and fill her head with something to keep them at bay.

That something was him.

The male moved in a blur and she gasped when she was suddenly on the busy dance floor, his hands on her hips and his body swaying against hers in an intoxicating rhythm. It took her a moment to catch up, but the second she did, she threw her arms around his neck and ground against him, rubbing up his thigh as he pressed it between her legs.

Gods, she needed this.

Her heart pounded, the frantic beat drowning out the music as she lost herself in the sway of his body against hers and the rich depths of his eyes. Her instincts whispered again, warning she was playing with fire, and this time she might get burned.

Screw it.

She had already been burned.

No one could burn her worse than *he* had.

Not even a vampire.

She threw herself into dancing with him, working up a sweat and burning off some energy as they writhed against each other to the beat of the music. She lost track of time as the songs faded from one to another and then another. He turned with her and she frowned briefly as a scar around his neck caught the sudden flash of white light that cascaded over him. It was thin, would be unnoticeable at a distance, but this close to him she could see it and she couldn't help wondering how he had come to have it.

And how he had survived the wound.

The silvery line stretched from below his left ear, around the front of his throat, over his Adam's apple where it was thicker and more pronounced, to below his right ear.

It looked as if someone had attempted to cut his head clean off and should have succeeded, but somehow he had escaped with his life.

She wanted to know how, but the way he was staring down at her when she finally drew her gaze away from the scar warned her to hold her tongue.

A couple of males bumped against them on the busy dance floor and the vampire turned crimson eyes on them and curled his lip, flashing a hint of fang that had them backing into the crowd.

He drew her closer, his scent surrounding her and stealing her focus away from the world, narrowing it down to him. She let it overwhelm her, let her guard down and gave herself over to the moment.

"What's your name?" she hollered over the music.

The man smiled, charming to the last, his eyes glittering dangerously with it. "Night."

"Aya," she said without missing a beat, sensing that he was waiting for her to comment on his name. If it was his real one, his parents had a bad sense of humour, but she couldn't deny that it suited him.

He was as seductive, beautiful and dangerous as the night.

A shiver prickled down her spine, setting her on edge and shattering the hold the vampire had over her.

Her silver-gold gaze drifted beyond him, towards the entrance, and her breath lodged in her throat.

The snow leopard male.

Aya fixed her eyes back on Night, trying to give him all of her attention again as they moved with each other, their bodies locked tight together. Her focus slipped, her eyes wanting to roam back to the other male, drawn to him even when she didn't want them to be.

She watched him in the corner of her vision as she looked up at the vampire.

The silver-haired male limped as he walked, favouring his right leg, but it didn't detract from the lethal edge to his gait as he prowled into the club. He was dangerous. Every instinct she possessed fired that warning across her mind, making it impossible to ignore.

He was more dangerous than the vampire grinding against her, pulling her closer to him, dipping his head to course his lips over her exposed shoulder.

The snow leopard's silver eyes narrowed and she shut hers, blocking him out as she twined her fingers in Night's dark hair.

Gods.

Her breath left her in a rush as she felt the snow leopard's eyes fix on her, the intensity of his gaze burning through her, drawing her into opening hers to look at him again. She resisted, tried to focus on the male dancing with her, using all of her will to pretend she couldn't feel the snow leopard's gaze drifting down her body as he passed. It lingered on her hips, on the point where the vampire clutched her, his fingers possessively digging into her black jeans as he lifted his head from her shoulder and growled.

A threat if ever she had heard one.

She held her breath, part of her expecting the snow leopard to respond.

He moved on, silent and stealthy, the epitome of a predator. He wouldn't rise to the threat of a lesser male. He would bide his time, study his opponent, and only make his move once he had discovered a weakness he could exploit and only if he decided he wanted her.

It had been so long since she had been around her own kind that she had forgotten how mature males behaved.

The air left her lungs in a whoosh again, her heart thundering against her breast as the vampire spun her in his arms and pulled her back against his front, grinding against her bottom and leaving her face-to-face with the snow leopard male.

Double gods.

It hit her hard as she stared across the open expanse of room between her and him where he casually took a seat at the bar directly in front of her.

She had chosen the vampire because he was the opposite of this male.

A snow leopard with an unruly shock of silver hair and pure silver eyes set in a ruggedly handsome face that sported numerous pale scars that immediately had her wondering what sort of life he had led.

What sort of Hell had he survived?

It couldn't be any worse than what she had been through.

He stared straight at her, stealing all of her focus away from the vampire, and this time she couldn't convince herself to look away. The coldness in his eyes entranced her. A snowy abyss that reminded her of her pride's village high in the mountains, far away from the mortal world. Stark. Dangerous. Liable to kill you if you set a foot wrong.

Whatever had happened to this male, it had turned him feral, had made him into a killer rather than a male from a species known for their calmness and desire to avoid conflict.

He looked as if he courted danger, sought out conflict, and enjoyed bathing his hands in blood.

His black t-shirt stretched over a firm body, his arms sporting more scars than she could count, and tight black jeans hugged his long lean legs. The fingers of his right hand flexed constantly, a restless movement she had seen many males do when they were on edge. Did he want to fight?

He was injured, but that didn't make him weak. He looked like the sort of male that would only be more dangerous when wounded.

His eyes remained icy as he shifted in his seat and she would have missed the twist of his lips that betrayed him if she hadn't been studying him so closely.

More than his leg was injured.

The way he held his left arm in his lap told her that it was wounded too. Her eyes dropped to his feet and narrowed as she spotted the black thick material encasing his left foot, at odds with the leather army boot he wore on his right. A cast. Had he broken his leg?

The vampire skimmed his hands forwards, brushing the apex of her thighs and providing a startling reminder that she wasn't alone. She gasped and tried to evade his wandering hands, but only ended up pressing harder against his front, rubbing his groin with her backside. He groaned against her shoulder and bit lightly with blunt teeth.

The snow leopard's eyes burned brighter, a flare of silver shining around his narrowing pupils, as if the sight of the vampire touching her had infuriated him.

Aya didn't belong to him.

She could do as she damn well pleased.

She turned in Night's arms, giving him the whole of her attention again as she resumed dancing. He pulled her closer, grinning at her as she rubbed against him.

She was pushing her luck.

It wasn't the vampire she feared either.

Her primal instincts warned that the snow leopard male was losing his temper and she was heading into dangerous territory.

Aya didn't want to get the vampire killed and she refused to drag innocents into what would amount to a bloodbath if the snow leopard lost his temper in the busy club. She glanced at the huge digital clock mounted on the black wall above the corridor to the exit. It was time she made her excuses and left.

"I need a drink," she hollered above the music as it began to fade and broke free of Night's clutches. "I'll be right back."

She heard a faint rumble of disapproval but he didn't try to stop her as she made a beeline for the bar, heading towards the end furthest from the snow leopard male. She could slip out the back through the door in the corner there, using her normal escape route she took whenever things got a little too hot and heavy for her liking.

The snow leopard tracked her as she made her way through the crowd, his gaze never leaving her.

It was going to be difficult to get away without him noticing.

What if he came after her?

Her pulse accelerated, cold sweat prickling down her spine at the thought of him catching her alone outside. Maybe it was better she slipped out the main exit. Rocky would take care of her, ensuring the male kept his distance. A snow leopard was no match for a bear shifter.

Aya turned her back to the bar, her eyes swinging past the male towards the main exit at the opposite end of the club.

She pushed away from the bar.

Panicked shouts filled the air, a rush of people coming at her confusing her senses as they sharpened and her instincts screamed at her to take the back exit and run. Several males bumped her as they raced in that direction and her eyes widened as she caught sight of the other end of the club.

People dressed in black combat gear surged into the busy room, driving the patrons in a wave towards her.

"Police," someone shouted.

"Raid," another yelled as they shoved their way through the throng, heading towards her in an attempt to flee.

Aya shook her head as she stared at the large group of males splitting apart and grabbing any shifter or fae they came across.

They weren't the police.

They were Archangel hunters.

CHAPTER 4

The mark was a female.

Harbin hadn't believed his eyes when he had set them on her in the grotty club in the suburbs of London. He had tracked her without ever realising what she was. None of his fae contacts had mentioned the gender of the snow leopard he had been asking questions about, but then he hadn't bothered to ask them about the sex of his mark either.

He had presumed it would be a male.

Sure, he had tracked and assassinated female marks in the past, but never a shifter. Females of the cat shifter species generally stayed within the boundaries of their pride homes, or at least within the limit of the law, keeping their heads down and tails out of trouble.

What had she done to make someone take out a contract on her?

He had been curious to know the answer to that question when he had discovered a snow leopard had a price on their head, but now he burned with a need to know. It played on his mind, constantly bouncing around in his skull and keeping him distracted. What could she have done?

Normally his marks were mercenaries, murderers or worse, but she didn't seem to fit any of those roles. Nothing about her said she was dangerous, and nothing he had gleaned from his contacts had pointed towards her being a killer or worthy of the bounty someone had placed on her.

Harbin stared across the room at the female in question, watching the way the vampire at her back pawed at her as they danced. The sight of the vile bastard's hands all over her caused his animal side to prowl just beneath his skin, restless with a need to separate them and then separate the vampire's head from his body. He despised their kind. Leeches, all of them.

He sighed as he caught his train of thought and derailed it.

Maybe Hartt and Fuery had rubbed off on him in the years they had been together.

Elves hated vampires with a passion, a dislike that ran both ways, born of the fact that vampires were distantly related to the elves. They were a wretched shadow of the elves, born from the corrupted ones left behind in this mortal realm millennia ago. The vampires had none of their forefathers' key abilities though, and the elves believed that was the reason they despised them so much. Harbin could understand that. He would be pissed if he discovered his kind were an offshoot from one that could teleport, use telekinesis, didn't go crispy in sunlight and didn't have to drink blood to survive.

The vampire slid his hands lower, startling the female, and a growl rumbled up Harbin's throat, rising from the pit of his belly as it churned with a need to sink his claws into the male.

Her wide eyes held Harbin immobile though, pinned to his stool, his mind filled with a constant cycle of questions.

Some of which bothered him, because for the first time in a long time, he was wondering what the hell he was doing with his life.

That niggling voice had started up the second he had set eyes on the female last night. A barrage of images had hit him, a horrifying replay of entering his pride village to find his mother and sister laying in a pool of blood on the crisp white snow. A rapid succession of memories had followed it, a rush of dark moments, all fragmented and blended together into a mind-numbing stream of pain, terror and bloodshed.

A twisted version of the events that had happened as he had tracked down the bastards who had attacked his pride.

Archangel.

He ground his teeth, his emerging fangs cutting into his gums, flooding his mouth with the bitter taste of blood.

It had all been his fault.

The deaths of his beloved mother and sister.

The deaths of so many of his kin.

Those deaths weighed his soul down and nothing he did lightened the load he carried.

It was his to bear, and he would carry the face of every victim with him until his dying day. He would recount them all whenever he crushed another Archangel member under his boot, giving them the same bloody end they had bestowed upon his beautiful kin.

Harbin closed his eyes and swallowed hard, fighting the pain that rose within him, pouring like acid into the hollow in his chest.

He deserved the pain. He deserved the exile his father, the alpha of the pride, had given him as his sentence. He deserved to suffer until Archangel no longer existed.

He deserved it because he had been the one to lead Archangel to his pride.

He could kill every member of Archangel, all across the world, but it wouldn't make a difference and he knew it. It wouldn't bring his family back, or the other snow leopards who had lost their lives because of him.

Harbin opened his eyes and fixed them on the female, catching her as she broke free of the vampire and started across the busy room.

What was he doing?

Had it really come down to this—tracking and killing one of a breed he had spent the past two decades trying to avenge in his own way?

His stomach turned, sickness brewing there as his mind supplied that he was no better than Archangel if he killed her.

He had hated seeing his kin attacked and murdered, had hunted and killed all but one of the Archangel members responsible to stop them from getting their hands on any more of his species. Now he was going to hunt one and kill it?

He was going to kill her?

Harbin stared at her, cold to the bone and numbed as the world around him dropped away. How far had he fallen? When had he lost sight of his true mission—the task of avenging his people?

That mission wasn't done.

He had never found the woman who had slept with him, using him for information before drugging him and ordering the attack on his pride.

A fragment of the man he had once been broke through the ice in his chest, whispering to let the snow leopard go and resume his hunt for the Archangel woman.

Whatever this female had done, it would be nothing compared with the sins of the Archangel huntress. That woman deserved death for the acts she had committed.

Images flashed across his eyes, a disjointed layer over the present, distorting and twisting the club into a forbidding yet breathtaking white landscape with the snow leopard female at the centre of it, her short black hair blowing in the frigid wind that scoured the treacherous barren terrain. She turned her head towards him and bright sunlight bathed her face, intensifying the gold in her eyes until they glittered like precious metal. Her soft pink lips parted, flashing a hint of straight white teeth, as she tipped her chin up and stared straight into his eyes.

For a heartbeat, a mere split-second of time that felt like a fantasy or foolishness as it fled, she was more breathtaking than the icy mountainous world around her.

She belonged in that world, a queen of all she surveyed, a beautiful and beguiling creature with whom few could contend.

A majestic female.

The mountains beyond her shook, blurring as they vibrated and rocked the earth, sending snow plummeting down their cragged faces. The air hummed around him. The bright sun faded.

The female dipped her head, raising her hands at the same time, and his stomach revolted when he saw the blood coating them.

He squeezed his eyes shut and shoved the heels of his hands against them for good measure, trying to shut out the horror he knew would come next. His left shoulder burned, the healing wound there threatening to reopen.

Again.

He breathed deep as he whirled into her place, staring down at his bloodstained hands. Images flooded his mind, replaying the night before, when he had watched the female for hours in the club before succumbing to a dark hunger that had ruled him, driving him into obeying and feeding it.

A hunger that was rising within him again now, demanding he head out just as he had last night and go on the hunt, using all of his skills to track down the hunters from Archangel that infested London.

It was a need born of the memories that surged within him whenever he looked at the female snow leopard. He had shut out everything that had come before the long dark months when he had hunted Archangel in the aftermath of the attack on his pride, sealed it away inside him and pushed it down deep. All of his softer emotions. Every shred of feeling he had ever possessed. He had thought all of it dead and gone, but he could feel it reawakening inside him.

He could feel it pushing at the walls he had constructed, and if they broke, it would be as if a dam had burst.

He wouldn't be able to handle the flood.

It would destroy him.

He needed to leave again, had to get away from the female and go out as he had last night, pursuing the cold calm that came in the moment before the kill. He craved it even more now, twitched with the need to bathe his hands in Archangel blood, satisfying his deepest, darkest hungers.

Three had died last night, and he could barely remember their faces.

Only had a series of brief images to remind him of what he had done, the rest of it buried deep within his subconscious, burned from his mind.

Screams erupted in the club and he sensed the swarm of signatures rushing towards him, crowding him and pushing at his control. He snarled through his short fangs, trying to warn them away, needing the space they were consuming in their mad panic.

Harbin flicked his eyes open and they settled on a male clad in black combat gear similar to what he wore when he was carrying out the final phase of a mission.

Only this male was no fae or demon.

He was mortal.

Archangel.

Emotions bombarded Harbin on seeing the two dozen strong mortal males surging through the room, firing on the fae in it with tranquiliser guns and crossbows, or lashing out with their black batons.

He pushed from his stool, his left leg aching under the sudden weight, and growled as he shoved the people attempting to flee away from him, clearing a space around him.

His claws lengthened at the same time as his fangs.

A young male demon went down hard at the edge of the dance floor, a dart sticking out of his left shoulder.

Harbin's blood burned, his heart labouring as he struggled to get enough air into his lungs. He shook with a need to unleash his snow leopard side and tear through the room, the urge stronger than it had ever been, fuelled by the constant awareness of the weaker female in the club with him.

His gaze sought her, locating her as she broke free of the throng of people to his left and made a run for it. She was agile and swift as she darted through the people, and he silently willed her to make it unseen to the main exit where a large male he recognised as a fellow shifter was stumbling into the club, shaking his head as he tried to rid it of the lingering effect of whatever dart the hunters had used on him.

They should have plugged him with more than one.

The big bear roared as he tore off his t-shirt and Harbin cursed him as all the hunters swung towards him.

Two males spotted the female.

Harbin pushed off, unable to ignore the pressing need to protect her.

One of the hunters hit her with a dart in her right thigh. She stumbled, a high shriek leaving her lips, but kept running, limping towards the bear as he started to shift. The second hunter pursued her.

Harbin growled and hobbled faster, cursing himself now. He needed to shift, his cat form being his stronger one in this situation, but he couldn't when his tibia was still healing. The shift would break the weakened bone, leaving him in a worse condition than he was now and making it impossible for him to fight.

The second male caught the female as she slowed, the drugs taking effect, and Harbin flinched as the hunter dealt a blow across the back of her head with his baton. She crumpled, hitting the floor in a tangled heap.

Pain pierced Harbin's right arm and hip, but it felt like little more than a brief sting as memories surged in response to seeing the female go down.

They rolled through him, ripping an agonised howl from his throat as he stumbled forwards, blinded by the pain and the fury, filled with a hunger to destroy every Archangel hunter he could see.

This was his fault.

He had hunted down Archangel members, all of them too young to have had anything to do with the attack on his pride. He had needed the kill though. He had needed the serenity of shutting down his feelings and focusing on a mission. He hadn't thought it would trigger an attack on the fae community, but it couldn't be coincidence that Archangel had targeted the very club where he had been seen two nights in a row.

Someone had witnessed the attack and survived to tell the tale.

Archangel had come after him for retribution and now innocents were being dragged into a living Hell again because of him.

The male grabbed her by her arms and hauled her into them, slinging her over his shoulder.

Harbin growled weakly and kept pushing forwards through the emptying club.

Several of the hunters left, carrying unconscious fae in pairs. At the exit, three were attempting to handle the bear shifter. Five darts stuck out of his bare chest and a nervous hunter embedded a sixth before a braver one dared to approach the slumbering brute.

A sudden sinking sensation washed through Harbin as he realised that the hunters were leaving, taking his quarry with them. His stomach squirmed, his instincts telling him to flee while he had the chance, to save his skin and escape whatever nightmare awaited the poor bastards at the hands of the Archangel hunters.

He pinned his feet to the floor and scrubbed a hand across his blurry eyes, trying to see the female as his body battled the effects of the drugs.

She hung limp over the shoulder of the hunter, her head lolling around and arms swaying with each measured step he took.

It would be easy to turn away, to slink into the shadows and wait for the tranquilisers to wear off. His body was already purging them, too strong for the puny doses they had used on him.

He sighed.

Shook his head.

He couldn't.

Not only because he had gotten her into this mess, but because he didn't know which facility Archangel would take her to and he would lose her if he let the hunters take her now. He might never find her again and he had promised Hartt that he would carry out his part of the mission.

He had vowed that he would remain close to her until Hartt and Fuery came to finish the job with him.

He had to keep that promise if he was going to keep his reputation as one of the best assassins in the guild. He had never lost a mark, and he wasn't going to start now.

Not even when it meant placing himself in the hands of the hunters he despised.

He scanned the room and spotted a lone male hunter at the back, struggling with a large unconscious male. His gut churned, every instinct he possessed screaming at him to run in the opposite direction. He couldn't. He had to get caught too.

A small part of him, a piece of him that refused to die now, whispered that his reasons ran deeper than a need to keep tabs on his mark and fulfilling his part of the mission. He wanted to get caught so he could ensure that she was unharmed by Archangel. He didn't want to let her be alone in that terrible place.

He needed to be there too.

Harbin roared and hurled himself at the young hunter. The male turned, wide brown eyes filled with panic, and swiftly raised his compact crossbow. Harbin saw the flash of the dart, felt the sting as it pierced his chest, and grunted as he stumbled a step. He pushed onwards, lumbering towards the male, desperate to force him into firing again. He needed the oblivion the tranquilisers offered. He would lose his mind if he had to do this capture and transport in a semi-drugged state. His memories would destroy what little sanity he had left.

A second hunter dropped his quarry and joined the first, lashing out with a baton.

Harbin staggered right as the blow connected with the left side of his head, pain ricocheting around his skull and turning the world hazy for a moment. He tried to retain his balance, his injured leg crumpled beneath him, and he hit the tacky club floor hard.

The two males closed in and every instinct he possessed commanded him to shift and fight. He shut his eyes and surrendered instead, allowing the hunters to crack their batons across his arms and head as he curled into a ball on his side. His snow leopard side pushed for freedom, writhing beneath his skin, wild with a need to attack and protect himself. It took every shred of his will to keep still and take the beating, to not retaliate and kill the males who were battering him.

He would find them and kill them, after he had fulfilled his mission.

His strength faded as the tranquilisers began to take hold, numbing him but not quickly enough to stop the need to escape the hunters and their vile clutches, and the thought of waking to find himself at the mercy of Archangel from driving him mad.

Shattered memory fragments bombarded him, filling his mind with a broken replay of blood on snow, crimson drenching white, and the black blur of the hunters who had attacked his kin. He saw their faces, heard their last gasps as he choked the life from them, staring into their eyes so he was the last thing they saw.

He saw *her*.

The blonde Archangel huntress mocked him with the pretty smile that had addled his lust-fogged alcohol-impaired brain, luring him under her spell in the small bar in the town nearest to the mountain where his pride had lived in safety for centuries.

A peace he had shattered because he had been too full of himself, as headstrong and hot-blooded as his father had always told him he was. He had been too blinded by lust to see the warning signs, had been too tempted by the sinful beauty and the thought of satisfying his carnal hungers.

His pain dulled as he slipped into a daze, the tranquiliser dose not enough to knock him out, leaving him at the mercy of his memories. They ran on a constant twisted replay, tormenting him, driving him insane with a need to hunt and kill, a hunger that he was powerless to satisfy in his drugged state. He weakly banged his head against the hard floor, seeking oblivion in order to escape his past, but he didn't have the strength to knock himself out.

He was vaguely aware of the hunters as they dragged him from the room, and the faint smell of gasoline as they loaded him into a truck. Lucidity came and went, giving him brief glimpses of holding cells in a darkened space, each filled with an unconscious fae or demon, before the past came rushing back to swallow him.

Each time it hit him, it drove him back under the violent tide of his memories. They battered him, turning him inside out with emotions that were still raw, his pain and fury yet to fade. He tried to growl whenever the blonde huntress flashed across his mind, tried to change the course of events whenever he saw her leaning in to kiss him, her emerald eyes glittering with desire, but no sound left his lips and nothing he did could alter the past.

The truck shifted, jostling him so he rolled against the cold metal bars of his cell. The feel of them pressing against his back and the thought of where he was heading combined to overpower him. Fear closed in despite his years of training and honing his abilities as an assassin, the emotion too strong to deny as it swept through him, swamping his mind and flooding it with images of what might await him and the other unlucky bastards in the truck with him when they reached the facility.

He tried to move, his instincts screaming at him to break free, to not allow Archangel to take him into a facility where he would be tortured and would possibly die. He hadn't survived this long, hadn't borne the pain for twenty agonising years for it to end here at their hands.

He wouldn't let them win.

He snarled and shuffled, managed to get his hands beneath him and convince his body to obey his foggy mind, but he didn't have the strength to push himself off the grotty floor. His arms gave out beneath him, his left shoulder hitting the floor hard enough to rip a pained yelp from his lips.

A hunter near the back muttered something and cautiously stalked forwards, heading in his direction.

He attempted to feign unconsciousness, but the pain in his shoulder was too intense, the fresh metallic tang of blood permeating the air telling him he had torn the wound open again. He gritted his teeth against it, his jaw muscles flexed, and the next thing he knew was a sharp sting in the right side of his chest as a dart impacted. Strange cold stole through him, numbing as it crept outwards from the impact point.

Darkness claimed him.

A brief, sweet moment of oblivion.

Followed by a rude blast of cold water.

Harbin snarled and tried to back away from the powerful jet, but a wall blocked his escape. He barked out his pain as the icy water thundered against his injured shoulder and then coughed as it struck his face, getting in his mouth and up his nose. He flinched away from it, curling against the wall, but it didn't stop his assailants. They kept up with their torment, hosing him down where he sat on the frigid tiles of what seemed to be a bright room.

As they ran the hose down his body, he barked again, fire and lightning rocketing up his leg bones as the jet reached his ankle. He growled a curse and swung his gaze towards them, narrowing his silver eyes on them as he breathed hard, struggling against his need to leap to his feet and rip them to shreds.

The two young male hunters lost their smiles, their dark eyes turning wary as they backed off in unison.

Without a word, the one with the hose switched it off and made a swift exit, followed by his companion.

Harbin panted through the pain and gritted his teeth as he looked down at his left leg. The bastards had removed his cast, exposing the deep bruises that marked his skin and leaving him in danger of re-breaking his tibia if he put too much weight on it. He wouldn't be fighting them any time soon, that was for sure. He needed a few more days before he could risk more than hobbling.

He huffed.

The bastards knew what they were doing. They knew what he was.

Who he was.

Not only had they taken his cast, which he would have easily stripped back to its base parts to get his hands on the metal rods to use them as makeshift batons, but they had taken his clothes.

They had removed everything he might have used as a weapon against them.

He flexed his fingers and smiled coldly as his claws extended.

Everything except his built-in arsenal anyway.

A shadow flickered out of the corner of his eye and he lowered his hands and looked towards the only exit in the white room.

A larger male blocked the door, his rugged face set in grim lines that Harbin felt matched his own expression. They had sent an assassin to deal with him, one of their finest no doubt. Only the best for him.

He bared his fangs at the male.

The bastard simply raised the dart gun in his hand and squeezed the trigger.

Four times.

Harbin grunted as each dart impacted in his injured shoulder and his chest. Cold swept outwards, turning his mind to mush and his limbs to rubber. He slumped against the wall, his head striking it hard, and his hands fell to his lap. He was vaguely aware of the hunter as he advanced, and the rough way he jerked him onto his feet. Icy tiles slammed against Harbin's face and cool metal encircled his wrists behind him, locking them in place. He struggled, one weak and pathetic attempt at fighting back that did nothing but make the Archangel hunter chuckle in his ear.

Harbin's hackles rose.

He would take pleasure in making this one suffer when he was free of this wretched place.

It rang around his mind as he stumbled through blurred corridors, beat deep in his blood as he heard the whispers and snickers of other Archangel members and felt their eyes on him.

Felt them mocking him.

The drugs the hunter had pumped him with were already fading by the time he smelled other fae and knew he was near the detention block. His new home for the foreseeable future. He bit back a growl as someone commented as he staggered onwards, feeling as if he had hit a tavern for a few too many beers and was paying the price.

"The mighty have fallen."

He hadn't fallen.

Not yet.

He would prove that to them when he escaped this Hell. He would show them all that he was as dangerous as the reputation that preceded him, as wild and feral as the legends told.

He would bathe in the blood of Archangel as he tore this facility to the ground.

He stumbled down a set of steps into a long white corridor and bumped off a wall. His escort shoved him in the back and he snarled over his shoulder at him. The male grabbed his shackled wrists and twisted. Harbin grunted, biting back the cry that tried to leave his lips as his shoulder caught fire.

The pain instantly faded, the anger that blazed within him dying as he felt eyes on him.

A familiar piercing that seemed to ground him and lift the haze from his mind, freeing him from the torment of his memories and his seething need for bloodshed.

His gaze swung towards the source of the soothing feeling.

The snow leopard female sat tucked in the back of a bright white cell with a thick glass front, hugging her black-denim-clad knees to her chest, her silver-gold eyes tracking him. His heart beat harder, an insatiable hunger instantly awakening in his blood, drumming fiercely in his veins.

His guard was down, stripped from him by the drugs and the pain, and he couldn't deny one thought as it speared his very soul.

She was beautiful.

And he was meant to kill her.

Fresh agony rolled through him, stirred by the thought of taking her life. It collided with the anger roused by the sight of her confined in a cell and at the mercy of Archangel.

He growled, flashing his fangs at her.

She continued to stare at him, unflinching in the face of his fury.

Brave female.

Would she be so brave when Archangel came for her?

The thought of her being dragged from her cell, pulled into whatever twisted experiments awaited her, churned his stomach until it boiled like acid and he wanted to take his claws to the male behind him, and every other person in the building.

He turned away from her and stared at the white tiled floor.

Would she be so brave when she faced him and knew her life was going to end?

What he had planned for her was surely far worse than anything Archangel could dish out, but perhaps it was more merciful. He liked to think so anyway. A wry smile curled his lips. He wasn't sure whether that made him fucked up or not. Was it better he gave her a swift death rather than her being subjected to Archangel's demented experiments?

A swift death was surely preferable.

He tipped his head back and stared up at the ceiling.

He certainly preferred it.

But the thought of Archangel doing anything to a snow leopard turned his insides and hollowed him out, scraping away all of the softer feelings she had stirred in him and leaving him raw with a need to butcher them all.

And he would.

The hunter shoved him into an empty cell and the glass barrier dropped from the ceiling before he could turn to attack him. The male stared coldly at him and pressed a button on a small black device. The shackles beeped and opened, dropping to the ground behind Harbin. He slammed his palms against the thick glass, right in front of the hunter's face, but the male didn't even twitch.

Harbin placed him right at the top of the list of people he would kill the moment he was free.

And he would do it with the very shackles the male had placed on him.

He turned towards them, a smile playing on his lips as he thought about using them to rip open the bastard's carotid.

A panel in the ceiling swished open, a hum sounded, and the shackles shot up into the dark opening. A tugging sensation in Harbin's left thigh had his fingers dropping to stroke the neat inch-long surgical scar there. Magnets. He should have known they would have a way of retrieving the shackles.

He hobbled across to the back of his cell, eased down to the floor, and kept stroking the scar, sensing the tracker buried deep beneath his skin.

Hartt would be coming.

Hartt would find him.

He had two days.

He could bear whatever Hell Archangel intended to put him through in that time.

He would survive.

And he would make sure his mark survived with him.

Harbin closed his eyes, seeking the rest he needed to heal his body and ensure he was fit to fight when the time came.

But only horror awaited him.

CHAPTER 5

The sound of screaming wrenched Aya from the tight grip of her nightmare. She breathed hard, sweat trickling down the valley between her breasts and her spine under her silver halter-top, her wide eyes fixed unseeing on a point across the room from her.

It took her a moment to remember where she was and realise that she hadn't been the one to scream.

The harrowed sound came again, a desperate bellow that made her shiver and chilled her to the bone.

The male snow leopard.

Whatever tormented him, it was infinitely worse than the nightmare she had been living in her sleep. Were the hunters hurting him?

Or were his agonised screams the product of a deeper suffering?

Aya hadn't failed to notice the darkness in him when the big hunter had marched him past her cell.

She had thought him more handsome in the full light, but there had been ice in his eyes that had made her cold inside.

One look into his pale silvery eyes had left her feeling he had no emotion in him, no shred of feeling, that whatever life he led, it had drained him of all light and left only darkness behind.

But the way he was screaming, each bellow speaking of agony and suffering, left her with a different feeling. Whatever emotions he had, they had been buried deep beneath that mountain of pain.

She could relate to that.

She had fallen into a violent abyss of nightmares shortly after seeing him paraded past her cell, stripped bare and exposed to the eyes of all, as if the hunters wanted to humiliate him for some reason. The twisted visions of her past had held her firmly in their grasp for the gods only knew how many hours, and mingled in with them had been images of the other captives being tortured by Archangel, experimented on as the scientists attempted to uncover their species' deepest secrets to use as weapons against their kind.

Rocky.

Aya pulled her knees up to her chest, rubbed her fingers over the smooth denim of her jeans, and brought her focus to the world around her.

Rocky was somewhere in this cellblock, trapped in a tiny white box just like her.

What would Archangel do to him?

The need to see him pushed her onto her hands and knees and she crawled to the glass front of her cell. She pressed her cheek to the barrier and peered down the corridor, but she couldn't see into the other cells. She could only see the one opposite her, and it was empty right now. She felt sure it had been occupied last night by an unfamiliar woman. What had Archangel done with her?

Had they released her?

Aya scoffed at that and her misguided hope. She knew Archangel and she knew better than to believe them capable of releasing their captives without a damn good reason. They said they merely studied species in order to understand them, to document them and discover methods of swiftly dealing with any from their kind who broke the laws and became a threat to the humans or other fae.

They lied.

She had seen the other side of Archangel with her own eyes.

She knew that most of the captives in the cells around her would never see the outside world again.

"Rocky," she whispered and laid her left palm on the several inches of glass, trying to reach through it to the other side so she could sense whether he was nearby.

Her stomach churned, hunger and fear combining to turn the acid into a bubbling pit. She closed her eyes and sighed out her breath, clinging to the fragile strands of hope, because she couldn't give up. She had to keep believing that Rocky would be fine and so would the others.

A hot shiver coursed through her.

Aya opened her eyes and lifted them, settling them straight on the male in the corridor.

Gods, he was handsome.

The bright lights made his sweat-soaked scruffy silver hair shimmer and his eyes almost glow as he hobbled along the stark white hallway, his lips firmly pressed together in a way that spoke of pain. He was trying to control it, but the edge to his gaze said that he was losing that battle. His expression twisted and darkened, and his shoulders and biceps bulged as he shifted his bound wrists behind his back, as if he was flexing his fingers.

Readying his claws.

The ice-cold look in his stunning eyes as they fell to her sent a warning arrowing through her, causing her instincts to fire back a response that told her to keep her distance from him. This male meant war.

She could almost read every dark fantasy running through his mind, could almost smell the blood of these hunters and see it splashing up the walls, streaking the pristine white with crimson. He wanted to kill the men behind him, and gods, there was a part of her that wanted to see him do it.

Profane lips peeled back off his short fangs as he growled and she instinctively lowered her gaze, obeying his command to avert her gaze from him.

Big mistake.

Taut square slabs of pectoral muscles, dusky nipples, and ropes of abdominals caught her eyes. She swallowed hard and tried to look away, but the way his muscles shifted with each step he took held her fast and fascinated her. Each bunch and stretch, each flex, spoke of power, and she couldn't stop her body from responding to it, heating and beginning to burn as her eyes betrayed her and slowly drifted down the length of his eight-pack to the dusting of silver hair that trailed onwards.

A stark reminder that he was naked.

One that had her eyes finally leaping away from him and fixing on the floor at his bare feet.

She frowned as he limped past, her eyes drawn to his left leg and the mottled skin above his ankle. He had broken it. How?

Her mind supplied that it had been in a fight, because by the looks of his body, he fought often. She might have been enraptured by his incredible physique, but that instant spark of lust he had ignited within her hadn't made her blind. She had seen the silvery streaks that covered his skin.

The sight of them stirred remembered voices in her head, whispers that had gone through the club the first night he had appeared in it.

He was an assassin.

Who was his target?

His gaze burned into her, but this time she felt only cold.

She knew the answer to that question.

The hunters weren't the only ones in this building that he was thinking about killing.

She was his target.

Aya lifted her head and pinned her gaze on the back of his head, refusing to let her instincts rule her. She wouldn't back down where this male was concerned. He had no power over her and she was going to show him that he had chosen the wrong female to target.

She was stronger than she looked.

Snow leopard females were weaker than their male counterparts, but what she lacked in physical strength, she made up for in mental. Males were ruled by their animal side, driven by it to get physical in a fight and tackle things head on. If he wanted to tussle with her, she would use all of her wits and agility to place him at a disadvantage and emerge the victor.

She watched him until he had disappeared from view and lingered for long minutes afterwards, her mind churning, a collision of wondering about the male's history and wondering what Archangel would do to him.

A weight settled in her stomach as she thought about him strapped to a black padded table in one of the small medical rooms, sedated and at the mercy of Archangel scientists.

Memories bubbled up and she fought to suppress them, tried to keep them shoved down deep inside of her where they couldn't hurt her. They were too powerful, easily breaking to the surface of her mind and swallowing her. The world around her faded, replaced by a startling splash of crimson on white tiles and the horrifying whirr of a bone saw.

Aya shoved away from the dark memory, pushed away from the glass and threw up.

A passing guard merely glanced at the mess she had made, and then her, and continued on his way down the white corridor.

She backed away into the corner of the room where she had slept and curled into a ball, wrapping her arms around her knees and bringing them up to her chest. Time trickled past as she stared at the corridor, not really noticing the guards as they came and went, or the fae they escorted. It was only when she felt the male snow leopard's eyes on her that she came out of her daze and lifted her eyes away from the spot on the tiled floor.

His eyes were even colder now.

Glacial.

They froze her with just a look.

Blood tracked down his bare chest from several dark marks, running in drying rivulets over his stomach, where they disappeared beneath a pair of black cotton trunks. Aya stared at them. It seemed Archangel had deemed him worthy of a little dignity. A reward for playing along and letting them run tests on him?

She would have done anything they asked had their positions been reversed and she had been the one stripped naked.

Just the thought was enough to have her trembling, memories of her previous time in Archangel's hands surging back to the surface to torment her. She hugged her knees harder and rocked as she fought the onslaught, refusing to let it own her. She was stronger now.

A survivor.

Nothing would destroy her.

The male's eyes narrowed, a flicker of curiosity breaking through the ice, and then he was gone, stolen from view as the two hunters dressed in black fatigues marched him back to his cell.

An assassin.

She still found that difficult to believe.

Whenever she looked at him, she saw a dangerous male, one that she knew she should keep her distance from, but one that she found impossible to put out of her mind. There was something about him, something held just beneath the surface, that told her he wasn't all he appeared to be.

He was more.

Maybe she had been wrong about him.

Aya lowered her head and squeezed her eyes shut. It didn't matter what feelings she had about him. He was an assassin and he was after her, and that was reason enough to keep her distance and remain wary of him. She had to stop thinking about him as anything other than an enemy.

A male who would kill her in a heartbeat.

She needed to get her mind off him.

A welcome distraction from her dark and worrying thoughts appeared in view from the right side of her cell.

A huntress Aya knew.

The pretty blonde led a group, her pale eyes fixed ahead of her along the corridor. Behind her, a large shirtless male trudged, his hands shackled in front of him and two guards at his back. Long rich brown hair laced with gold and held at the nape of his neck by a leather thong, and the smooth but sculpted contours of his face, painted a picture of sinful perfection.

An image even she wasn't unaffected by as his wicked lips quirked and he briefly glanced her way. Heat speared her, spreading outwards from her chest, and she muttered a curse.

An incubus.

The effect he had on her, and the lines of markings that ran up the underside of his corded forearms and snaked over his biceps and shoulders were definite traits of an incubus, but it was his eyes that were the dead giveaway.

No other fae species had eyes that swirled gold and blue like his were.

He shifted them back to the woman in front of him and Aya couldn't miss the brief tensing of the huntress's shoulders.

His markings shimmered with hues of bright gold and cerulean.

Was he using his charms on the huntress?

Aya had seen her more than once in the city, but had never seen her shaken as she was now. She wasn't the usual confident and cold female Aya knew. Her face was a mask of cool and collected, but her eyes betrayed her.

They edged to her left, as if she wanted to look back at the incubus behind her.

Maybe he had already used his charms on the huntress and she was still fighting the effects.

Aya's gaze drifted back to the incubus.

The way he was looking at the huntress though, and his calm demeanour, left Aya feeling that something was going on and stirred her curiosity. She uncurled and leaned forwards, eager to study the male as much as she could before he too disappeared from view.

There wasn't a scratch on him, and the relaxed way he walked said he was comfortable with his situation. He hadn't fought Archangel when they had captured him.

Why?

She frowned.

Because he had wanted to be captured.

Aya glanced between him and the huntress and back again. She knew that look he was giving the female. It spoke of hunger, but also of a deeper desire, one not born from lust but from the heart.

He knew the huntress.

Aya went to look back at her but she moved beyond the left wall of her cell and the incubus soon followed.

Was there more to the huntress than met the eye?

She'd always had a suspicion that there was something different about her. Her scent wasn't quite right. It wasn't quite… mortal.

Another group moved into view and she studied this one with even deeper curiosity.

Speaking of not mortal.

The black-haired huntress held her head high, her amber eyes focused and intense, but Aya could sense the flicker of fear that she was trying to hide as she stormed along the corridor. This one didn't belong here. She had heard the rumours about her.

Sable was the hot topic of conversation in every fae bar and club in the city, and beyond.

Aya didn't know what blood ran in her veins, but the rumours said it was mortal mixed with something powerful.

The dark huntress's lineage wasn't her only reason for being on her guard.

The great big brunet bare-chested male stalking the corridor behind her, an unconscious blue-haired male slung over his thickly muscled broad shoulders, was her number one reason.

A demon king.

The rumours were true.

Sable was mated to the Third King.

The brute snorted and shifted the male, jostling him. Aya wasn't sure what breed the unfortunate male was, but she pitied him.

It was wrong of a female and male of the fae world to assist in the capture of one of their own.

Aya's stomach squirmed, her anger immediately dissipating as a quiet voice whispered through her mind and chilled her blood.

She couldn't pass judgement on the couple.

Because she had committed the same sin.

CHAPTER 6

Whatever cocktail of drugs they had given him, it really fucked with his control.

Harbin prowled his white cell, attempting to work off the adrenaline caused by the nice round of 'studying' he had been subjected to in the grim operating room that had been his own personal Hell for what had probably been several hours but felt like several days.

He had been a damned good boy in that wretched torture chamber, behaving himself so Archangel wouldn't have reason to get feisty and do more damage than necessary. As much as he wanted to rip all their heads off and piss down their necks, he needed his strength more if he was going to make it through the next two days.

Surviving until Hartt came for him and the mark was priority one, but the longer he spent in the white-washed Hell of this facility, the closer he danced to losing his mind and the harder it became to deny the base urges welling up to consume him.

The worst of which was the itch to fuck.

Being a snow leopard male on the cusp of sexual maturity blew most days, but it was made infinitely worse by the presence of the female.

He hadn't noticed the effects when he had been back at the club, surrounded by the swirling thick scents of the other fae and unable to see the female clearly in the flickering piercing colourful lights.

But, fuck, did he notice it now that he had seen her several times under bright clear light, all of her damned beauty and lush plump curves revealed to him.

And, fuck, did he really notice it now that his senses had honed in on her particular scent.

She was all he could smell.

Even when Archangel had been working him over, prodding and poking him while questioning him about Hell and everything else he had seen in his short life, he hadn't been able to smell anything but her. Not the disgusting stench of antibacterial products, nor the rank odour of the sweaty little humans so eager to divulge his darkest secrets.

He could only smell the sweet, subtle scent of mountain air that he now associated wholly with her.

Gods, she smelled like home.

And it was playing havoc with him.

He turned and slammed his fist into the glass of his cell, pain ricocheting violently through his bones in response. The fiery zing gave him sweet respite from his turbulent feelings for a second, a brief moment in which he felt calm again and steady.

Centred.

A hiss sounded and he jerked his head up, his eyes narrowing on the pale vapour as it descended into the cell from above the door.

It seemed Archangel employed nefarious tactics to deal with naughty prisoners.

Harbin didn't back away from the gas as it rolled towards him like a menacing fog. He closed his eyes, kept his head tilted back, and inhaled, taking the foul tasting toxin deep into his body.

He wanted oblivion.

He wanted to sleep through this nightmare.

His legs wobbled, turning to jelly beneath him, and gave out a second later, sending him crashing into a heap on the ground. Sound spiralled around him, voices blended together into nothing more than a blur of noise. Darkness encroached and he welcomed it, reached out to pull it closer as his body succumbed to the effects of the gas.

Sweet, sweet fucking oblivion.

He smiled as he slipped into it.

A sharp bang rattled him from the gentle cradle of darkness, its tender arms slipping free of him as light washed back into his mind.

He groaned and rolled onto his side, curling into a ball for a moment before stretching out, reaching his limbs as far as they could go. Every muscle lengthened and warmth burned through him, a satiated feeling that could only come from a deep and restful sleep. He kept his eyes closed and assessed his condition as he continued to stretch, unable to deny his base instincts as pleasure rolled through every inch of him. There really was nothing like a good stretch. Most days, he denied himself that unearthly pleasure, but this time he indulged it. Revelled in it.

Gods, it felt good.

But not quite good enough to erase his awareness of his surroundings.

Or of his new neighbour.

The male muttered to himself and it took Harbin a moment to regain enough of his faculties to decipher his tongue and understand what he had said.

"What is this magic?"

Harbin snorted, managed to convince himself to stop with the fucking stretching, and sat up. "It's called glass, Dumbass."

There was a deep pause, and he wondered whether the male had heard him.

"Are you dragon?" The words came from his left, muffled by the white wall between them, but clear enough that they could have a conversation.

He had to be going mad if the thought of conversing with someone actually made his day look bright and sunny when in reality it was stormy and dangerous as all fuck.

But still, the guy was a dragon, and dragon shifters were damned powerful.

They also didn't belong in the mortal realm, which Harbin decided the male hadn't quite figured out yet since he seemed rather calm.

A softer banging sound told Harbin the male was tentatively exploring his surroundings. If they were going to have a conversation, then he would have to move closer to the dragon. He lumbered onto his feet and placed a little more weight than usual on his left leg. It ached less, the throbbing barely noticeable now. The sleep caused by the gas had done him some good, helping rejuvenate his tired body. If only Archangel knew. He grinned to himself. The bastards wouldn't have knocked him out, that was for sure. They probably wanted to keep him nice and weak, easy to manage, so he would behave himself whenever they decided to take him from his cell and prod at him.

He ran his thumbs around the elastic waist of his black trunks. At least his good behaviour had given him back one item of his clothing. Maybe he could get the rest back if he continued to play nice. Not that nudity bothered him. Plenty of his captors had stripped him bare in order to leave him with only his built-in weaponry, and he had managed to kill them all and escape. Even the ones who had attempted to pull his claws out had met with a grisly end.

Harbin limped to the left wall of his cell and leaned there near the glass front.

"Nope. Not a dragon… but it helps in my line of business if you know your languages." He had met enough dragons in Hell to know it paid to speak their tongue. Their English was often more than rough around the edges and the last thing he wanted was a sixty foot reptile with a temper misunderstanding him.

No assassin crossed a dragon.

Well, none that lived to tell the tale anyway. He was sure some idiots thought they could tackle a mark of that magnitude and that their target ate them and used their bones as toothpicks.

"Where am I?" The male's voice grew louder and Harbin could almost sense him on the other side of the wall, resting close to him.

He was powerful. Too powerful for the cell to hold if he lost his temper?

The thought of escaping and grabbing the female snow leopard in the panic had his heart leaping in his chest, and he had to draw a deep breath to settle himself. He wasn't in any danger. He didn't have to fear Archangel or give in to a need to escape that only made him weak and pathetic.

Hartt was coming.

And, fuck, for once Harbin couldn't wait to see Fuery.

The mad bastard would tear Archangel a new one when he popped into the facility with their boss, and Harbin wanted to see the dark elf rip through the mortals with his sword.

He wanted to put them to his own blades too.

Harbin pushed the pleasing image aside and focused on his neighbour. Maybe he could get some information out of him or use him to his advantage in some way. He just had to push his buttons a little.

"A complex filled with bastards. From the twittering I've heard during the past day, they're quite excited about you." Lies, but probably the truth. Archangel got excited about anything rare landing in their hands, and you didn't get rarer than a dragon shifter.

Which led Harbin to wonder how the hell they had gotten their dirty paws on him.

"Where is Anais?" There was desperation in those three words, and it gave all of the dragon's feelings away.

He felt deeply for whoever Anais was and the maturing side of Harbin could appreciate that, his screwed up instincts finding it sweet and appealing. He didn't need a damned mate. There was no time for love in his life, and bitches definitely didn't deserve a drop of affection from him. Females were traitorous, backstabbing whores.

"She a dragon too?" Harbin ground the words out as politely as he could manage given the anger churning in his gut, the fury roused by the thought of the female who had betrayed him.

She had used her wiles on him, had seduced him into believing she was attracted to him and desired to be with him. He had been stupid enough to think she was being honest, that she might be more than a tumble in the hay. The barbs of her lies still stuck in his heart, slowly working deeper, tearing it apart.

He growled under his breath and clawed at his chest, struggling for air as he tried to regain control of his mind and shove her from it.

"She is mortal."

Those three words sent him back over the edge and he stumbled away from the wall, mind reeling as he stared blankly at the other side of the cell.

Mortal.

A cold shiver ran through him followed by a hot blast of anger.

They had done it again. They had sent a female to seduce a fae male, no doubt in order to capture him for one of their studies.

He snarled through his fangs, ploughed his fingers into his silver hair and yanked on it as the anger inside him coiled tighter, burned hotter. The flames ate away at his control, shattering his mind and turning his heart to ash in his chest as everything came flooding back.

The bar. The beauty. The betrayal.

He collapsed to his knees and curled forwards, unable to breathe as those terrible memories washed over him, racking his tired body and tearing him to pieces. He tried to hold himself together, scrambling to gather each broken piece of his soul before the memories leaped forwards, but he wasn't swift enough.

White snow. Red blood.

His beloved mother and sister, their sightless eyes staring at the heavens, to the place where they roamed free with their ancestors.

Stolen from him too soon.

Hot tears rolled down his face as he grimaced, clenching his teeth against the pain ripping him apart. Still raw. Still killing him slowly twenty years on.

The blood of his kin. The cries of those who had survived the brutal attack on the pride. The look in his older brother's eyes as he lifted them from their dead mother and sister and set them on him across the frigid square.

Gods, Cavanaugh had known it had been his fault.

Harbin had seen it then. He had seen the disappointment and disgust. The anger. The pain.

He had done the only thing he could. He had gone after Archangel, mad with a need to make them pay. He remembered little of what had happened in the aftermath of the attack. Only the taste of blood, the feel of bones breaking and skin rupturing beneath his claws, and the overwhelming urge to keep fighting.

Until all were dead.

That urge still lived within him.

It still took him whenever he crossed paths with an Archangel hunter, and he still lost his mind when he killed them, remembering only fragments of what happened, engulfed by his rage and his pain.

Harbin growled and fought the dark need as it rose inside him, threatening to drive him insane. He could smell the Archangel hunters, could sense their presence around him, but he couldn't reach them. If he succumbed to his urges, he would only lose his mind, unable to satisfy his deep craving to spill their blood. He had to retain control.

Voices blurred around him, a female and the dragon's. The huntress had come to him, but Harbin was too deep in the grip of his memories to make out what they were saying to each other. He breathed deep and clawed back control, focusing on his need to hear what was being said, because it might end the attack ravaging his mind and body.

If he could only hear she hadn't betrayed him.

He needed to hear.

A different male voice joined the blur and he caught the words 'study' and 'shift'. He twisted his hair in his fingers and focused on those two words. They wanted to study the dragon. They wanted to see him shift.

It wasn't possible.

No dragon could shift in this realm. The curse placed on them millennia ago made it impossible. It also made the male's time limited. If he didn't escape, he would die here. Not because of Archangel's experiments, but because this realm would kill him.

"I'm sorry." A soft female voice rang through the glass and Harbin heard the hurt in it, pain that spoke to him and softened the harder parts of him for a heartbeat before he closed himself off again.

A female could easily sway a male with a few sweet and well-chosen words. It meant nothing.

Harbin only hoped the dragon could see through them too.

"I am sorry too." Those four words, spoken by the shifter, carried a weight of bitterness, hurt and hatred, and Harbin breathed easily at last.

The male was wiser than Harbin had hoped.

He wasn't sorry the bitch had betrayed him. He was sorry he had ever met her.

The huntress who had used and betrayed Harbin wouldn't receive such a simple ending. His closure needed blood and death, and he wouldn't be sorry about it.

Harbin closed his eyes. "Escape... the mission... and then revenge. He's coming. He's coming. He's coming. Escape... the mission... and then revenge."

He lost himself as he chanted those words, so focused on them that they filled his mind and left no room for any other thoughts. They consumed him, drove him, and no matter how much he tried, he couldn't stop saying them. A passing guard looked in on him and Harbin lifted his head, bared his fangs and kept chanting. The hunter gave him a look that said he had gone mad.

Mad. Yes. Definitely mad.

But not insane.

Driven. Obsessed. A madness that kept him walking forwards, forever onwards in search of the one elusive female, the one death that would free him of the compelling urge to butcher Archangel hunters and make them pay for their sins that was beginning to consume him again.

He had lost sight of his true mission, but now a need to fulfil it ruled him, had him in its grip again. This time, he wouldn't set it aside for anything. This time, he would complete it and the huntress would die.

It ended now.

He shoved onto his feet and began pacing, taking swift agitated strides across his cell as the thought of finding the bitch who had betrayed him and killed his kin spawned a thousand more thoughts, an account of all the knowledge he had gained during his search for her across all of the continents of the mortal realm. Somewhere in that knowledge was the seed that would bear fruit and give him her location. He just had to find it.

His fingers flexed, twitching with the need to sink his claws into her.

Escape. Fuck the mission. Get revenge. That was all that mattered now. Escape and revenge.

It was time she paid for her sins.

He sharply turned towards the wall separating him and the dragon and banged on it. Time to sow some seeds of his own, ones that might just get him out of this white-washed Hell.

"That the woman you were looking for?" he said.

"Yes."

Harbin snorted. "They sent a woman to trick you, too?"

Silence greeted that question and he could almost hear the dragon's thoughts, could almost taste his freedom. He was close. He just had to push the male a little more. He had to play on his feelings, both the good and the bad.

"Did she sleep with you and then betray you?" He pressed his palms to the wall and waited.

The dragon growled. "Yes."

Harbin spat out a foul curse. "They did the same thing to me... and then they attacked my pride. They killed my sister and mother."

Silence again, and this time Harbin knew the reason. The dragon was thinking about his clan and the danger it was in now. Dragons valued their clan above everything. Well, everything except their treasure.

A low snarl rumbled through the wall, the sense of power Harbin got from him increased tenfold, and then the dull sound of fists slamming against glass sounded. The dragon was pissed. Just how Harbin needed him.

The banging ceased and he felt the dragon move closer.

"What is your name?" Those words were laboured, spoken between hard breaths if he had to guess.

"Harbin."

"My name is Loke. You heard my conversation with the huntress. I cannot be here. I must escape these fiends... and therefore I need your help. I need your knowledge of this facility."

Bingo. He had just secured his ticket out of here. Now he just had to give the male what he knew, and escape and revenge would be his.

Escape. Revenge.

He hadn't realised he had relapsed into chanting about those two things until the damned dragon was roaring down the house and pummelling the glass again. Fuck.

"Bad move," Harbin called, but he knew it was already too late. "They don't like it when we're rowdy."

Loke stopped the banging but the deathly silence in the other cell told Harbin that they were already releasing the gas. He didn't have much time if he was going to convince the dragon to break him out.

He growled as he gave the dragon the information he needed, his voice deeper and more vicious than he had ever heard it as thoughts of finally achieving his revenge rolled through him.

Atonement.

It would finally be his.

"Two scientists. Bonds are weak. Shatter them. Scalpels are weapons. Four guards. Two observers. Eight throats to cut. Kill the fuckers and come get me."

Harbin grinned and sealed the deal by placing a cherry on the top.

"I know a portal back to Hell."

CHAPTER 7

Harbin couldn't wait to see what the scientists had in store for him this time. He had expected the two male hunters at his back to escort him into the same cramped medical room as before, but they had continued along the stark white corridor, leading him deeper into the facility. The shackles they had placed on him were cold against his bare lower back, irritating him. He flexed his fingers, fighting the itch to stroke the surgical scar on his thigh where his implant sat deep beneath the skin. Escape. That instinct rode him now, strengthened by the conversation he'd had with the dragon shifter.

It was within his reach.

He had been set on escape and revenge until he had passed the cell of the female snow leopard and had seen it was empty. A pressing need to see her again had welled up inside him, startling him with its intensity. Curiosity drove questions through his mind, a hunger to know where she was and what Archangel was doing with her.

That hunger filled him with a dangerous need, one that had little to do with his mission and everything to do with his need to atone.

He couldn't leave without her.

He needed to see her and see she was safe, and know that she would be in her cell when the time came to escape this Hell. Whether that escape came at the hands of Hartt and Fuery, or the dragon.

He wasn't leaving without her.

His fingers itched with another need as he cursed himself, a desire to plough them through his wild silver hair. What the fuck was wrong with him? What had happened to the cool and collected killer?

He growled a curse out loud this time.

He had been unravelling from the moment he had set eyes on her.

He had bottled up everything, every softer feeling or painful memory, and now it wanted to come out.

It couldn't have worse fucking timing.

He needed to be on his A game right now, at peak strength, with his wits about him. He didn't need to be mooning over a damned female just because his hormones were out of whack and the need to mate was strong. The urges he had been suppressing for the past few years rose to overwhelm him whenever he thought about her, riding him harder than ever.

Ninety-nine years old.

It taunted him.

Crossing paths with the female couldn't have come at a worse time.

He hadn't believed his teachers or his family when they had told him that as a male he would hit sexual maturity at a century old. He had thought it bullshit, a rough estimation of the time he would awaken as a fully matured snow leopard adult, able to breed. He had never thought it possible that they were right and it would hit him at dead on a hundred.

It certainly felt as if it was going to, and if the rollercoaster ride he had been on the past few years was anything to go by, it wasn't going to be much fun.

He had been keeping his urges under control, never straying close to women when they were at their strongest, trying to rule him, but now they were owning him, pushing back whenever he attempted to wrestle them under his command. His instincts were too powerful, and gods only knew it was because of the presence of the female.

How the ever-living fuck was he going to escape with her when his condition was worsening, degrading to a point where whenever he thought about her lush curves and feeling her flesh cushioning his fingers he got a raging hard on?

He looked down at the front of his black trunks and grunted. It wasn't as if he could hide the damned thing with his current clothing shortage either.

Maybe it was better he let Hartt and Fuery handle her, but that meant handing over control to them. It would place her in danger. Hartt and Fuery would want to carry out their mission.

He snarled at the thought and bared his lengthening fangs. No fucking way. He wanted nothing to do with females, especially not a snow leopard, but he couldn't let them take her from him. He couldn't sign her death warrant.

He had to handle her himself.

The hunters shoved him into a room, pushing him right out of his thoughts and back to the present. The moment he realised his wrists were unbound, he turned back to lash out at the mortals, but a solid steel door slammed in his face. Great. Another cell.

He turned around and dread slithered over his skin as his eyes took in the new room. What the hell were they up to now?

Everything in the large rectangular room with him looked rather unthreatening. Blue plastic barrels, ropes, and boxes were strewn across the white tiled floor. Did they think he would be tempted to play with the stuff?

"Make yourself at home." The male voice barked over an intercom on the left wall, above which was a small camera.

They were watching him.

He spotted more cameras on the other walls, and in the corners of the room too.

They honest to gods wanted to see what he would do when faced with all the shit in the room with him.

Fuck all. That's what he was going to do with it.

Instead of surrendering to his natural curiosity, he started pacing the room, cataloguing everything about it. There was a deep gully across the middle of it, cutting it into two squares. He glanced up at the ceiling, at a dark band there. He would bet his left nut that there was a barrier up there, ready to slam shut and divide the room into two.

Harbin casually strode away from his end of the room, towards the place where the barrier was hidden in the ceiling, curious to see what would happen.

He was within a few paces of the gully when the scent of male snow leopard hit him. His nose tingled, his primal instincts firing and seizing command. He peeled his top lip off his teeth and dragged the air over them, tasting the male's scent.

A snarl rose up his throat and he stalked towards the first item that smelled of the male, a barrel just over the gully on the other side of the room. He halted a few feet from it, stealing back control of his body and refusing to give in to the need to rub the damned thing to erase the male's scent from it.

Archangel were fucking with him.

Maybe they wanted to see how long it would take him to cave and let the need to scent mark everything seize control of him.

He huffed and forced himself to turn around and walk away, back towards the end of the room that didn't smell of the male.

It was a dangerous game they were playing. This close to sexual maturity, the scent of another male affected him deeply, triggering a primal need to fight and fuck, and gods help anyone who was on the receiving end of either of those needs because he felt like a feral bastard, liable to rip apart an enemy or a bedfellow.

He stormed to the steel door and banged his fists against it. He needed to get out. He needed to escape. Fuck waiting for Hartt. Fuck the female mark. He had to get to the dragon and get the hell out of this place. He couldn't do it. He couldn't handle any more.

The matching steel door at the other end of the room opened, jerking his gaze in that direction, and his stomach dropped as the female snow leopard was shoved into it with him.

Clad only in a strapless white bra and panties.

No.

The twin urges to fight and fuck combined into one seething hunger and he roared as he launched himself in her direction, unable to claw back enough control to stop himself. The terrible urge to escape overrode them all, filling him with a black need to fulfil his mission. He could only watch himself running at her, determined to wrap his hands around her throat and choke the life from her, convinced that he would be free then.

He would be free.

The glass panel dropped and he slammed into it, cracking his nose on it. The taste of blood coated his tongue, worsening his hunger to fight. He shook his head and gathered his senses, and growled as he attacked the barrier that kept him from his mark.

The female shrank back, her gold-silver eyes filling with fear as she brought her hands up to her chest and swallowed hard. Those wide doe eyes pinned on him, burning into him and wrenching him in two directions, tearing him between the hunger to kill and the terrible need to kiss her.

Fear.

He frowned and looked down at the barrier, and snarled as he spotted the holes in it. He could smell her. Sweet mountain air.

His knees weakened, threatening to buckle and send him crashing to the ground as that scent curled around him, seeped into his skin and made him heat from the inside outwards. He shuddered, his body swiftly hardening in response to her tempting smell, his primal instincts hijacking control and leaving him at their mercy.

The darker part of himself that had been established in the blackest pits of Hell, born of bloodshed and violence, and a constant fight for survival, rose against it, pushing back and flooding him with a terrible need to escape.

Kill the mark.

Secure his freedom.

That was all that mattered.

He attacked the glass again, alternating between slamming his fists against it and clawing it. Nothing he did left a mark on the five-inch-thick barrier. He growled and kept up his assault, but it strengthened the hold his primal instincts had on him. The more he fought the barrier, the harder he breathed, and the deeper he took her scent into him, until it filled him completely and the thought of killing her was replaced with pleasing images of killing whatever male had marked the items in the room with him.

In the room with *her*.

His deepest instincts seized control again at that thought, telling him that there was a male in the room with his female, even when the logical part of him could see that there wasn't. It didn't matter how much he told himself that she was alone and they were the only two snow leopards. He couldn't stop himself from pushing away from the glass and tearing into every item on his side of the room that smelled of the male.

A male that wanted his female.

He roared.

He wouldn't let the male have her.

She belonged to him.

He was vaguely aware of the danger of his thoughts, but nothing he did could douse the needs coursing through him. His more human consciousness was just a passenger as his animal side drove him to destroy everything. He ripped apart the plastic barrels and boxes, and raked his claws down the ropes, erasing the male's scent as he left a wake of carnage behind him. When everything on his side of the room was in pieces, he stalked back to the barrier and growled as he attacked it.

He had to reach the things on her side.

He had to kill the male that wanted his female.

The female backed away from him, towards the white wall at the opposite end of the room to him, her fear a palpable thing that beat in his veins as she stared at him through striking wide eyes.

He needed to get to her.

Blood smeared the barrier as he clawed at it, wild with that need, and he growled weakly as it consumed him, together with a sense of hopelessness and despair that sank its fangs into him and refused to let him go.

He needed her.

But he couldn't reach her.

"Lift the barrier."

Harbin's eyes narrowed on the intercom and then the female.

She gasped and shook her head, her eyes darting around as she looked for an escape route. Her black hair swayed, brushing pale cheeks that he wanted to stroke to feel their satin softness beneath his fingertips. Desperation flooded her scent, jacking up the fear in it.

The barrier started to lift.

Harbin didn't wait.

He rolled under the gap as soon as it was large enough and sprang to his bare feet on the other side. The primal part of him that wanted to erase the male's scent from the room decided it wanted something else even more.

Her.

Harbin launched himself across the room, leaping the gap between them in one bound, and slammed against her. He grasped the back of her neck, pressing his short claws into her flesh to hold her in place, and kissed her, swallowing the gasp that left her lips.

Her fists struck his bare chest, punching one moment and shoving the next, desperate noises escaping her as she tried to break free of his hold.

He kissed her harder, her taste flooding him with pleasure as he dominated her, obeying every instinct he possessed.

She tasted forbidden and sweet.

Cold washed over his skin and snow rushed down his neck and back like a waterfall. The stillness of the mountains surrounded him. Her warmth met his, penetrating his skin and sinking deep into him together with this kiss.

Etched on him forever.

He groaned and tightened his grip on her, not wanting this to end, intent on taking more of her into him.

He needed more of her.

Her claws raked down his right cheek, the stinging fire and the tang of blood forcing his primal instinct to have her to recede, replaced by an instinct to defend himself.

It was enough to shatter the hold of his hunger.

A sickening awareness flooded him and he staggered backwards, reeling from the mental blow delivered by the horrific realisation of what he was doing.

Forcing himself on her.

He didn't stop moving until the wall at the far end of the room struck his back, stopping him from placing more distance between them. He stared at her, breathing hard and shaking. Gods, what the fuck had he been on the verge of doing?

The female curled into herself, her head lowering as she turned her side to him and pressed against the far wall, her fall of black hair obscuring her face. Her bare shoulders trembled and the salty scent of tears reached him, making him feel even more like a bastard.

He raised his hand, paused and lowered it, sure that whatever words he could muster wouldn't be enough to apologise for what he had done. It would be all too easy to blame his hormones, but it would be a lie, because they weren't wholly responsible for how he had acted.

He wanted her. He had wanted her before he had smelled her scent or seen her clearly. He knew that now. He had wanted her the moment he had set eyes on her. She rocked him as no other female had, and that frightened him, because he couldn't do this again. He couldn't allow a female to have that sort of power over him.

Never again.

Harbin spat out a curse as a trickle of red ran down the back of her neck and swallowed hard as he lowered his gaze to his bare feet, guilt and shame flowing through him at the same time as a feral need to sink his fangs into that same place and pin her while he mated with her.

He laughed, the sound out of place in the strained silence.

He was so fucked up.

Killing her wouldn't have bothered him at all, but the thought of taking advantage of her had him tied in knots and disgusted with himself. Gods, Hartt would be pissing himself laughing if he knew just what twisted shit was going on inside his head and in this room.

He pinned his back to the wall and breathed slowly as he waited for Archangel to remove the female from the room.

When close to thirty minutes must have ticked past, he realised that they weren't coming to help her.

Bastards.

They were leaving her at his mercy even after witnessing what he was capable of doing to her.

He curled his fingers into fists at his sides as she shuffled slowly and carefully towards the door on her side of the room, moving as quietly as possible, as if that would stop him from noticing how desperately she wanted to escape him. She pressed one slender hand to it and remained there, tucked close to the cold metal that kept her dangerously within his reach.

Another eternity ticked past and then everything changed.

She changed.

She turned her head and slid her silvery-golden gaze his way, and she was different now. Darker. Angry. Was this what Archangel wanted to see?

Is this why they had kept her in the room with him?

They wanted to see how long it would take for her to turn from fearful female to dangerous woman.

She pushed away from the door and came to face him, her posture no longer meek and afraid. She clenched her fists at her bare hips and fixed her unflinching gaze on him. Her chin tipped up and her eyes brightened, turning more silver than gold, her snow leopard side emerging as her emotions grew stronger. Darker still.

"I know who you are."

Harbin stared at her, having trouble taking those five words in and making them stick. He had to be hearing things.

Her eyes didn't shift from his and the look in them sent a chill creeping through his chest. He had heard her right. She did know who he was.

Which meant, holy shit, that she was part of his pride.

He staggered a step towards her, senses reeling and mind racing. "How long have you been here?"

A confused crinkle formed above her silvery eyebrows and then she frowned. "Only as long as you have… this time."

This time. His stomach dropped and his blood turned to ice. He had meant how long had she been in London, but she had taken his question to mean how long had she been in Archangel's hands. He shook his head, not wanting to believe what he was thinking because it would break him, but she nodded slowly, confirming his worst fears.

Archangel had captured her twenty years ago.

They had put her through hell because of him.

She snarled, flashing little fangs, and her eyes turned to liquid silver as fur rippled over her exposed skin. "I hope they give you what you fucking deserve. It took a lot for me to return to this place, but I had to do it."

That hit him like a tonne of bricks and he couldn't breathe as she smiled viciously across the room at him.

Victoriously.

She had lured him into a trap. She had known he was tracking her, knew who he was, and she had gotten herself caught because she had known he would have to do the same in order to stay close to her and fulfil his mission.

Son of a bitch.

She calmly walked to the steel door of the room and rapped her knuckles against it, and he was unprepared for the deluge of raw emotions that crashed over him when the door opened to reveal no one to escort her on the other side.

She wasn't a prisoner.

But he was.

Harbin roared and kicked off, intent on reaching the traitorous bitch before she slipped beyond his grasp forever. He leaped over every obstacle in his way but the door slammed shut before he could reach her. He rained blows down on it and a panel slid open, revealing glass and the female. She donned a robe, wrapped it tight around herself, and glanced over her shoulder at him, not even a flicker of guilt in her eyes.

"Why?" he barked, even when the question felt redundant because he already knew the answer.

He just needed to hear her say it.

Her smile faltered and something akin to guilt or possibly sorrow entered her silvery eyes.

"I wasn't the only one Archangel captured that day, but I was the only one left alive when Archangel was placed into the hands of a person with a more noble vision, one where humans and fae could live and work in harmony." She pressed her hands to her chest and screwed her eyes shut. Tears slipped down her cheeks, and a stupid part of himself he couldn't quite kill ached with a need to wipe them away, proving just how fucked up he was. "I'm doing it for the ones I had to watch die during my three years of captivity, whether it was a slow and torturous death of the spirit that took them or a corporeal one through vivisection or poison testing for weapons."

Gods, it had been hard enough when he had only had the weight of the deaths of those at the pride village on his shoulders, swift ends by steel and bullets. He couldn't bear the weight of what she was placing on them. He pressed his hands to the metal door, his arms shaking and his knees threatening to give out as what she was saying slowly sank in.

She lifted her head and looked into his eyes, and he could see that she might have been strong enough to survive whatever horrors Archangel had inflicted on her, but she was haunted by the things she had seen and endured.

Things that were his fault.

"The people around you were the ones who killed your kin by experimenting on them and killed the others back at our pride," he bit out and her expression didn't change, didn't reveal one single emotion to him. It remained flat and cold. He snarled and slammed his fists against the steel that separated them. "Archangel are the ones who fucked up both of our lives.

They were the ones who sent a huntress to seduce me, drug me and betray me… and they were the ones who killed my sister and mother."

Shock flitted across her face before she schooled her expression again. She hadn't known the whole story, he could see that now. She hadn't known that he had been used by Archangel. What twisted spin had Archangel put on what had happened back then to make her believe that he was the one who had orchestrated everything?

His stomach dropped as the answer hit him.

They had told her and the others they had captured that he had sold them out.

Her lips parted but two male hunters appeared before she could speak, ushering her away. He stared at her as she walked down the corridor, wedged between the two mortals, her arms wrapped around herself.

At the last second, before she was stolen from view, she looked back over her shoulder at him.

A touch of regret shone in her gaze.

Harbin's legs gave out and he crashed to the ground, still reeling from everything that had happened and what she had told him. She had lured him into a trap. She had wanted revenge and for a moment, he felt sure that she had thought she had it, but then he had driven a spike into the perfect image that Archangel had painted and made her believe, fracturing it and leaving her doubting the hunter organisation.

He couldn't take any pleasure from that, not while his mind was filled with thoughts of everything she and the others Archangel had taken from the village that day must have suffered because of him.

Not while his mind kept whispering to him, filling his heart with a suspicion that he couldn't shake.

The female had taken out a contract on herself in order to entrap him and have her revenge.

He had been betrayed again.

CHAPTER 8

Aya needed air. She couldn't breathe as she rushed through the maze of bright corridors in the palatial sandstone building belonging to Archangel. Hunters eyed her as she hurried past them, her head bent and her short black hair concealing her face.

And the tears streaking her cheeks.

The events of the past few days had finally caught up with her, the male snow leopard dealing the final blow that sent them all crashing down on her and rattling her.

Harbin.

Gods, what was she doing?

Had he been telling her the truth, or was it just another deception, a lie spun to shake her trust in Archangel?

She shoved the flat of her palm against a glass door and sweet night air washed over her, the coolness of it sending a wave of calm through her as she could finally breathe again. She strode out into the welcoming darkness, heading for the spot in the centre of the courtyard where the amber glow of the lights emanating from the rows of windows on the walls of the quadrangle barely reached.

Aya tipped her head back and breathed deeply, trying to centre herself again and settle her turbulent thoughts and feelings. Her fingers stroked over the soft material of her silver halter-top, a methodical rhythm that slowly calmed her.

What had she done?

It was her fault that Rocky and the others were in the hands of Archangel, and while she had been able to meet with a senior member of staff before her encounter with Harbin and secure their release, she didn't fully trust Archangel to hold true to their word.

Not anymore.

All because Harbin had shaken her.

She had thought herself prepared to handle facing him and finally having her revenge, making him pay for the years she had suffered at the hands of madmen and the close to two decades of reliving those nightmarish times that had come afterwards.

She had been wrong.

With only a handful of words, backed up by the pain that had shone in his silver eyes, hurt that had called to her deepest animal instincts and had made her want to soothe him, he had punched a hole in her beliefs and ripped them apart.

She paced the small patch of darkness, the gravel crunching beneath her black boots. Her hands still shook, but not as violently as they had been when she had returned to the small room where her clothes had been waiting for her and had dressed. She had barely been able to fasten the button on her black jeans. It had taken her close to ten attempts before she had finally managed it.

It wasn't only Harbin's words that had shaken her though.

Her lips tingled and she pressed trembling fingers to them, her breath hot on their tips as she thought about the kiss.

She'd had a deal with Archangel, a plan they had agreed on, and they had changed it. Twice. When she had contacted them about Harbin, they had agreed on a plan, one where they would wait until two days after her call and capture both her and Harbin together, taking them into custody when they were alone outside the club in order to maintain her cover as just another member of the fae community.

They had promised to do things quietly, and that only the two of them would be captured.

The senior member of staff she had met with tonight had apologised, stating that it was another operation that had seized her and the others the night after she had contacted Archangel, and she had foolishly believed him.

Until they had changed the plan again.

They had sworn the barrier would remain in place, keeping Harbin separated from her. They had lied, and that only weakened her trust and made her feel they had been lying to her from the start.

Harbin had been so swift to enter the room, to cross it and reach her, that she hadn't had time to react. She had been in his arms, her back pressed to the wall and his powerful body caging her before she could move, and then his lips had captured hers and she had been thrown back close to forty years to a fumbled first kiss in a snowy mountain village.

Aya spat out a curse and dragged her fingers away from her lips.

That kiss had meant nothing. He had made that perfectly clear to her then. He felt nothing for her, but that hadn't made it hurt any less when he had betrayed her.

She looked back at the doors she had exited.

If he had betrayed her.

He hadn't been lying when he had said that Archangel had killed his sister and mother, and part of her believed he hadn't been lying when he had said Archangel had used him too. She had already known he had told them the location of the village, but the tale she knew differed from that point.

When Archangel had changed hands, and she had been set free, a huntress had been sent to speak with her about everything. The pretty blonde female had told her about that night and that she had been there, and that Harbin had been given money and his pride given protection in exchange for three males and a female. Archangel hadn't intended to spill blood, they had only fought to defend themselves when the males in the village had attacked them.

Aya had believed her.

She had been alone, afraid and angry, and she had needed someone to direct that fury at and the huntress had given her a target.

She had directed Aya's anger away from Archangel and made her focus it on one of her own kind.

Aya slumped to her knees and stared at the golden gravel, reeling as everything clicked into place.

The huntress was the one who had seduced Harbin.

Aya could easily see the bastard falling for her beauty, with her glossy blonde waves, shapely figure and stunning green eyes, and it hadn't exactly taken much convincing for him to fall into bed with anyone back then. A pretty smile and a little flattery, and any female could have had their way with him.

Except her.

Gods, she hadn't realised just how bitter he had made her, and it only churned the guilt already brewing in her stomach, making her sick. She had believed Archangel because she had been upset with him, filled with jealousy and anger that she had held on to for twenty years after they had kissed. Jealousy and anger that had only grown with each female she had seen him cavorting with in the village, and each trip he had taken down the mountain to slake his lust with the mortals.

Maybe she was doomed to place her faith in the wrong people.

Forty years ago, she had believed Harbin had felt something for her, and he had crushed that belief.

Yet no kiss had ever stirred heat in her veins as his had.

She wished with all of her heart that when he had kissed her in the room that she had felt nothing but cold fury, but that kiss had melted the ice in her veins and the thick glacier that encased that heart, making her burn for him all over again.

Damn him.

She knew why he affected her so deeply too.

It had hit her the second she had stepped into the room and he had looked at her, his eyes bright silver with hunger, need that she felt sure he was probably blaming on his impending maturity, but she knew stemmed from something else.

She was his mate.

The feeling had drummed through her, an awareness that she had found hard to shake during her time locked in that room with him, and that was impossible to escape even now that she was free and he was probably back in his cell.

How long would it be before he realised it too?

Would he come after her when his instincts finally told him that she was his fated female?

Her heart beat harder, and the walls around her closed in, the darkness choking the air from her lungs as her instincts roared at her to run. She needed space and time, needed to escape and taste the fresh air of freedom in her lungs. She couldn't do this.

She shoved to her feet and eyed the archway cut into the side of the building at the opposite end of the courtyard.

Freedom beckoned but she couldn't convince her feet to move.

She had already tried running from him, had fled to this courtyard, but she hadn't been able to outrun her desire for him. It still drummed in her blood, quickening and setting fire to it. Nothing she did could douse those flames now, not with the memory of his kiss branded on her mind and her lips.

Gods, she needed to speak to Rocky. She needed to talk to someone. She was going to drown in her thoughts if she didn't.

The things Harbin had said kept her pinned in place, and the need to know whether he was telling the truth warred with a desire to pretend those words had never left his lips.

She couldn't face the thought that Archangel had lied to her.

She had trusted them for too long.

After her release, she had begun to work with them as a sort of informant, feeding them information about dangerous immortals. She had believed that by working with them that she had been protecting the fae, shifters and other immortals who wanted to live in peace. She had spent fifteen years assisting them.

The thought that they might have lied to her to gain her trust, just as they had apparently spun lies of a more wicked nature to Harbin in order to gain his twenty years ago, hollowed out her insides and left her cold.

Archangel had put her through three years of Hell, but the tests they had run on her had been nothing compared with the experiments they had done on the males they had captured with her. While the scientists had put the males through a more physically painful course of experiments, they had labelled her as a more valuable asset because of her gender, and had instead inflicted a round of studying on her that had been invasive and had left her emotionally scarred.

She closed her eyes and shut out the images that wanted to bombard her, the memories she did her best to keep contained to her nightmares. That time was in her past now, but some days it still felt as if it had been just yesterday that they had laid her on inspection tables and invaded her body, studying how she differed from a mortal female.

The need to run overwhelmed her again, this time born of a deeper fear, one she couldn't brush aside.

She couldn't face the pain of rejection all over again. No snow leopard male would ever want her as a mate, could ever feel anything for her, because she had overheard the scientists that had studied her and the one thing mature males of her species desired was the one thing she couldn't give them.

She couldn't bear offspring to help the survival of their species.

Aya looked back over her shoulder again, unable to ignore the urge that beat within her, drawing her back to the cellblock.

Back to him.

The need to run from him clashed with another need, one that began to grow, becoming strong enough to subdue the urge to flee.

She needed to know the truth about everything.

She needed to speak with Harbin again, but she wasn't sure he would be rational. He was too different to the male she had known for most of her life. The coldness in him, the darkness that seeped from him and warned her to keep her distance, set her on edge and made her want to obey her instincts and do just that.

Was this what life as an assassin did to people?

The male she had known back in the village had been filled with life and light, with easy smiles and quick wit. He had been a little wild, but he hadn't seemed capable of cold-blooded murder, and she knew from her research that he had done some terrible things during their time apart.

What had driven him to step into such a dark and dangerous life?

Her heart whispered the answer to that question. It had shone in his eyes when he had told her that Archangel had murdered his mother and sister, and now she knew of that event, she could see that the times he had been escorted past her cell, his eyes filled with icy darkness, that he hadn't been plotting her demise. He had been fighting his need to attack the Archangel hunters who guarded him, and possibly every other mortal in the building.

Archangel had set him on the dark path to becoming the cold, emotionless assassin she had met in the nightclub.

A male who was nothing like the one she had fallen in love with forty years ago.

She needed to speak with him.

She turned back towards the doors and the high shrill of an alarm sounded. The lights from the windows on all three floors of the building surrounding her flickered as hunters rushed through the corridors and her heart kicked off at a pace. What was happening?

She listened hard, tuning out the wailing alarm in an attempt to detect what had triggered them.

Someone screamed. Another joined in, a shriek of agony that was cut short and made her cold inside.

It was an attack.

Her stomach dropped.

She pushed off hard, sprinting towards the glass doors.

Harbin.

CHAPTER 9

Harbin paced his cell, his bare feet silent on the cold white tiles. Only the sound of his breathing and soft swish of his newly reinstated black jeans filled the tense silence. The return of more of his clothes wasn't a good enough exchange this time, not as payment for what Archangel had put him through.

Hell, if he was honest with himself, he didn't deserve the damn clothing. They should have stripped him bare again and put him in solitary for what he had done to the female.

The darker part of himself rebelled at that thought, pushing back against it, pointing out that she was the reason he was trapped in his own personal Hell. She had betrayed him. She had lured him to her, had tricked him into falling into Archangel's hands, and had orchestrated a meeting that had rattled him.

All for the sake of revenge.

He wouldn't have been as pissed if she had been in the right and events had followed the path that she believed they had taken.

But they hadn't, and he was furious.

He would never have knowingly betrayed his kin, and the fact that she believed he had sat in his gut like acid-coated lead. What sort of male did she think he was?

He huffed and strode back across the small cell as his mind flashed images from his past at him, reminders that he hadn't been the most stellar member of his pride. He had never embraced his duties as the son of their alpha, or taken on any form of responsibility, or done anything that benefitted his people. He had been lapse in his studies, lazy in his work, and had spent most of his days in the lead up to being exiled in the arms of whatever female would satisfy his latest itch to fuck.

Gods, he hoped she hadn't been one of the many he had bedded at the pride, but it would certainly help him understand the weird rush of sensation he'd had when he had been kissing her and would go some way to explaining why she hated his guts and had been happy to swallow the bullshit Archangel had fed to her.

He doubted she would have believed them if they had said his brother, Cavanaugh, had sold her out or anyone else at the pride.

The devious bastards had probably overheard something she had said about him during her captivity and had used him all over again, painting a big target on his chest for her knowing full well that she harboured some sort of resentment towards him and would take the bait.

Now she was taking her best shots at him, trying to bring him down and make him pay.

He wanted to be angry with her, wanted to hate her for what she had done to him all for the sake of revenge, but part of him felt he deserved it. He hadn't sold her out, but he had betrayed her and the rest of his kin in a way, and he knew that everyone from the village probably wanted him dead too and some would probably be happy to do the deal themselves if they ever crossed his path.

Fuck, he would probably hand them his blades and let them do it.

It was part of the reason he had kept his head down and had spent most of his time in Hell. His death wouldn't bring back the dead. It wasn't a big enough price to pay for the things he had done. Living was that price. He had to stay alive, live with his sins, and keep walking the path towards whatever scrap of redemption he could find.

He had to finish the job he had started twenty years ago.

He needed to end the female who had betrayed him and set in motion the events that had turned his life upside down and destroyed the ones of many of his kin.

Harbin growled and clenched his fists.

First, he had to escape Archangel's hands and find the snow leopard female. He needed to make her believe that she had placed her trust in the wrong people, even when he knew it would only hurt her. Her striking silver-gold eyes had shown a wealth of pain and guilt when he had tried to make her listen to him, telling her the short version of the real course of events that had taken place that day at the village. He couldn't imagine the pain she would feel when he told her everything that had happened and convinced her that Archangel had lied to her.

He was certainly going to feel more like a bastard than ever, that was for sure.

He paused mid-stride and stared at the blank white wall opposite him. How the fuck had she softened the hardest parts of him so quickly, pulling down all of his barriers and setting his emotions free? A week ago, he wouldn't have been concerned about hurting her. Fuck, he wouldn't have been concerned about telling her the truth.

He would have been focused on killing her as payment for her betraying him.

What was it about her that had him going against his darker nature and his training as an assassin?

She was a mark, by her own choice since she had clearly taken out the contract on herself to entrap him, but she was a mark nonetheless. A target. A mission. Nothing more than a job.

But she had done nothing wrong.

She hadn't killed anyone, or stolen anything, or done anything worthy of him taking her life. The only sin she had committed was the sin of betraying him, born of a need for vengeance that probably burned as fiercely in her heart as the one that blazed in his.

And hadn't he really betrayed her in the first place?

Hadn't he betrayed all of his kin with his constant straying from the village to sleep with mortal females that must have drawn the eyes of Archangel to that town and his pride in the first place?

Hadn't he betrayed them when he had used his position within the pride, albeit in a coded manner, to impress the huntress Archangel had sent to squeeze information out of him?

He had told her that he was in charge, a male in position of power, because his father was out of town. He had basically given her the green light to attack his pride by revealing they were vulnerable, without their alpha to protect them.

Gods. He screwed his eyes shut and dug the heels of his hands into them, his head hurting with the collision happening in it, a twisting and churning relentless stream of thoughts that tore at him.

He deserved whatever the female snow leopard had in store for him, and if it would take away some of the pain she held locked inside her, born of her years of captivity in this terrible place, he would willingly subject himself to it. Whatever pain she wanted to deal to him, he would take it. He would do all he could to atone for his sins.

But first he needed to get her away from Archangel.

He needed to tell her everything and convince her to allow him to track and put an end to the huntress who had brought them both so much pain and changed their lives for the worse forever.

He touched the three jagged marks on his right cheek.

He had to save her.

He couldn't deny that need. It pounded in his blood, a deep visceral ache that owned him. He couldn't leave her here, where she was in danger.

He needed to protect her.

He wouldn't fail her again.

He turned back towards the glass front of his cell.

The lights dropped, plunging the entire floor into darkness, and a siren wailed. A moment later, red lights began to flash, giving him glimpses of his surroundings. He covered his ears and grimaced, struggling to focus as the assault continued. Guards rushed past his cell and the other prisoners grew loud enough for him to hear over the shrieking pulse of the alarm. Something was happening.

Harbin cursed.

Had the dragon escaped his captors? If he had, the bastard had better be on his way to him to take him up on his offer. His cursing turned into a long growl. There was no way he would be able to convince the dragon to take a detour to search for the snow leopard female. He doubted she would return to the cell where she had been held if she was working with Archangel, and he wasn't sure how big the building was or where to begin looking for her.

The need to protect her warred with a need to escape.

He had her scent now. He could track her and find her.

But the building was swarming with Archangel hunters, and all of them had probably armed themselves the moment the alarm had sounded.

He slammed his fist into the glass front of his cell as a sense of futility swept through him. As much as he wanted to save her, he couldn't. The number of hunters he had seen during his captivity was only a small percentage of the total number that occupied this building. Any attempt to find the female would end in him being captured again.

It was no use.

He had to take the opportunity to escape when it came.

He would return for her. He swore that under his breath. He wouldn't allow Archangel to poison her mind any longer. He would set her free.

Noise in the corridor drew his attention there. He caught a glimpse of a mortal male dressed in black fatigues and a flash of blue-leather-clad legs. The dragon. They were dragging him back to his cell. Dammit.

If he had been the cause of the alarm, they would have shut it off the moment he had been rendered unconscious and placed back in containment, which meant someone else was responsible.

He tried to focus through the noise, honing his senses, seeking out anything fae or immortal in origin. The sense of power emitted by the dragon interfered with his search, making it hard for him to tell whether someone equally or more powerful had launched an attack on Archangel. He focused harder, determined to understand what was happening.

He had a brief sensation of power, strength the magnitude of which he had only felt in Hell when fallen angels were near him, and then it was gone.

What the hell was going on?

He strode to the wall that separated him from the dragon and banged on it.

"What's happening?" he hollered and waited, willing Loke to respond. He wasn't sure whether the male was merely drugged or actually unconscious, but he hoped it was the former because between the irritating siren and the growing hunger to escape, he wasn't sure how long he had before he completely lost his shit.

His animal form prowled beneath the surface of his skin, making him itch with a need for freedom and cool night air, a desperate hunger that made the cell seem to shrink around him, until it felt too confined, closing in on him and stealing the air from his lungs.

He had to get the fuck out of this Hell. He couldn't wait for Hartt to come. He couldn't. He had to get away, whether it was with the female in tow or left behind for him to rescue later. Right now, he just needed air and space.

Freedom.

He pressed his palms to the wall, focusing on the male in the cell beyond, and whispered, "Come on, Loke."

The dragon was his shot at escaping during the insanity happening around him. Even dazed by drugs, the shifter male would be strong enough to beat his way out of the cell if he put his mind to it. He had to be.

He felt Loke move at last and sensed him coming closer.

"I do not know." Loke's deep voice rumbled through the wall and the alarms fell silent. Sweet fucking mercy, Harbin could hear himself think again. The dragon huffed. "I sensed a strong presence near me and then the infernal lights began flashing and that noise began."

"It's called an alarm. They raise it when something bad happens." How little did dragons know about the mortal world? Harbin knew they couldn't be in it, but surely they could keep up to date somehow. He didn't have time to explain everything to Loke, not when the crushing need to escape was growing stronger by the second, and not when each of those seconds that ticked by stole more of the dragon's power.

"Then something bad has happened." Loke moved closer still.

Now that Loke was nearer to him, Harbin could feel that he was already drastically weaker than when he had first arrived in his cell. Too weak to break the glass and aid Harbin in his escape?

That thought had his throat closing, his stomach twisting, and his snow leopard side pushing for freedom, wild with a need to run free.

Harbin shoved away from the wall and started pacing again, breathing hard and fast, struggling against his animal form as it rippled over his skin. No good would come from changing. It wouldn't give him the added strength he needed in order to escape the cell, but he couldn't stop the urge that ran rampant through him, stronger than he had ever felt it.

He had to shift.

He snarled, his canines lengthening and his claws emerging. He couldn't take it anymore. He had thought he was strong enough to survive a few days in Archangel's hands but he wasn't. Being here, being near the female and discovering what he had done to her and what Archangel had done to her and others because of him, was too much to bear. His heart couldn't take it. Not when the female had softened it, leaving it vulnerable once more.

He clawed at his chest, punching holes in his black t-shirt.

Fur rippled over his skin, a flash of silver marked with darker spots.

The alarm started again, the red flashing lights stinging his sensitive eyes and making him growl through his fangs.

A shriek pierced the wailing noise, not mechanical but made by a living creature. The scent of blood crept into his cell. Was Archangel under attack?

His claws grew longer as more grunts sounded and the metallic clash of weapons reached his ears. A battle. He itched for freedom for a different reason as the noises grew louder, coming closer to his cell. He wanted to fight too. He wanted to make Archangel pay for everything they had done.

He prowled closer to the glass, his breathing turning heavier and harder, his chest heaving as he struggled for control and fought for patience. His time would come. Archangel would pay in blood for the things they had done to him and his kin.

They would pay for the things they had done to the female.

The need to avenge her burned hot in his blood and he couldn't contain the feral roar as it rose up his throat, his primal instincts forcing it from his lips as every inch of him coiled tight, ready for the coming battle, itching for it. He would avenge her.

"Can you see anything?" He managed to push the words out, more growl than syllables when his animal side was at the helm and he was barely suppressing the shift, holding himself in mortal form by sheer will alone.

"Nothing." Frustration laced that word, speaking of Loke's deep desire to escape.

A desire that matched his.

The sounds grew closer, the fight near enough that a splash of blood landed on the pristine white tiles outside his cell. Whoever had invaded Archangel this time meant business.

He pressed his palms and his cheek to the cool glass front of his cell, desperate to catch a glimpse of the fight and the ones responsible for shedding so much Archangel blood so swiftly.

The alarms ceased and the lights stopped flashing, the brighter white ones coming back so suddenly that Harbin flinched.

When he opened his eyes again, they widened.

Clad in skin-tight obsidian armour, his blue-black hair dishevelled by the violent clash and crimson splattered across his pale skin, and his violet eyes filled with displeasure and irritation, his boss was a formidable sight, but Harbin's heart leaped in his chest all the same.

"Hartt!" he barked and the elf slid him a thoroughly unimpressed look as he strode towards him.

"What the Devil made you toss yourself into this predicament?" Hartt stopped outside of Harbin's cell and he was about to answer when he felt the familiar and unsettling sensation that only one person caused in him.

He looked off to his left, to the other elf standing there, glaring into Loke's cell, his jet black eyes no doubt narrowed on the shifter.

Fuery curled his lip at Loke, flashing a hint of fang, and then waved his hand in the air, producing a cloth. He methodically wiped his long black blade on it, cleaning the blood from the metal, the look in his eyes relaying the dark thoughts in his mind. He wanted to kill Loke too, and probably every other poor fae, immortal or vampire in the cellblock. Fuery didn't distinguish between friend and foe, because he saw only foes.

Tainted bastard.

Harbin felt sure that Hartt was the only one capable of keeping Fuery in line, and that without his boss holding the mad bastard's leash, the elf would have killed Harbin and every assassin at the guild a long time ago.

"Fuery, get your backside in gear and deal with those guards." Hartt pointed towards the end of the corridor they had come from.

Fuery grinned, sick excitement flashing in his black eyes as he turned to face his new enemies and crooked his armoured clawed finger, beckoning them to their doom. His pointed ears flared back against overlong blue-black hair that he had drawn back to reveal them, securing the top half into a ponytail with an elegant silver clasp but leaving the rest down to curl around the neck of his obsidian armour.

He bared his fangs and disappeared in a flash.

Hartt watched him go, his carefully schooled expression not hiding the wariness he felt. The regret.

Harbin growled, regaining his attention. Hartt could be as cold as Fuery when he needed to be, but the elf still had a little too much heart at times, was swayed by it when he should have been stronger. Archangel deserved what Fuery was dishing out to them and if Harbin were free of his cell, he would be fighting alongside the elf, no trace of regret or pity in his veins.

Hartt sighed out his breath and slowly slid his violet gaze back to Harbin, and this time the compassion in it was for him. He bared his fangs at his boss, reminding him that he didn't need his pity and that he had sworn to keep everything Harbin had told him to himself. If Fuery caught Hartt looking at him as if he was a special snowflake and needed someone to take care of him, it wouldn't be long before the entire guild was talking about him behind his back, trying to figure out why Hartt treated him differently from the rest of them.

"Stand back." Hartt pulled a small black device from the air, twisted it and pressed it to the glass of Harbin's cell. He flicked a look at Loke. "I suggest you move back too."

Harbin did as instructed, striding to the back of his cell and curling into a ball in one corner, covering his head with his arms as he tucked it close to his knees. He sensed Hartt move and braced himself. A bright flash, a deafening bang, and then a shockwave rocked him and a thousand needles stung his flesh as pieces of the glass hit him. He grunted and grimaced, his ears ringing and the tiny lacerations stinging for a few seconds before his body began to heal them.

In the distance, Hartt muttered several curses in the mortal tongue.

Boots crunched on the fragments of glass.

"I suggest you escape this place." Those words weren't directed at him. Hartt was speaking to Loke.

Harbin had to do something. He couldn't leave the dragon behind. They could all escape together. He pushed onto his feet and carefully crossed the treacherous span of glass-littered tiles to the front of his cell, grimacing whenever a piece cut into his bare soles.

"Desist!" The deep commanding voice had Hartt whipping his head in the direction of the end of the corridor and Harbin's stomach dropped as he sensed the wave of power that washed through the cellblock.

There would be no escaping that way, not when the newcomer was blocking their path. Whoever he was, he was too powerful for them to fight, and Hartt seemed to know it. Even worse, Fuery seemed to know it too. The elf was suddenly beside Hartt, a stunned expression on his face that quickly morphed back into dark lines that said he was ready to challenge this new foe, even when he wasn't sure he would win the battle.

Mad bastard.

Harbin reached the front of his cell. "Take the dragon."

Hartt flicked him a look that made his stomach sink lower. "I cannot teleport three. I am sorry."

His boss dropped his violet gaze to his boots, a sorrowful edge to his expression, and then drew in a deep breath.

Harbin didn't have a chance to argue with him. Hartt grabbed him with one hand and collared Fuery with the other. He caught a flash of a bare-chested male with bright blue hair standing beyond the cracked glass front of a cell, and then darkness swallowed him whole.

Dammit.

He shirked Hartt's grip the second they landed in an unfamiliar dark city street and paced away from him, the cuts on his feet stinging with each stride across the wet tarmac. Hartt's steady gaze followed him, and he could sense the elf's desire to apologise. He shot Hartt a look that told him it wasn't necessary, because he knew that if he could have, he would have taken Loke with them. Hartt would have seen it as a golden opportunity to add a dragon shifter to their ranks.

Hartt drew down another deep breath and slowly sank to his haunches. He rested his elbows on his bent knees and stared straight ahead, his violet eyes turning unfocused. Harbin knew better than to ask if he was feeling alright. Teleporting three took a lot out of him when one of the three was Fuery. As mad as the elf was, he was extremely powerful, and that meant he drained Hartt's strength. The rule with teleporting went that the more powerful a being an elf teleported with them, the bigger the drain on their power, and the longer it took them to recover.

They would have to wait for Hartt to recuperate and they would have to do it somewhere in the mortal realm.

Carrying both him and Fuery just a short distance from Archangel would have sucked the strength from Hartt. There was no way he could teleport all three of them back to Hell without killing himself.

They needed a place to hide, and Harbin needed answers, and there was one place they might find both of those things.

Underworld.

CHAPTER 10

Harbin was sure he was about to make the biggest mistake of his life yet.

He stared at the black steel door of the closed nightclub, his heart thundering against his ribs, slowly building up the courage to knock on the damn thing and accept whatever fate awaited him. Whatever happened once that door opened, it was going to be tough to handle and he wasn't sure he was ready.

He wasn't sure he would ever be ready.

He had spent the time it had taken to locate the nightclub and then the long walk to it mulling over everything and gathering the balls to go through with the plan, but now he was here, that strength had fled him and he wanted to forget it and find somewhere else to lay low and discuss everything he had discovered about his mark.

The two elves staring at him as if he had gone mad propelled him into action when they both stepped forwards, their armour peeling back from their hands in unison as they raised them to knock.

He growled at both of them and they glared at him, but relented when he blew out his breath and approached the door.

He could do this.

How bad could it be?

Images of his older brother killing him sprang to mind.

Or worse, Cavanaugh looking bitterly disappointed to see him again.

His hand fell, his stomach dropping with it. He couldn't do it. It had been too long and Cavanaugh probably blamed him for everything that had happened and hated his guts, and he wouldn't blame his brother one bit, but he didn't think he could take seeing the anger and resentment in his brother's eyes.

Not again.

"For the love of the gods." Hartt grabbed him before he could move a muscle and darkness swallowed them.

When it evaporated, all three of them were standing in the middle of the closed nightclub with several fae and some mortals staring at them. A slender mortal female near the long black bar that lined the wall opposite him turned towards him, her blonde hair swaying across her shoulders as she shifted and pinned him with large dark eyes. His own eyes widened when he saw beyond her, catching sight of the unconscious blue-haired male laid out on the bar top, the coloured lights rotating above him washing him with sombre hues.

Loke.

Harbin looked back at the female. Was this the one who had betrayed Loke? He would have growled at her had the male standing beside her not been staring at him so intently, radiating familiar power that had him carefully considering any move he made.

The one who had commanded Hartt and Fuery to halt their attack.

Another elf.

The male's violet eyes glimmered with keen intelligence and his blue-black hair was preened and perfect, neatly clipped at the sides and back, revealing his pointed ears. Black scaled armour hugged a lithe physique that belied the power this male held within his grasp.

It wasn't only physical power. He radiated power of another nature, his regal bearing and confidence speaking of a male who commanded respect and seemed to have it from all those around him—a mortal female, a jaguar shifter, an Archangel huntress and a demon king.

Even Harbin's two elf companions seemed at a loss and unable to bring themselves to look at the male, which led Harbin to suspect he was some sort of leader of their kind.

The elf's pure violet gaze darkened and the hand he held against the blonde female's neck tensed. "Ignore them. Thorne and Sable will deal with them."

That didn't sound good.

The blonde female nodded and returned her focus to Loke, and the black-haired Archangel huntress and her burly russet-haired bare-chested companion advanced on him. The big demon grunted, his red eyes glowing like embers as he rolled his thickly muscled shoulders and his dusky horns began to curl from behind his pointed ears.

The huntress Harbin might be able to handle, but the demon was going to prove a problem, especially since he had the sinking feeling the pair were bonded. If Harbin tried to take out the huntress, the demon would lose his shit, and an enraged demon was far too powerful for him to take down, even with two elves on his side.

A door to the left of the black bar shot open and Harbin's breath rushed from his lungs as his gaze shot towards it and landed on another tall male clad in just a pair of pale grey sweats.

Fuck, maybe letting the demon kill him wasn't such a bad idea after all.

The new male's silver eyes verged on wild, his equally silver short hair mussed on top, as if he had been sleeping just seconds before.

Just seconds before he had smelled Harbin in the club.

The male stormed towards him and Harbin struggled to breathe, fighting to settle his heart and his nerves, and find a sliver of strength and courage to face the male who was looking at him as if he was staring at a ghost but was throwing off dangerous vibes that had Harbin's animal side prowling and ready to push for freedom and attack.

The big snow leopard male was pissed as all Hell and Harbin could hardly blame him.

But at odds with the anger rolling off him in tangible waves was something that gave Harbin the courage and hope he needed.

Incredulity filled the male's pale eyes.

The sandy-haired jaguar shifter moved into the path of Sable and Thorne and folded his arms across his chest, causing the dark grey t-shirt he wore with his paler grey sweats to tighten across his back. "I have a no fighting policy in this club, as you're well aware. At least until I know what the fuck they want."

Sable's golden eyes darkened and Harbin had the impression she wanted to ignore the shifter and attack them anyway. She looked like the type that loved to fight. Maybe the almighty train wreck that was about to hit him and spill the story of his life would provide enough entertainment for her and everyone else in the room.

Harbin sucked down a breath and blew it out. "Brother."

Everyone turned to look at him, but the jaguar shifter's stunned expression won first prize. "You know them, Cavanaugh?"

His brother nodded, his silver eyes locked on Harbin. "I like to think I knew one of them anyway... it's been a while since we've seen each other. I might be wrong."

Those words cut him and he dropped his gaze to his bare feet, clenched his teeth and tried to weather the hurt that welled up inside him. He cursed the softer part of him, the emotions the female had unleashed, breathing new life into them, because they only caused him pain. They were the source of so much agony and he had kept them contained, had locked them away to spare himself, and now he couldn't so much as breathe without feeling as if he was dying, each gulp of air scraping in his lungs.

He sensed Fuery and Hartt flanking him, and silently thanked them for their support. Hartt knew the story of his life, but Fuery didn't, and Harbin hadn't expected him to care enough about him to have his back.

Although, the mad bastard probably just wanted to fight everyone else in the room, and forming an offensive line with him and Hartt was a good way of pushing someone into attacking first.

Harbin lifted his head and looked back at Cavanaugh, and the low-lit club and everyone in it fell away as he stared into familiar silvery eyes, at a face that took him back to better times and only made the pain in his heart grow fiercer.

Sable shouted something and Hartt retaliated, but Harbin didn't pay them any attention as he looked at his brother, fighting to find the right words to say.

He had been keeping track of Cavanaugh's movements over the years, using his network of contacts like spies to keep an eye on his older brother. It had surprised him when Cavanaugh had left the pride and come to London, but it hadn't surprised him when he had learned that his brother had finally found his mate and brought her back to Underworld with him. He was glad for them in a small way, one he didn't want to acknowledge, not when he knew that such an ending wasn't on the cards for him. It was rare for a snow leopard shifter to find their mate, and Cavanaugh's had been right in front of him from the start.

Eloise.

Harbin had always known his brother's feelings for the female, even when Cavanaugh had failed to see them for himself. It was about time the idiot noticed how mad he was for her, and how in love she was with him. Cavanaugh had a big heart, had always been the better male, and he deserved a happy ending.

Himself on the other hand, he only deserved the anger he could see building in his brother's eyes as Cavanaugh came to terms with what he was seeing and that it was really him standing in the middle of the closed nightclub, causing another fight to break out because trouble had always followed him everywhere.

Cavanaugh continued to stare at him in silence and Harbin wasn't sure how much more he could take. He hadn't seen him in two decades, and he wasn't exactly the brother that Cavanaugh remembered. He doubted that his older brother could see a single shred of the male he had once known in him now.

Maybe he could change that at least, although the desire that ran through him would possibly just show Cavanaugh how much he had changed, because he couldn't remember ever apologising for anything in the eighty years they had lived together in the mountains.

But he needed to do it, he needed to tell his brother how sorry he was before Cavanaugh turned on him and hit him with both barrels.

He opened his mouth and didn't have a chance to get the first word of his apology out.

Cavanaugh grabbed him and Harbin tensed, prepared to take a blow, but then his brother's arms wrapped around him like steel bands, crushing him with the strength of his embrace. The warmth of his skin, the familiar scent of him, sent all of Harbin's strength flooding from him and he sank against Cavanaugh, feeling as if he was dreaming or had maybe finally lost his mind, because it felt too good to be real.

"Gods, I've been looking for you for five fucking years, you little bastard… where the fuck have you been?" Those words, growled in his ear with so much anger and affection, drained the last of Harbin's strength and he couldn't find his voice to answer.

He closed his eyes and hoped to the gods Hartt and Fuery were too busy arguing with Sable and Thorne about what had happened back at the Archangel facility to notice how pathetic he was acting, stripped of his strength by nothing more than a tight bear hug from his brother. The guild would laugh their arses off at him and his reputation as a merciless assassin would be shot if word got out about this.

The darker side of him said to push his brother away and remember what he was now, he was that merciless assassin with blood on his hands, but the softer part wanted to stay a little longer, absorbing what it felt like because he couldn't remember ever experiencing this. He felt wanted. Loved. Even when he knew he didn't deserve it.

Cavanaugh cleared his throat, released him and scrubbed a hand around the back of his neck. "We should probably go somewhere private to talk."

The awkward edge to his brother's pale eyes drew Harbin's focus back to the others in the room with them and he barely stifled his cringe as he realised that Hartt had witnessed the public display of affection. Thank the gods that Fuery was too busy growling and flashing fangs at the demon king, practically nose-to-nose with the massive brute.

The door in the back wall banged open again, throwing a brief burst of white light across the room.

"Hartt?" Silence descended as a soft female voice rose above the din and the tension already filling the air grew thicker.

Cavanaugh swung towards the source of the voice, shifting to one side of Harbin and revealing the female to him. Another elf. It was rare to see a female outside of the elf lands in Hell, and even rarer to see one stand with her head tipped up, radiating confidence in the company of so many males. Strength. This was one female who knew how to handle herself and the look in her violet eyes said she was considering dealing out some punishment to his boss for some reason.

If Harbin had to guess, he would say they had a history and that it hadn't ended well.

The elf female stepped further into the room, her fall of black hair brushing her shoulders and melting into the long black satin negligee she wore.

Harbin was about to look to Hartt for an explanation when all Hell broke loose.

The jaguar shifter roared, the strange sound echoing around the expansive nightclub, and launched himself at Hartt. Harbin swiftly sidestepped out of the path of the male, moving closer to his brother and readying his own claws. The jaguar slammed into Hartt, knocking him back a few steps, but his boss was quick to defend, blocking each fierce blow the sandy-haired male dealt.

Hartt teleported and appeared right in front of the female elf.

Harbin cringed. Was his boss insane? Was he trying to get himself killed? It was obvious to Harbin that the jaguar was mated to the female elf, and he was fairly sure Hartt knew it too. He was provoking the jaguar on purpose, but Harbin didn't have a damned clue why.

The jaguar roared again, the sound deafening in the heavy silence, and sprang towards Hartt, landing right behind the taller elf male, his eyes glowing dangerously in the low light. Hartt ducked to his left, dodging the blow the jaguar aimed at the back of his head, and twisted to face him.

Hartt actually smiled at his enemy.

Maybe Fuery wasn't the only mad bastard in the guild's ranks.

"How the hell do you know my mate?" the jaguar snarled and slashed with his claws, frustration rolling off him as Hartt dodged again, nimbly strafing to his left and coming around behind him.

"We were engaged once," Hartt said and it explained a lot, and also made the whole messed up situation reach boiling point.

"Kyter," the female elf snapped in a firm tone but her mate wasn't listening.

Kyter roared and kicked off, hurling a hard right hook at Hartt's face. Hartt went to dodge to avoid it and the jaguar moved with speed beyond what was possible for his species, catching the elf with a swift left that had him staggering sideways and growling. The noise level in the room rose as Hartt finally stopped evading Kyter and attacked him, landing several blows but receiving just as many as he dealt as they danced around the room.

Cavanaugh backed off and Harbin joined him, giving the two room to work out their differences.

The bitter scent of anger and frustration rolled from the blonde mortal female at the bar with the elf leader, growing stronger as the room grew louder. Whatever she and the elf were doing to Loke, they were trying to help him and the fight wasn't helping them concentrate. He looked back at Hartt and Kyter as they grappled with each other, tempted to intervene and give the mortal female a shot at helping the dragon shifter. He could sense Loke weakening and, as heartless as he tried to be, he didn't want to see the male die.

"You must stop disappearing like this, my prince." A male dressed in the black armour of the elves appeared close to the one Harbin had pegged as some sort of leader of their species and answered one of the questions that had been plaguing Harbin.

The male was a prince.

The prince.

The prince's hand tensed against the back of the mortal female's neck and she squawked. "I am sorry."

The new elf male huffed, but there was no anger in it, nor frustration. If anything, it sounded teasing to Harbin. Was this male a sort of babysitter for the prince? The two had to be close if the prince accepted the way he had spoken to him, chastising him in front of others in a manner that almost challenged his authority.

The female in the negligee pinned him with wide violet eyes. "Bleu?"

The male looked over his shoulder at her, his wild blue-black hair parting to reveal the pointed tips of his ears as he brushed it back from his face. Lights flashed over that face, and Harbin recognised it. Not a babysitter, but a commander. Harbin had crossed paths with the elf in the past and each encounter had left him with new scars.

He smiled grimly. He had given as good as he had got though, adding a few new scars to the male's collection. Elves weren't the only ones with weapons capable of cutting through their armour. Harbin's blades were made of the same material, a gift from Hartt the day he had proven himself as a member of the guild by eradicating three powerful fae and protecting injured comrades.

Bleu frowned at the female, and then turned on the spot, his gaze swinging towards the source of the commotion. It landed on Harbin, a brief flicker of recognition lit his violet eyes, and then he shifted his focus to Kyter and Hartt where they fought in the centre of the massive room.

Harbin sidestepped again when Kyter went flying past him, stumbling but not managing to keep his footing. The sandy-haired male landed on his back on the black floor, pressed his hands to the ground above his shoulders, and flipped back onto his feet. Golden fur rippled in waves over his arms, and he flashed fangs as he growled at Hartt, his eyes bright in the darkness.

Hartt was pushing his luck. If the male shifted, it would be difficult to defeat him.

"What did you do this time to get in deep shit with assassins, Io?" Bleu barked and the female elf looked mortified.

"I am not in trouble." She folded her arms across her chest and glared at Bleu. "Hartt is not here because of me."

Kyter landed a hard blow on Hartt's jaw and the elf staggered sideways and snarled at the jaguar through bloodied fangs.

His boss was going to end up needing to see the dentist if things continued, and Harbin wasn't sure it would end there. Fuery was prowling the side lines of the fight, his claws flexing as he watched the two males go at it. The Archangel huntress and her demon escort both looked as if they were considering joining in for the hell of it.

But most worrying was the look slowly dawning in Bleu's violet eyes, one that warned he was close to dealing with Hartt himself.

Harbin wasn't sure what would happen if Bleu made a move, but pandemonium sprang to mind. It would be all out war as both sides took it as a cue to join the fight.

"Oh, that is enough." The female elf huffed and disappeared in a burst of green-purple light, reappearing right between Kyter and Hartt, her long negligee swirling around her legs like black smoke.

She pressed her delicate palm to Hartt's armoured chest and he sailed across the room, slammed into the black wall to Harbin's right and landed with a grunt on the floor.

Kyter breathed hard beside her, each laboured one shifting his grey t-shirt and causing the long claw marks in the soft material to open and reveal flashes of bloodstained skin. His bright golden eyes locked on Hartt and then her. The dark abysses of his pupils widened, and Harbin could see the hunger in him.

His own animal side rose in response to it, the primal needs that had seized hold of him back at the Archangel facility coming back full force to fill him with a maddening need to shift and track the female snow leopard.

He *needed* her.

His chest heaved with that need and he struggled to remain where he was, battling his body as the ache to shift grew stronger and the voice deep within him commanded him to find the female. She was vulnerable and alone, left at the mercy of an organisation that had done terrible things to her.

He had left her there.

He had left her behind.

His brother's gaze landed on him, intense and focused, pulling his away from the exit. Cavanaugh's silver eyes questioned him and he knew his brother could sense the struggle within him and knew the source of it. It was his impending transition into sexual maturity that was triggering the need to find the female and nothing more.

Cavanaugh frowned at him, a flicker of something in his eyes that Harbin didn't like.

It was nothing more.

He looked away from his brother, unable to look at him when he was fighting the urge to hunt for the female.

Gods, he wanted to hunt her.

He wanted her.

The compelling need ran deeper in his blood than the usual urge to fight and fuck, and no matter how much he wanted to pretend it was otherwise, he knew it stemmed from more than hormones.

This need ran soul deep.

Cavanaugh's gaze on him intensified and he paused as he realised that he had been rubbing his chest through his t-shirt, soothing the aching spot directly over his heart.

Hartt pulling himself up off the floor gave his brother something else to focus on, releasing Harbin from the hold of his knowing gaze. Harbin dragged his focus back to the current situation too, aware that at any moment the fight might escalate and he would have to step in to help his friends. He had brought them to this place, and he was fucking damned if they were going to end up hurt because of him.

They were navigating dangerous waters, and he doubted there was a way to settle the dispute without more violence. He was always the first to pick a fight over diplomacy, but he also knew when to pick a fight. He scanned the gathered immortals, fae and mortals. The odds were against them.

His side were highly trained, and highly skilled, but then so was the enemy. An elf commander, an elf prince, a demon king and two huntresses from Archangel, were more than a match for him, Hartt and Fuery. When he added Kyter and the elf female, the scales were tipped in their favour.

He doubted Cavanaugh would fight on his side.

This nightclub was his home now, and snow leopards protected their homes and their prides.

Darkness welled in Harbin's stomach at that and he swallowed hard in an attempt to settle it as he tried to pretend that thought hadn't cut him to the bone and left him reeling. He had failed as a member of his noble species, but he wouldn't fail again.

Hartt and Fuery were his pride.

The guild was his home.

He would protect them both.

Bleu stared at Hartt, a troubled edge to his eyes that Harbin liked even less than the one that had been all about violence. He was trying to place Hartt, and Harbin knew enough about family to know that he was going to lose his shit when he realised who Hartt was.

Hartt locked his gaze on the female, wiped the back of his hand across his mouth, smearing blood over his cheek, and proved to Harbin that he was as mad as Fuery and had a death wish to boot. "If I had known you would turn out so damned beautiful, I might have married you after all."

Bleu's eyes widened in recognition.

Kyter roared and hunkered down, his muscles coiling and fur flashing over his exposed skin as he prepared to launch himself at Hartt.

Bleu was there before he could move a muscle, teleporting right in front of Hartt as he walked back towards the female. Harbin grimaced as Bleu's fist slammed into Hartt's face with so much force that the crack of bone was audible in the strained silence and Hartt flew across the room again. His boss growled and teleported, reappearing right in Bleu's face.

The male didn't even flinch.

He grabbed Hartt by the throat and shoved him away.

"Focus," the elf prince said to the mortal female and Harbin willed her to do it, because they were going to lose Loke if she didn't. Whatever they were doing, it had been making the dragon stronger, but now he was growing weaker again. "Bleu will handle this mess. Will you not, Bleu?"

"Yes, my prince." Bleu gave a stiff jerk of his head and a black blade appeared in his right hand.

Hartt flexed his fingers, his black scaled armour covering them and turning them into deadly claws.

This was not going to end well.

Bleu launched himself at Hartt and the two clashed, Hartt swiftly blocking Bleu's arm as he brought it down, his sword a black blur slicing through the colourful lights that filled the room near the bar where the elf prince and the mortal female worked on Loke.

The elf commander leaped back and attacked again, quicker this time, and Hartt didn't have time to block Bleu's arm with his own. The blade struck Hartt's forearm instead and he growled as it sliced through the armour, cutting into his flesh.

Harbin snarled and stepped forwards, and Cavanaugh's hand came down hard on his shoulder. He wanted to shirk his brother's grip, but he planted his bare feet to the floor instead, heeding his warning not to intervene.

Not yet anyway.

But if it looked as if Bleu would seriously injure Hartt, he was going to take the elf down and he wouldn't be alone. Fuery paced in the darkness, prowling there like a wraith, a terrible shadow ready to bring bloodshed and death to any who dared to stray into his path.

Bleu shoved Hartt in the chest and Hartt flew across the room. His back slammed into the bar near the mortal female, shaking the black wood and jostling Loke.

The female turned and pinned him with a furious look before sweeping her gaze around the room, her anger flowing from her in warning waves. "Will you all go in the other damned room or something. I'm trying to fucking concentrate!"

Hartt's violet eyes gained a guilty edge and he wasn't alone in his feelings. Everyone had stopped to look at her and all of them were now looking elsewhere.

All of them except Bleu.

"Take the fight elsewhere, Bleu," the elf prince snapped.

The male didn't listen to him. He glared at Hartt, his violet eyes darkening to a dangerous degree.

"Stay away from my sister, you assassin scum. I hear even a rumour that you merely looked at her in the wrong way and I will kill you. Tainted bastards like you deserve to be put down."

Shock washed across the female elf's face. "Tainted?"

"It's nothing." Hartt shoved away from the bar, avoiding her steady gaze.

His words had no effect on her. She continued to watch him with worry in her eyes and Hartt continued to pretend she didn't exist. Harbin had never seen his cool and collected leader so flustered. It didn't show on the surface, but he could see beneath that practiced façade. Bleu's words had rattled him, hitting too close to the mark.

Hartt shot him a glare. "Get a move on, Harbin, or we're leaving you behind."

Harbin could understand his sudden desire to leave. It wasn't only for his own sake, it was for Fuery's. Elves viewed the tainted as something that needed to be exterminated, a stain on their race. Hartt wasn't even close to being tainted, but someone else in the room was and his boss had just realised the danger that male was in.

Hartt teleported and reappeared next to Fuery in the shadowy side of the room, drawing Bleu's gaze there.

Harbin's muscles tensed, coiling in readiness as he waited for the elf to mention how tainted Fuery was and attempt to kill him. Not on his watch. He would take the elf out of action if he tried anything.

Bleu's violet eyes widened and the words that left his lips weren't ones filled with anger or hatred, but ones holding a wealth of shock that seemed to deal a blow to the elf who uttered them. "Commander Fuery? I thought you were dead."

Fuery's expression shifted on hearing his name, turning darker than usual, and the sensation of danger he radiated increased, warning that he was on the verge of attacking.

It didn't stop Bleu from taking a step towards him, the surprise that had been in his voice slowly painting itself across his face as he stared at Fuery.

Fuery snarled, hunger sparking in his black eyes, a dark need to spill blood. Bleu recognised him, but Fuery didn't seem to have a clue who he was. How did the elf commander know Fuery? Harbin looked to Hartt for an answer but his boss averted his violet gaze, fixing it on Fuery, a flicker of concern in it.

"How did you survive Vail's attack?" Bleu whispered and the elf prince turned to face the room, his hand falling away from the mortal female's neck as he stared across the room at Fuery, his stunned expression matching Bleu's.

Fuery remained silent, glaring at the two elves now, his fingers twitching at his sides. He wanted to attack, but he wasn't, and that stunned Harbin. Normally Fuery attacked first and asked questions later, a policy that Harbin had difficulty with since it usually meant they were trying to question a corpse. Why wasn't he attacking now, when Harbin could see he was desperate to lash out?

Did he know Bleu?

"What happened to you?" Bleu ventured another step towards him.

This time, Fuery reacted, but not as Harbin had expected. Rather than attacking, he backed away a step and threw a panicked look at Hartt, his black eyes gaining a wild edge as he shook his head, causing the longer strands of his blue-black hair to brush his neck. Hartt closed the small gap between them and placed his hand on Fuery's shoulder, and Harbin could only stare as the touch calmed him and he drew down a deep shuddering breath.

"The elf is tainted," the prince said and Bleu looked back at him. "The male you knew no longer exists, Bleu."

Bleu looked as if he didn't want to believe that, and it only left Harbin with more questions. Had they been close once, before whatever attack Bleu had mentioned? Vail. The name was familiar. Harbin racked his brain, trying to place it, and frowned when it came to him. Vail was the mad elf prince who had turned on his people. Hartt had told him about the male once, but he had made Vail sound more like a legend told to scare young elves than a real person.

The elf commander took another step towards Fuery.

Fuery responded by pulling his black blade from the air and snarling at him. Hartt shifted in front of Fuery, partially shielding him with his body and placing his hand over the one Fuery held his blade in, stopping him from attacking.

"Do you not recognise whose company you are in?" Bleu snapped and Fuery's dark gaze danced to the elf leader and back again. "Do you not recognise your prince?"

Fuery narrowed his black eyes on Bleu and growled words in the elf tongue. Harbin didn't know the language, but he caught a name.

Vail.

Bleu's expression twisted into darkness, long white daggers flashing between his lips as he snarled, "Your prince is standing in this very room, not roaming Hell bent on bloodshed and destruction. That wretched male is not your prince."

"Watch your tongue, Bleu!" the prince snapped, and it seemed Fuery wasn't the only one who still felt affection for a male that was apparently mad and evil, driven to kill all who stood in his path.

Bleu lowered his head, his unruly hair falling down to brush his forehead, and pressed his right hand to the black scales covering his chest. "My apologies, my prince."

Loke groaned and shifted, and Harbin's gaze leaped to him. The big dragon shifter stole all of the attention away from Fuery, but only held Harbin's for a few seconds, as long as it took for him to sense that he was stronger now. Safe.

He looked back at Fuery, focusing on him as Hartt worked to calm him. He had never realised before today just how much affection Hartt held for the tainted elf, but he could see it now as the male stroked his shoulder and hand and spoke to him in a low voice, slowly coaxing him back from the brink.

Was Hartt the only reason Fuery wasn't roaming Hell like the prince he admired, wreaking havoc and leaving a trail of blood in his wake?

Fuery lowered his hand and his shoulders sagged, his lips parting as his breath left him and the tension seemed to wash from his limbs. His black blade disappeared and Hartt glanced down to where it had been and then back at his face, saying something in the elf tongue that Harbin wished he could understand. He had always wondered about Fuery, but now he had more questions and now he needed to hear the answers to them. He wanted to know what had happened to push Fuery so close to the brink and propel him into life as an assassin.

"Harbin?" Hartt caught hold of Fuery's wrist. The elf lowered his eyes to it, the black slashes of his eyebrows rising as he stared at Hartt's hand, a distant look on his face. He blinked slowly and Harbin had the impression that he wasn't quite with them.

Hartt had told him once that sometimes Fuery lost the fight against the darkness, but that he always came back. Harbin could see now that his boss had been putting things too simply, skimming over some of the facts.

The darkness had swallowed Fuery, but it had been Hartt that had drawn him back to the light, and now Fuery looked lost and confused, as if he couldn't recall what had happened during the time he had been consumed by the darkness that lived inside him.

The worry shining in Hartt's violet eyes warned the calm wouldn't last, that Fuery would remember everything that had happened, and that was the reason his boss was suddenly so desperate to leave.

"I might be a while. Go on without me. I need to finish my mission and then I'll meet you," Harbin said, and nodded when Hartt looked relieved.

Hartt tossed one last look towards Bleu where he now stood beside his sister with Kyter at his side. Silvery light chased over him and Fuery and then he was gone. Bleu muttered something in the elf tongue, his gaze sliding towards Harbin, filled with a dark desire that Harbin recognised because he had felt that same hunger running in his blood countless times.

Bleu wanted to force him to leave too.

He wanted to attack him.

The prince responded, his tone equally black and threatening.

Harbin stepped forwards but Cavanaugh suddenly blocked his path. He looked up at his brother, expecting to find him protecting his friends.

He wasn't.

He stood with his bare back to Harbin and growled at the two elves, baring huge canines.

He was protecting him.

A wave of tingles raced over his skin, shooting down his spine, and he wasn't sure how to process everything that had happened in the last thirty minutes. He had come to this place expecting to find a bitter, angry male who wanted nothing to do with him. He hadn't expected to find a male who was unchanged by their years apart, still quick to defend him despite his failings.

Still protecting him. Still loving him after everything he had done.

"Enough. No more fighting." Kyter scrubbed a hand down his face and then over his wild sandy hair, his expression filled with weariness.

The elf female sidled closer to him and caressed his arm. He turned a frown on her but it melted away, softening as he lifted his hand and stroked her cheek. Her smile caused his eyes to darken, hunger surfacing in them, desire that had the female snow leopard dancing back into Harbin's mind.

His gaze strayed back to the exit as need flooded him again, a deep ache to find her.

He stared at the doors as the night called to him, his primal instincts urging him to seek her and see that she was safe. He needed to protect her. He needed her. She was vital to him, a piece of him that he had been missing his entire life, and with her he knew that he would be complete. A ridiculous notion, one he wanted to dismiss but found he couldn't. She was more than just another female. She was beautiful. No. She was breathtaking. She was power and vulnerability, grace and deadliness, and a whole range of entrancing impossibilities rolled into one incredible female.

He took a step towards the doors, driven to hunt her.

He would find her.

She would be his.

CHAPTER 11

Cavanaugh snagged Harbin's arm and he heard his brother talking, but couldn't make out the words as he was dragged across the low-lit main room of the nightclub, his eyes constantly fixed on the doors and his heart pounding with a need to find the female.

It was only when they passed through a door and it slammed shut, stealing the exit from view, that the urge shattered. Harbin looked around the bright white expansive back room of the club, slowly coming back to the world as the need to hunt faded.

Cavanaugh stared at him, a keen edge to his silver eyes, one that unsettled Harbin.

He would rather his brother exploded with anger and raged about the things he had done, and how he had disappeared for two decades, than face what he felt with a certain sense of impending doom was about to happen.

Conflict he could handle. Discussing the obvious reason behind why his focus kept slipping and drifting towards a specific location, he couldn't. He preferred to hold his personal business close to his chest, and his feelings even closer, beyond view of anyone, especially now they were coming back to life, roused by the female snow leopard.

He had expected meeting his brother again to cause the rising tide of his emotions to overwhelm him, bursting the barrier he had built around them. What he hadn't anticipated was the calm he felt in Cavanaugh's presence, a soothing sensation that eased him and seemed to ground him, instead of pushing him over the brink.

Rather than being swallowed in a dark flood of emotions, he floated on calm waters, drifting in the light.

Harbin glanced back towards the door, his thoughts returning to the female snow leopard.

She had the same effect on him, and he wasn't sure how to process that.

Even when he had been in the grip of the darkness that lived inside of him back in the Archangel facility, one look into her eyes, even the briefest of glances, had poured light into his soul and soothed him, giving him back control.

Cavanaugh took a step towards him, stealing his focus away from the female, and he caught the look in his brother's silver eyes, one that warned he was on the verge of bringing up something that Harbin couldn't bring himself to speak about, because that would mean acknowledging it.

That would make it real, and he wasn't sure he was ready for that, because it would cause a war to erupt inside him, a battle between the darkness born of his past and his vendetta, and the part of him that secretly strived towards the light.

A familiar smell sent relief coursing through him but it lasted only as long as it took the pretty snow leopard female to descend the staircase against the far wall of the white room.

Eloise rubbed her mussed chestnut hair, her golden-brown eyes hazy with sleep as she carefully took each step. "What was all the noise about?"

She reached the bottom step, yawned and tripped, her bare toes snagging in her loose baby blue pyjama bottoms and sending her tumbling forwards.

Cavanaugh was across the room in a heartbeat, catching her in his arms and drawing her close to his bare chest. She curled into him for a second before lifting her head and welcoming the soft press of Cavanaugh's lips against hers.

Harbin looked down at his bare feet and turned his cheek to them, trying to shut them out as the war he had feared erupted inside of him, flooding his mind with images of the female snow leopard who had betrayed him. The torrent swept him along, one moment flashing a replay of her as she spoke the words that had cut him to his soul, telling him that she had betrayed him, and the next making him relive the moment when he had kissed her.

She had tasted so sweet.

Had felt so fucking good in his arms.

He needed to know about her, and that was the real reason he had come to see Cavanaugh. He had wrapped it up in another cause in order to make it easier on himself, pretending he had come to Underworld purely to give his friends a safe place to rest and recuperate, because the darker part of himself still wanted to lash out whenever he thought about the female in any way other than as a mark.

A mission.

She had him twisted in knots, and he hated it. He had become accustomed to the darkness inside him, the emotionless state he had embraced in order to survive, in order to keep his past locked away and stop it from destroying him. Now she had awakened the light, had unleashed his emotions from their cage, and he was no longer sure how to proceed. That darker side wanted to destroy her instead now, hungered to take her and the Archangel huntress down.

He wanted to protect himself.

He couldn't handle what she had done to him. Luring him. Trapping him. Betraying him. He tunnelled his fingers through his silver hair and pulled it back, tugging so hard that it hurt. Gods, why couldn't he hate her as he hated the Archangel huntress?

Why did he feel as if he was walking towards his doom and he couldn't change his course, couldn't avert the disaster looming ahead of him, one that would annihilate him?

If he let her sneak into the heart he defended so vigilantly, she would have the power to destroy him.

Fuck, the part of him that wouldn't shut the hell up said that she had already done it. She had broken through that barrier. He couldn't stop thinking about her, couldn't control the craving he had for her or his need of her. Not even the terrible thing she had done was enough to make him hate her.

He wanted to hate her.

He wanted to shield himself from the pain he could feel coming and it was safer to hate her than to love her and have her take that and break him with it by throwing it back in his face.

Cavanaugh's steady gaze on him was joined by Eloise's, and he fought to pull himself out of the mire of his thoughts and regain his focus.

He needed to know about the female he had encountered, but that didn't mean he was going to let his guard down around her. He couldn't deny his need to know who she was, or the one that drove him to find her and set things straight with her so she would know the truth about Archangel and would be safe, but he could deny the urges running rampant through him and protect his heart.

Harbin lifted his head and looked at his brother, grimacing as he caught Cavanaugh petting Eloise again with a stupid sappy look on his face.

If anyone would know the members of their pride, Cavanaugh was that male. He had cared enough about his kin to take the time to know everyone, to understand the smallest things about them, all so he could converse with them on a daily basis. Cavanaugh had been born to be a leader of their pride, a male worthy of the role of alpha.

A male worthy of the mate he now held gently in his arms, whispering tender things to her that Harbin wished he couldn't hear, because they only stirred the primal need that had taken root within him, making him want to hunt the female he had left behind at Archangel.

He needed to find her, but first he had to understand more about her.

He needed to know who she was.

"Cavanaugh..." He waited for his brother to finally release his mate before sucking down a deep breath and pushing the words out. "I have to talk to you about someone."

"Someone?" Cavanaugh frowned and shifted to face him, and Eloise remained on the step beside him. Her hand slipped into his and Harbin glanced at them, feeling a sharp pang in his chest as he watched his brother's larger hand curling around hers, holding it tightly.

Gods.

Even something as stupid as that made him ache to see the female again. What the hell was wrong with him?

The voice that had been constantly whispering in his mind since first setting eyes on her murmured that he knew what was wrong with him, he was just afraid to acknowledge it.

He shut it out. The female was a mark, by her own choice, and had orchestrated a plan to capture him and put him into Archangel's hands. She wanted revenge and that made her dangerous. He had escaped, thwarting whatever plan she'd had for him, but he doubted he had seen the last of her. He needed to know more about her if he was going to convince her that she didn't want his head on the chopping block. She wanted Archangel's.

"A mark," he started.

Apparently that word didn't sit well with his brother because Cavanaugh's eyes darkened rapidly.

Maybe his brother hadn't believed the elves when they had called him and his friends assassins, or maybe he had thought only Hartt and Fuery operated in that line of business. It would be just like his brother to try to see some good in him and refuse to believe he was capable of spending his days killing others for profit.

"She's a mark... but she placed the contract on herself. Archangel captured her twenty years ago," he stumbled when Cavanaugh's expression shifted, pain flooding his handsome face as his silver eyes brightened, and shook off his own hurt in order to continue. "They harmed her and others, and then they fed her lies and she believes them. She thinks I sold her out."

He waited for either Cavanaugh or Eloise to say that he had in a way, but both of them remained silent as they looked at each other and then back at him.

"I need to know who she is… and I thought maybe you could help." Although, he wasn't sure that coming to Underworld had been such a great idea, because being around his brother was playing merry hell with him. Being near the female had been bad enough, reawakening the softer emotions that had no part in an assassin's life, but being around Cavanaugh was infinitely worse.

It took him back beyond twenty years, to a time when they had lived together in peace, enjoying life to the full. A brighter and better time, one he hadn't realised he missed until he had seen Cavanaugh and Eloise together again.

How many times had they all trekked from the village together, heading high into the mountains to shift and play chase, to burn some energy? How many times had they all crashed in front of a blazing fire afterwards, spent and tired from the exertion, and aching and sore from laughing so hard as they talked?

Gods, those days felt like a distant memory that belonged to someone else.

Something beautiful he had witnessed from the outside rather than experienced.

"Did you get a good look at her?" Cavanaugh's deep voice rumbled through the room and Harbin pulled himself back to it.

He nodded, keeping his features schooled and emotions locked away, because his brother was watching him closely and any slip would give away that he had done a lot more than just get a good look at the female in question.

"Jaw length silver hair, but she dyes it black. I'm guessing she wants to blend in and lay low. Silver-gold eyes. About this tall." He held his hand at around shoulder-height to him.

"She give you those?" Cavanaugh pointed at Harbin's right cheek.

He was touching the marks before he could stop himself, his focus slipping as he recalled her taste on his tongue and how warm and soft her body had felt against his.

"You're on the cusp."

Harbin snapped back to the room, ice blasting through his veins and cooling his hungers as his brother's words sank in and he met his silvery gaze.

It challenged Harbin to deny it, and he wanted to, but the words refused to leave his lips.

Cavanaugh sighed. "I wish I could help, but several females at the village had eyes like that and silver hair. I'm guessing you got more than a good look at her, so did she have any scars, any marks of any kind that would give me more to go on?"

Harbin frowned at the floor and pictured her. It didn't take much effort. The moment he thought about her, she popped into his head, wearing just her white underwear. Damn. He had loved the feel of her curves beneath his hands.

He hadn't realised he had growled until Cavanaugh was right in front of him, his left hand clamped down on his right shoulder. His brother hadn't done it to soothe him. He had done it to anchor him in place in order to protect Eloise. The slender female was tucked behind Cavanaugh, a wary look in her golden eyes.

She was safe. He wasn't interested in her. Fuck, he wasn't interested in any of the females he could smell in the club. There was only one that he wanted.

Her.

"She had a scar... here." He ran his index finger across his right collarbone. "It was old."

Cavanaugh turned pensive, silent for so long that hope began to build in Harbin's chest.

It faded when his brother shook his head. "I don't remember anyone with a scar like that. Maybe she picked it up after leaving the pride or kept it hidden."

Harbin exhaled hard. It was a lost cause then. He had been banking on his brother being able to tell him more about the female in the hope that he would be able to place her and remember her. His memories of his time at the pride were fragmented now, churned up so much that unless he had a specific one he wanted to recall, he couldn't get them to fall into order. Maybe he hadn't known the female before, but if he hadn't, why had she felt so familiar?

"She kept it hidden." Those words leaving Eloise's lips had him staring at her in stunned silence. She came out from behind Cavanaugh, moving to stand beside her mate. "I know her."

Gods, had his heart just done a ridiculous jump in his chest? "You do?"

Heat flooded him, hope carried with it, and he couldn't stop himself from inching closer to Eloise, eager to hear what she knew of the female.

"We played together and she got that scar falling out of the rafters of the barn when we were small." Eloise's soft pink lips tugged into a wistful smile. "Her name was... um..."

Harbin barely stopped himself from grabbing her shoulders and shaking the answer out of her.

"Aya."

He stumbled back a step as that name hit him, dragging him back beyond twenty years, to another twenty before.

It transported him to a small classroom and a boring lecture about snow leopards that he had been itching to escape. Cavanaugh had promised to take him into the mountains to hunt after his lessons and he had spent the day caught up in fantasising about it, eager for the day to be over.

He had been the snow leopard equivalent of an adolescent, appearing in his late teens to mortal eyes, but sixty years of age in reality.

He hadn't taken in much of what the teacher had been saying, talking about the phases of a snow leopard's life, from birth to sexual maturity and beyond. None of the class had been close to that stage in their lives, all of them at least four decades away from maturity.

He remembered her.

He remembered the fresh-faced and freckled daughter of their teacher and how her eyes had always sparkled like the pale sun suspended above their mountain home.

He remembered because she had been the first girl he had kissed.

Well, she had kissed him.

The bell had rung to signal the end of the day and they had been walking together. He could still feel the sun on his face and smell the crisp fresh snow on the ground. It had been one of the rare times she had walked with him back towards the village square, and she had talked to him this time rather than shuffling along in awkward silence.

She had asked whether he thought that not being sexually mature meant they couldn't have sex or wouldn't enjoy it.

She had blushed, he remembered that, because it had made him blush too. She had worded it in a way that had made it sound as if she had been talking about them having sex.

He hadn't given any thought to that sort of thing before that moment, but fuck, had he started thinking about it then.

They had walked a little deeper into the village, along the narrow alleyways between the older buildings at one end of it, with their pale stone ground floor and their upper floor with its crisp white panels surrounded by elegant carved dark wood. The mountain peaks that surrounded three sides of the village had shown between the low-angled wooden roofs of the buildings, reaching towards the clear blue sky and stealing the focus of his eyes, allowing his mind to wander a different path to his feet. When they had come close to the square, he hadn't been able to hold his tongue.

He had asked whether she thought they would enjoy anything intimate before they had matured.

She had countered his question by asking what sort of things.

And gods, he had said kissing, because kissing had been on his mind. There had been numerous couples in the village, and he had seen many of them kissing and his natural curiosity had always focused on it, making him wonder what it would feel like and why they did it.

He hadn't quite known what to do when she had looked around them at the empty alleys and then grabbed his hand, dragging him behind the stone base of the nearest building and pressing him against it. Her hands had scalded his chest through his jacket when she had leaned into him and tiptoed, and he hadn't been able to take his eyes off her lips as they had neared his.

His heart had been racing, blood thundering, and then she had set him on fire with a clumsy kiss that still had him burning forty years later.

It hadn't taken him long to find his feet and have her pinned against the wall, his body caging hers as he kissed her harder, desperate for more of her.

That time he had kissed her, she had welcomed it, wrapping her arms around him and tugging him closer.

He had bumped against her and snow had rained down his back, the icy chill nothing when he was burning from the fumbled kiss, losing himself in her.

Only the crunch of boots on compacted snow had broken them apart and she had hurried ahead of him down the alleyway. He had followed her home, seeing her there safe, before returning to his own one, still lost in a daze from the feel of her kiss and the urges she had awoken in him.

Fuck, he had dreamed of that kiss for weeks. He had wanted to do it a thousand times over again and had gone to school every morning filled with the hope he would see her again and she would let him kiss her.

She had avoided him though, always fleeing whenever he found her alone, and in the end he had been nothing more than a typical teenage boy. She hadn't wanted to kiss him, she had made that clear with her behaviour towards him, and so he had found a female who did.

He had embraced the passion she had unleashed in him, working his way from kissing and fumbled touches to bedding the females who approached him, all of them eager to attempt to secure a place of power within his family by securing him as their mate. He hadn't been interested in a mate, or anything resembling a relationship. He had been consumed by lust and a desire to learn more, to sate his needs, and he had. Being immature, he hadn't been able to impregnate the females, so he had slept with them freely, not thinking about whether they were interested in more than sex with him because he wasn't interested in anything beyond fucking them.

When he had grown bored of the females in the village, he had started heading down into the town, sleeping with the mortal females there, knowing he couldn't impregnate them either so he could do as he pleased with zero consequences.

Or so he had thought until the fateful night the Archangel huntress had set her sights on him.

Harbin scrubbed a hand down his face and groaned as he realised that Aya had spent twenty years seeing him chasing other females after she had been the one to give him his first kiss.

He hadn't really given any thought to how it might hurt her but he suspected now that it had, and that hurt had made her an easy target for Archangel's lies.

Gods, she had to hate him.

Despise him.

It was a lost cause, but he couldn't deny his need to find her and explain, to make her see that he hadn't sold her out. He couldn't deny his need of her.

It was primal and deep, the call of the wild, and it demanded things of him that he had no right to feel or desire.

Not when there was zero hope.

He had made sure of that by whoring himself in the village with the pride females and down in the town with the mortal ones.

He had made his bed and now he would have to lie in it, alone, forever.

A female like Aya would never want a male like him. She could never forgive his sins. She could never love him.

Because he didn't deserved to be forgiven or loved.

Harbin watched as Cavanaugh tucked a rogue strand of hair behind Eloise's ear and lingered with his fingers on her neck, his silver gaze soft with love and flooded with warmth. Eloise lifted her hand and placed it over his, holding it against her as she turned her head, closed her eyes and pressed a kiss to the heel of his palm.

Harbin shut his eyes and tried to stifle the pain as the past and the present clawed at him, ripping away the softer parts and leaving his chest hollow and cold again.

He didn't deserve what Cavanaugh had.

He didn't deserve a fated female, the one female in the universe meant solely for him, and the only one he could truly bond with to forge a connection that most snow leopards could only dream of because finding your mate was more than merely rare. It was almost impossible.

Male snow leopards searched the globe for their fated one, and most never found her.

His had been in front of him all along and he had been too blinded by lust, too overwhelmed by desire, to see her, and now she was lost to him.

His animal side cried out and he couldn't contain the pained roar that left his lips, a call filled with the yearning that had been growing inside him, one he felt sure was going to consume and destroy him.

A call for his mate.

A call for Aya.

CHAPTER 12

Aya paused mid-step and looked back along the alleyway between the brick buildings, sure she had sensed someone behind her. No one was there. She waited a few seconds more, studying the shadows of the quiet London side street, and then started walking again, heading towards the main road that would take her to her small apartment. She pulled her thick grey wool jacket closed over her mulberry jumper, folding her arms across her chest, and kept her head down as she walked, her leather boots loud in the silence of the night.

It wasn't the first time she'd had the unsettling sensation since making her excuses and leaving the Archangel facility.

The first time had been that same night, a few hours after Harbin, the dragon, and many other prisoners had escaped, Rocky included. She might have had a hand in helping some of them, but Archangel didn't need to know that. They had been a little too happy for her to leave after questioning her, and she suspected they were going to be watching her for a while, so she had been keeping her distance from Switch and any of the escaped fae and immortals.

At first, she had put the odd sensation down to them tailing her, but she had sensed no one near her. When she had studied the feeling, setting aside her fear that Archangel were coming for her and those she cared about, she had discovered something unsettling.

It wasn't a sense that she was in danger. It didn't stem from the feeling that someone was stalking her.

It tugged at her animal side, making it restless, and that was why she had automatically associated it with her being in danger.

When it was quite the opposite.

Her snow leopard side was drawn to the source of the sensation, so much so she had awoken last night to find herself standing at the window of her bedroom, on the verge of lifting the sash.

She had wanted to shift and drop to the pavement below, had ached with a need to seek the origin of the call that drummed in her blood and lured her to it.

Harbin.

Gods damn him.

She hadn't anticipated this. It was a complication she didn't need, not when her head was already tied in knots, her thoughts still tangled. It felt impossible to find the end of the right thread, the one she could pull to make the whole ball unravel so she could finally know what to believe.

She hadn't found the courage to question Archangel about what they had told her all those years ago or the huntress who had been the one to meet with her, but she was beginning to believe Harbin. Little by little, day by day, that belief grew and the faith she'd had in Archangel weakened.

Little by little, the need for answers grew too, and more than once she had found herself standing outside Underworld, staring at the sign and considering going in. She hadn't lied to Rocky when she had said she avoided the club because a snow leopard shifter worked in it and she had wanted to stay away from him, but she hadn't exactly told him the entire story.

Harbin's brother was the snow leopard shifter, and until recently he had been the alpha of her pride.

She wasn't sure that he would recognise her, but she feared that he would or that Harbin had been in contact with him and that he would try to detain her.

Harbin was still in London.

She knew it because if he had left the city, she would no longer feel drawn to him. The compulsion to find him would have faded as the distance between them had grown, until it had finally died completely.

He wasn't staying at Underworld though, or at least he hadn't been there the times she had ended up outside it, because she hadn't felt him nearby. The closer she came to him, the stronger the pull towards him grew. It was part of the reason she couldn't face him in order to get the answers she needed. It was too dangerous. The pull she felt towards him was already strong while the distance between them was no doubt great. If she was in his presence, it would be unbearable.

She wasn't sure she would be able to control her primal urges and she was damned if she was going to surrender to them and to Harbin.

His kiss had rocked her, shaken her world all over again, but she wasn't going to make the same mistake twice and believe it had meant anything.

The last time she had stood outside Underworld, she had caught his scent though.

Aya paused again, the memory of his smell flowing through her, the masculine mix of spice and snow warming her despite her best efforts to not allow it to affect her.

Gods help her. She wished Harbin would leave the city and release her from his wicked spell, because she wasn't sure how much more she could take. She hadn't been prepared for how deeply seeing him again would affect her, turning her world and her feelings on their axis and leaving her thinking about him almost constantly.

Dreaming about him.

The nightmares of her past no longer haunted her sleep. He did. A vision of sensuality and danger, an alluring and tempting male that she never quite found the will to resist. If she couldn't resist him in her dreams, how could she expect to do so in reality if their paths crossed?

His kiss had shocked her, had made her realise just what he was to her, and she had wanted to flee in that moment, to run and not look back. She still wanted to run away, even as the rest of her wanted to run towards him. She wasn't strong enough to deal with this turn of events. He had crushed her heart once and it had never completely recovered from that blow. She wouldn't risk it again, because she feared this time the damage would be devastating and permanent.

But she still needed answers, or she was going to go mad. She had to know whether he had been telling her the truth and Archangel had used and betrayed him.

Maybe she could call Underworld and ask to speak with Cavanaugh. That way she would get her answers, and she would remain safe.

Although, she wasn't sure how honest Cavanaugh would be with her. He had been her pride's alpha, a position where he had been responsible for being truthful to his kin and open with them, but he was also Harbin's brother. There was a high chance that the behaviour towards his kin that had been ingrained in him wouldn't stop him from doing all in his power to protect his brother. There was a chance he would lie in order to pull her into the web of deceit Harbin had spun and snare her so that male could find her.

Because he was hunting her.

She knew it in her heart, sensed it during the times she felt compelled to find him. He had been close to her every time.

Watching her from a distance.

She was his mark, but more than that, she had hurt him and she was beginning to understand that he had grown into a male who embraced vengeance over walking away. The pride had taught the latter, instilling a desire for peace in all of its members, and Harbin had turned his back on that.

He had changed dramatically, transforming into the dangerous male now after her.

An assassin.

Because of Archangel?

She had to know the answer to that question, because she felt she was going to go mad if she didn't get it. She couldn't allow her fear of Harbin finding her and what she might do if it happened to control her moves and her thoughts. Cavanaugh was a good male, and as much as he loved his younger brother, he wouldn't hand her over to him. He had proven himself a male who preferred to take the peaceful route over the violent, and a male who would never place a member of his pride in danger.

He would protect her from whatever plan Harbin had for her if she went to him.

He was no longer the alpha, but he was still the male she had known her entire life, one dedicated to protecting others.

She hoped.

The tiny seed of doubt took root in her mind and began to grow. Cavanaugh had left the pride. She had heard the rumours. He had left it in the hands of a male unworthy of the position of alpha and many had suffered. He had allowed his people to come to harm.

A chill went through her.

He might do the same to her.

She pushed back against her doubts and drew down a deep breath to steady herself.

She also knew that Cavanaugh had had a good reason for wanting to free himself of the role of alpha, one she couldn't hold against him.

Although, phoning the nightclub still sounded more appealing than risking her neck.

Or her heart.

Aya mounted the steps of her apartment building, slid her key into the lock of the main glass door, and twisted it at the same time as pushing it open. A low lit hall greeted her, not the cleanest of spaces, but it was home. She trudged up the stairs to her floor, her thoughts stuck on repeat, replaying the terrifying moment when Archangel had broken with their plan and had lifted the barrier between her and Harbin, allowing him to charge into her side of the room.

She had thought her number was up, that he was going to kill her, and then he had been kissing her.

Gods, he had kissed her.

It had been almost forty years since their first fumbled kiss, and she had been close to many other males in that time, but no kiss had made her burn as Harbin's did. He set her body on fire with only a brush of his lips and had her resolve melting, her limbs turning to rubber, when he turned up the heat and his kiss grew more demanding.

She warmed inside and lost herself for a moment, forgetting where she was, transported back to that room and the way his hard body had caged her and his lips had mastered her—body and soul. Gods help her.

She shook herself out of her daze and pushed on, striding down the narrow dark corridor to her apartment door. She opened it, stepped inside and pressed her back to the door as it closed behind her, her breath leaving her on a sigh. She had to pull herself together. She was stronger than this.

Harbin was an enemy, a danger to her, and the quicker she realised that, the better. She couldn't trust him. He made a living deceiving people in order to kill them. He wasn't the male she had grown up with, the one who had never stopped smiling and had relished every challenge the mountains had thrown at him, tackling it with glee. He was no longer carefree and full of light and laughter.

He was darkness embodied, dangerous and deadly, a shadow of the male he had once been.

He would kill her, because she was a job to him. That was the only reason he had followed her into Archangel. It hadn't been to protect her and ensure that she was safe, not as a male of his status should have behaved. It hadn't been to be near to her and comfort her to ease her fears, as a lover would have chosen.

It had been to be near to her so he could find an opportunity to end her.

Aya turned, flicked all the locks and slid the chains into place, and kicked off her boots. She shirked her jacket as she turned away from the door in her dark apartment and tossed it over the back of her couch to her left, and tugged her jumper off. The air was chilly in the apartment, her grey t-shirt offering her little protection from the cold, but she didn't care. She was used to temperatures far below what London felt even in deepest winter.

Her gaze roamed to the clock above the TV on the far wall, her sensitive eyes able to make out the hands in the darkness. It was late, already creeping into the next day. She yawned as her strength faded, the constant adrenaline rush of walking the streets and being on alert for both Archangel and Harbin leaving her drained and weary.

She glanced at the couch and TV to her left, and then at the door in the wall to her right, and couldn't stop her feet from carrying her towards it. Bed was too appealing, even when she knew she wouldn't find the rest she needed. Harbin would haunt her sleep, and she would wake feeling more fatigued than ever, but it would end tonight.

Tomorrow, she would call Cavanaugh and she would make him tell her everything.

She would finally discover the truth.

She stripped off as she walked into her bedroom, leaving her clothes in a trail on the floor, and grabbed her small cream satin nightie as she passed it where it lay strewn on her dressing table. She slipped into it, yawned again, and flopped onto her bed. The thick duvet was a comfort, cushioning her and immediately making the tension flow from her limbs.

Another yawn pushed free and she sank into her bed, her focus slipping as sleep caught hold of her and pulled her down into the darkness.

She would talk to Cavanaugh tomorrow, she would learn the truth about that night twenty years ago, and then she would ask him to speak with his brother and convince him to drop his mission.

The comforting arms of sleep wrapped around her and she drifted in them for a time, suspended in the peaceful darkness, her mind slowly emptying.

Harbin refused to leave it.

He wavered in front of her, staring at her as he had in the room, dressed in only a black pair of trunks, his body on full display for her eyes. They delighted in roaming his compact muscles as they flexed beneath his skin, barely an ounce of fat on him, all lean power that called to her most feminine instincts.

Wild silver hair begged her fingers to brush through it, to tease it with a soft caress before tugging on it, giving him a brief flash of pain and her strength.

Sharp silver eyes locked on her, intense and focused, drilling into her and heating her wherever they touched. They drifted over her, the black chasms of his pupils growing wider as he lowered his focus to her breasts and then the swell of her hips.

Hunting her.

Her every instinct screamed it at her, but it didn't make her scared this time.

It thrilled her.

There was desire in that look, hunger that matched her own, or maybe even surpassed it. It was need that spoke to her, coaxed her into taking a step towards him. His eyes darted up to hers, widening slightly before narrowing into a wicked look, one that made her heart skip a beat and then thump ever harder against her chest, until her head swam and she felt sure she would pass out.

He advanced on her, each slow step ratcheting up the heat flooding her veins, fanning the embers of her desire back into an inferno that burned her resolve to ashes.

Long, powerful legs easily ate the distance between them, each stride coming faster, until he was running at her.

She pressed back against the cool wall, her breaths coming quicker too, until she was panting, aching for him to reach her.

He stretched out a hand to her and disappeared as the room melted away, blinding white light drowning it out.

Aya turned, breathing hard, her eyes darting around as she searched for Harbin.

Only empty white greeted her wherever she looked, blurring together into nothingness.

Hot breath fanned across her neck, a thousand tingles dancing down her spine in response and making her shudder in pleasure.

She tried to turn but strong hands clamped down on her upper arms, freezing her in place. She struggled and then gave up the fight, moaning as he stepped into her, his lean muscular body pressing against her back, his groin nestled against her bottom.

Naked.

She felt exposed and vulnerable, but it lasted only a heartbeat, the time that it took for him to lower his lips to her neck and press a kiss to the nape.

A groan escaped her as her eyes slipped shut, hot pleasure rolling down her spine. He moaned with her, his breath moist on her skin, cranking up the bliss flowing through her. His fingers tightened against her arms and he moved closer, and her eyes shot open as she felt the hot, hard press of his cock against her lower back.

His deep, guttural groan of pleasure as he dipped his body and rubbed himself against her had her eyes falling closed again and her breath rushing from her as her body heated, burning at a thousand degrees. Fire blazed in her belly and lower, and she couldn't stop herself from arching her back and grinding against him.

One callused hand slid around her front, coming to cup her left breast, and she gasped and then moaned as he palmed it before thumbing her nipple, sending sparks shooting outwards from the stiffening peak. The heat travelled lower, turning her body liquid. She wriggled her hips, feeling the slide of desire between them, her need that she knew he could sense, because she could feel his too.

It wasn't just the demanding press of his cock between her buttocks that told her of it. It ran deeper. In her blood.

In her soul.

Her male hungered, and gods, she hungered too.

He growled, the sound sending another thrill through her, and she didn't stop him when he grasped her hair with his right hand, lifting it away from the nape of her neck and pinning it against her head, forcing it forwards. She whimpered as he tongued her nape and teased with a swift brush of blunt fangs. The slickness between her thighs grew with each sensual glide of his mouth over that spot, each wicked tease that tortured her and had her writhing against him, aching with her need.

His left hand dropped from her breast and trailed lower, and she willed it onwards, over her rounded belly to the point where she needed him. His masculine groan of pleasure as he sucked on her neck, thrust his thick cock between her buttocks, and skirted the thatch of silver hair between her legs made her knees weaken and her breath come quicker still.

She opened her mouth to utter his name, to beg him to give her what she needed from him.

His fingertips brushed lower, briefly dipped between her wet folds and pressed against her aroused nub.

She barked out a moan as bliss rippled through her and then growled as he stole it away, removing his hand from between her thighs.

His answering growl made her quiver and melt, and rub against him, desperately coaxing him into surrendering to his desire.

She gasped when he grabbed her left thigh and yanked it up, exposing her to the air that had suddenly turned frigid.

She opened her eyes and they widened as she took in the familiar mountains towering over her and the endless pristine snow. She didn't feel the cold as she stared at her frigid homeland. The heat of his body kept it from hers. His hips slid lower and her breath hitched as his lips stilled against the nape of her neck and she felt the press of his fangs. Her primal instincts warned what was coming, and a trickle of fear ran through her.

The blunt head of his cock nudged between her thighs.

The sharp points of his fangs pressed against her neck, in the spot where he would bite when he claimed her as his mate.

He growled.

Aya shot up in bed as her instincts blared an alarm, and it took her a moment to gather her senses and realise that it wasn't the threat of Harbin claiming her as his mate that had awoken her.

She shrieked and rolled off the left side of the bed as a man clad in black made a lunge for her, landed hard on her knees on the floor and shot to her feet.

Another male closed in on her, and neither smelled of Archangel.

They smelled of death.

Aya's heart burst into overdrive and she turned towards the sash window and shoved it up so hard that the glass fractured. She didn't hesitate as the cold night air rushed into the room. She pressed one foot to the sill and leaped out of the window, plummeting towards the hard tarmac in the alley below.

The shift was swift to come, fur rippling over her skin as her bones distorted, pain rushing through her as they shrank or grew, cracking as they formed new shapes. Her tail sprang from the base of her spine, her nose flattened and grew wider, and her ears turned rounded and moved upwards as her shift completed, turning her into a sleek snow leopard.

She twisted in the air, the wind whipping through her thick silver fur as she dropped, seeking a perfect landing.

She wasn't quick enough.

She cried out as she landed hard on the quiet road, fire sprinting up her limbs.

She had to run.

Aya kicked off and whimpered again as her right hind leg protested. She gritted her sharp teeth and growled through the pain. She couldn't let it slow her down. The men would be coming for her, and death would be swift to follow.

Witches.

She would know their rank scent anywhere.

Many of their kind used hers in potions and spells, claiming their parts made the most potent ones.

The most dangerous ones.

She had learned to identify witches for that reason, not wanting to cross paths with them. She left whenever one ventured near her, slipping away before they noticed her, and avoided the fae towns where they peddled their spells.

Aya looked back up at her window.

These two felt different to the ones she had run into before though.

Darker.

More dangerous.

She had to move fast.

She lowered her gaze to the alley and froze.

The two males stood before her, identical in every way, from their long black coats that concealed their bodies to their inky black hair, and their faces and haircuts.

Twins.

No wonder her instincts were screaming they were more dangerous than any witches she had encountered before.

Twins shared magic, able to tap into each other, doubling the vast power at their disposal. They were feared by all, even other witches. When one twin was injured, the other only grew stronger, siphoning more of their sibling's magic. The magic wanted to save itself, and would desert the weaker host, seeking the stronger one, making them even more formidable. In an attempt to protect itself, it would end up giving the stronger twin so much power that they would be able to heal their sibling without weakening themselves, giving them the ability to attack with multiple spells at the same time as they tended to their twin. Once the injured sibling was healed, the magic would split evenly between them again, until the next time one was wounded.

It was a terrible cycle of power, an infinite circle that couldn't be broken, not even through death.

Twins had the power to become necromancers.

Raisers of the dead.

The two males stared at her, blue eyes glowing faintly in the darkness, a shimmering corona of blood around their jagged pupils warning her that she was dealing with such witches.

Aya turned tail to run the other way.

A third male stood before her.

His red eyes narrowed on her.

Her body shifted against her will, her bones blazing with crippling fire. She cried out again, the sound more human now as her face morphed back despite her attempts to hold her snow leopard form. Pain ricocheted through her, stealing her breath, and she shook from head to toe as the shift completed. She tried to move her hands but they felt as heavy as her head and all she could do was breathe and stare at the male with the red eyes.

Triplets.

It wasn't possible.

The magic they shared would be vast. Infinite.

She managed to press her right hand to the tarmac but her strength failed her as she attempted to push herself up off it.

The male made a clucking noise with his tongue, as if her feeble attempts displeased him.

What did he want with her?

Footsteps sounded behind her, the other two males closing in. She kept her focus on the one in front of her, because he was the one in command.

The look in his eyes said that whatever they wanted, it would make the three years she had spent in captivity at Archangel look like a picnic.

Her eyelids grew heavy and fatigue rolled through her, swiftly followed by panic as she tried to remain awake. She couldn't let them take her. She had to escape somehow.

She just wasn't sure how.

Her eyes slipped shut again.

A scream pulled her back to the world and she stared blankly at the fight in front of her, a frenetic blur of black and silver that she found hard to follow when her mind was foggy and heavy, and sleep kept tugging her back towards the darkness.

A male bellowed in agony and she smelled blood, rich with a tang of magic. Witches. Twins. They were fighting someone. She had to escape the twins before they noticed. Her primal instincts whispered to her, correcting her and rousing her from her stupor.

Not twins.

Triplets.

If two were fighting, one was elsewhere.

She pushed back against the desire to sleep and screamed when she saw male hands on her, pulling her onto her back and revealing a face to her. Handsome and lean, topped with neat dark hair. Shadows played in the contours of his face, but the darkness that clung to him couldn't hide one thing from her.

Red eyes.

The leader.

A burst of strength went through her and she lashed out, slamming the flat of her palm into his face with as much force as she could manage. He grunted as it connected with his jaw and knocked him backwards, forcing him to release her.

She sprang to her feet and ran for the wall, the pain in her twisted ankle forgotten as she made a break for it. He spat out something dark in the language of the demons and his boots sounded on the tarmac. Her pulse accelerated and she leaped, hitting the brick wall ten feet up. She kicked off, twisted in the air and shot towards the other building across the narrow alley.

Her bare feet struck it first and she kicked off again, propelling herself upwards. The roof was close now. If she could reach it, she might be able to escape.

Freedom was so close that she could taste it.

She hit the wall, twisted and leaped again, gliding effortlessly towards the top of the second building. She sailed over the low wall surrounding the flat roof, landed and rolled, coming up onto her feet.

Freedom looked a lot like death.

Tall, wicked and terrifying.

Aya had a flash of her dream, felt a ghost of fangs against the back of her neck, and her body betrayed her, heating in response, aching for the male stood before her.

He breathed hard, his chest heaving beneath his tight black t-shirt. The black fatigues and boots he had paired his top with caused him to blend into the night, little more than a deadly shadow. Only the moon outlined him, highlighting his wild silver hair and turning his skin pale. His right cheek bore more scratches than the ones she had placed on it when he had kissed her and a trickle of blood ran down to his jaw as she stared at him.

Her eyes widened. Silver and black. He had been the one fighting the two witches in the alley.

Her breath left her in a rush. It wasn't possible that he had come charging in like some white knight to protect her. He wanted her dead.

Didn't he?

"I killed one... but they'll be coming back for you," he growled in a thick deep voice that did funny things to her insides, making her quiver and forget that she was meant to be afraid of him.

He was her mate. Her male. Her fated one.

Hers.

She shoved that stupid notion and the instinct that had birthed it away, determined not to become a victim and lose her life because she had been muddled by the primal needs coursing through her. Harbin was her mate, she couldn't deny that, but he wasn't hers.

He was just an assassin looking to claim her head and probably a nice fat pay off in exchange for it.

That was the only reason he had stopped those witches. He was protecting his interests, not her.

He shattered that belief.

"You're not safe here anymore."

Aya could only stare at him, struggling to take that in and make sense of it. He wanted her safe?

He had been watching over her and had revealed himself the moment she had been in trouble, rushing in to protect her, battling males who could have easily killed him and sold him for parts on the black market.

For her.

She shook her head, wanting to deny it, but it was there in his silver eyes. His expression was devoid of emotion, revealing nothing to her, as cold as a glacier and just as forbidding, but his eyes betrayed him and told her everything. He had wanted to protect her.

He still wanted to protect her.

"I'm sorry," he whispered and she frowned.

She was about to ask what part of the Hell she had been through he was apologising for when he raised his hand to his mouth.

She heard a soft puff of air.

Felt the sharp sting in her neck.

Saw the world twirl into darkness.

The last thing she knew before oblivion swallowed her was Harbin's scent of spice and snow, and the warmth of his arms around her.

A muttered curse.

And the soft press of his lips to the spot on her neck where the dart had struck.

CHAPTER 13

Harbin had been tracking Aya for the past two nights, watching her from a distance and studying her every move. She followed a routine, leaving late in the evening and heading towards the Underground station close to her small apartment in what he could only describe as one of the more unsavoury regions of London.

That was being kind.

He had visited places in Hell that were safer and cleaner.

The first night he had hunted her down, locating her in what he now knew was her favourite restaurant in the neighbourhood, he had wondered what the fuck had made her move into such a rough area.

It hadn't taken him a long time spent perching on the corner of the roof of a building and watching the locals moving around the streets below to realise why she had come to this place.

Fae and other species lived here.

Her instincts as a snow leopard were driving her to find others similar to her in an effort to feel as if she was part of a pride. That instinct rode him sometimes too, when he was away from the guild for weeks on end, driving him to return to the place his primal side had decided was home now and the people it viewed as his new pride.

He sighed and tracked her as she walked, huddled into her thick grey coat, braced against the cold.

Odd that she felt it so keenly having been raised in the mountains.

He canted his head and hunkered down, balancing on his toes and resting his elbows on his knees. Life in the mortal cities had made her soft. It had changed her.

Life in Hell had changed him too, but where she had softened, he had hardened. He could walk naked in the snow and not feel the cold. He could walk across fire and not feel the burn. He had mastered his body, had gained complete control over his emotions and decided what he felt.

But she had broken that hold, and now he found himself coming to this same rooftop every night to watch her carrying out her life, running through her routine.

First a stop on the steps of her red brick apartment building to button her coat over a heavy wool jumper, the colour of which changed each night.

Tonight, it had looked like blood to him.

Then she moved off, heading towards the central hub of the area she called home, stopping at her favourite restaurant.

He hadn't realised she was partial to Italian food.

But he did remember now that she was fond of food in general. It was the bane of his species. Living in a freezing climate meant they would have had to consume vast amounts of calories if they had been mortal, but they were shifters. Their metabolism ran at a faster pace, meaning they had to eat almost double the amount a mortal in such low temperatures would have to consume to remain alive.

He had shaken his instincts to eat hearty meals when he had moved into the guild, slowly adjusting to the warmer climate.

It seemed Aya hadn't quite adjusted enough.

She made her way through a huge plate of pasta each night, together with bread and other accompaniments.

And dessert.

He smiled.

She always had loved sweet foods.

His smile faded as that thought came out of nowhere, hitting him head on and rattling him. What the fuck was he doing?

Why did he come here every night to watch her?

He scrubbed a hand down his face.

Because he couldn't stay away.

He tried every night, heading out in a different direction, mixing up what he did when he was out in the city, even ending up in front of one of the portals that would take him back to Hell if he uttered the right words.

No matter what he did, he always ended up back here, watching her.

Fuck, he had even tried hitting a fae strip club.

That had lasted around a minute.

The amount of time it had taken him to glance at every female present and realise none of them were a patch on Aya.

He growled and shoved his fingers through his hair, tugging it hard. How many times was he going to have to remind himself that she had tricked him into tracking her down by placing a contract on her own head, just so he would end up in Archangel's hands?

She had betrayed him.

He had vowed that he would talk with her, ensuring she knew the truth about the people she had trusted, the ones who had tortured her for years and poisoned her mind with their lies, and then, well, he wasn't sure what happened then.

Either he killed her or he gave her a chance to cancel the contract and walked away.

He was sure that once he was back in Hell, his arse on the line in another mission, that he would soon forget about her and his life would return to normal.

Killing, healing and then fucking whatever piece of arse took his fancy. Rinse and repeat.

His heart whispered treacherous words and he tried to ignore them, but they refused to go away, circling his mind like vultures bent on picking at a carcass.

His carcass.

The one that had been devoid of a soul for years, following a meaningless routine. The death and the pain had been glorious, had made him feel alive. Screwing a stranger in some grimy back alley just to scratch the biological itch that rode him ever harder as he came closer to sexual maturity while avoiding experiencing even a hint of intimacy? That had left him feeling dead inside.

Females were bitches though. Betrayers. He had learned that lesson and he wasn't going to put himself through that again. Never. He couldn't control the urge to fuck, but he could control how it went down, and it went swift, hard and without any intimate contact. Just the way he liked it.

A flash of Aya in the room at Archangel, her white strapless bra and panties stark against her creamy skin, and her entrancing eyes fixed on him, had him instantly hardening in his trousers. He palmed his rigid cock, cursing her name and his lack of control. He wouldn't get involved with her. Never.

He couldn't trust her. She had proven that to him. She had set a trap for him and he had fallen right into it. She had given him over to the people who had destroyed his life without hesitation, and he would make her pay for that.

He gritted his teeth and pressed his palms against his knees, his fingers curling over and claws digging in. His eyes narrowed on Aya as she walked the main road of her neighbourhood.

She had played him, and now he would make her regret it. He would show her how wrong she had been about Archangel and he wouldn't stop telling her all the gory details of his past, all the horror he had witnessed that night, until she broke down and showed him she regretted what she had done.

Just as he regretted his actions.

If he had to live with his sins, then she had to live with hers.

He might have accidentally placed her into the hands of Archangel twenty years ago by allowing one of their members to play him for a royal fucking idiot, but she had turned around and done the same to him.

And she had known exactly what she had been doing when she had thrown him to the wolves.

Cavanaugh's deep rumbling voice echoed around his mind. Harbin focused on it, allowing the words to soothe his darker side now just as they had when his brother had spoken them during a private talk back at Underworld. Cavanaugh had been kind to him since he had walked back into his life, treating him gently and with great care, but he had been firm about one thing.

Giving Aya a chance.

It had taken some convincing to get Harbin to agree to that, his brother countering every point he tried to make, forcing him to look at it from the other side. Her side. Cavanaugh had given him a lot to think about, and in the long quiet day that had followed it, when he had been alone in his temporary quarters in the nightclub, Harbin had done just that.

It had led him back to the feeling he'd had in the Archangel facility, the need to make Aya see the truth and free her from Archangel's clutches, breaking their hold on her mind.

He sighed and watched her. Small. Weak. She needed his protection, and as much as his darker side wanted to punish her for what she had done to him, he couldn't allow his bitterness to stop him from seeing to her safety.

He couldn't allow himself to think of her actions as a betrayal.

Archangel had deceived her. It had deceived him.

He had to stop following her, watching her from a distance, and confront her. He had to face the fear that he might not be strong enough to control himself around her, unable to suppress his need to retaliate and lash out to protect himself, or kiss her again.

Gods, he was messed up, still torn between punishing her and kissing her.

He had hoped that in time those twin urges would fade to a manageable level, but they only seemed to be growing worse the longer he delayed talking with her.

He tried hard to push away the feeling that she had betrayed him, but it was difficult. Whenever he managed to subdue it enough to head out to hunt for Aya, it came back again, rising inside him like a black tide, an oil slick that smothered the softer side of his heart that she had brought back to life. It pushed him to lash out at her, filling his mind with poisonous thoughts, telling him that she had hurt him.

She had.

But gods, he had hurt her first.

"What the merry hell are you doing?"

The deep male voice coming from behind him had Harbin on his feet and facing the owner in a flash, his claws at the ready and a growl leaving his lips. How the fuck had the male snuck up on him? He had been absorbed in watching Aya, but he had still been alert, aware of his surroundings.

The only plausible answer was teleporting.

But the male was mortal.

"I didn't hire you to stalk the female to death," the male said, his English accent bearing a regal edge that left Harbin aware of what this male thought of him.

The bastard thought him lowly and disgusting, and that speaking with him or being in his presence was beneath him.

Harbin bared his fangs on a snarl, concealing the intake of breath that he pulled over his teeth to catch the male's scent.

A witch.

No wonder the bastard had been able to sneak up on him. Harbin despised witches. He curled his lip at the wretch, feeling it was only fair he let the male see what he thought of him since he had been so kind as to make his feelings about Harbin clear as day.

The witch narrowed red eyes on him. Everything about this male was darkness incarnate, from his black trousers and the long black robe he wore over the top of them, to his black hair, to the scent and sense of magic that bled from him. "Well?"

It took Harbin a moment to recall that there had been a question, and when he did, he barely hid the shock that rippled through him.

Aya hadn't hired the guild to kill her.

This male had.

He stared the male down, swiftly studying him and putting everything about him to memory. Why would a witch hire him to kill Aya?

He took another deep breath and stilled.

It was subtle, but hidden amongst the scent of death and magic, was one that was all too familiar to him.

A scent that was branded on him and one he could never forget.

The scent of the Archangel huntress who had betrayed him.

A growl rumbled up his throat but he caught it in time, holding it inside, and schooled his features to hide the emotions running riot inside him. The male was allied with the bitch he had been searching for since that night twenty years ago.

He was being played all over again.

"I'd love to kill her… but I'm under strict orders to wait for my boss and a fellow assassin to get their arses here." Harbin folded his arms across his chest, positioning his fingers on his biceps in such a way that the male would see his claws were out and he was ready for a fight if he made a move.

The witch's eyes narrowed into fiery slits. "You require three males to kill one little female? Perhaps we have hired the wrong guild."

We. Either there was more than one witch involved, or he was talking about the Archangel huntress he was in league with.

Harbin snorted. "My part of the job is purely tracking. Fuery wants the kill, and I don't tend to deny Fuery anything. He has a tendency to kill people for that sort of thing."

The way the male's skin blanched told Harbin that he was aware of Fuery and knew the legends that surrounded him.

Legends that were all true.

The witch stared at him for long seconds, a calculating edge to his red gaze, and then nodded stiffly. "Very well."

He disappeared.

Harbin's shoulders sagged and he looked back towards the place where Aya had been, but was now gone. He didn't trust the witch. The bastard's eyes had slid towards where Aya had been walking just before he had nodded. Was he going to go after her?

Was he on to him?

Harbin was sure that he hadn't revealed his surprise to the male, or the anger that had washed through him on realising who the male was working for and that he was being set up again, but what he didn't show on the surface could easily be detected by a spell.

He stared at the spot on the street where Aya had been, focusing on her scent and drawing deep breaths of air down into his lungs to catch it again. She would be heading home now, having passed the evening meandering around the late night shops and some cafes that stayed open into the small hours.

The Archangel huntress had hired him to kill her.

The thought of finally getting his hands on her and having his vengeance reawakened the colder, emotionless and lethal part of himself that had been in command for the past twenty years, filling his mind with pleasing images of luring her to her death.

The woman wanted him to kill Aya, because she knew Aya was connected to him.

He could use Aya to draw the woman and the witch out, and eliminate them both in one fell swoop.

His deeper primal instincts pushed back against that idea, focusing on what would happen to Aya if he walked down that dark path.

The huntress must have known Aya back when she had been a captive of Archangel and now she was using her to get to him. He couldn't use Aya in the same way. His every instinct demanded that he protect her and keep her close to him, and did nothing that might endanger her.

She was his mate.

It was imprinted on him, unshakable and undeniable, even when he wanted to pretend otherwise. The instincts as her male ran deep in his blood and his bones and he couldn't ignore them. They were stronger than the new instincts that had been born in the bloody aftermath of that night two decades ago, the ones he had honed until they were as sharp as the blades he favoured as an elite assassin.

More powerful than the ones that whispered this was a golden opportunity to put an end to the bitch who had haunted him for twenty years and finally lay his ghosts to rest.

He stood at the edge of the rooftop as a war raged inside him, the two sides of him battling as he struggled to see the right path to take. Could he really allow this opportunity to pass him by?

He had been waiting twenty years to face the Archangel huntress, had searched for her across all the continents, following even the smallest breadcrumb in his desperation to redeem himself and shed the weight of his sins from his shoulders.

He growled and tore his eyes away from the direction of Aya's apartment, fury curling through his veins and mingling with the guilt there.

What kind of a sick son of a bitch was he?

He knew Aya was his fated female, yet there was a part of him that was willing to risk her life in order to finally have his vengeance, sating the need that had been burning inside him for twenty long years and had kept him marching forwards through a dark existence, treading a path that could only do him harm towards a future that grew blacker the longer he kept walking it.

He couldn't turn back though.

It was too late for that.

He didn't care about saving himself from whatever harm life as an assassin was doing to him. He didn't care that it was killing him, stripping him of feeling and making him disconnect from the world he had once loved, leaving him feeling that he couldn't trust anyone. Not even Hartt.

He only cared about avenging his family and his pride.

He only cared about righting his wrongs.

He only cared about protecting her.

Once Aya was safe and the huntress was dead, he would return to his life as an assassin and he would never see her again.

A scream rent the night air and Harbin's head snapped up, his gaze instantly zeroing in on the direction it had come from.

A chill ran through him and he was moving before he had even thought about what he was doing, driven to reach the source of that terrified shriek.

Aya.

He knew it in his blood as it thundered through his veins, felt it in his blackened soul as he leaped the gap between two buildings and sprinted across the flat roof. She was in trouble. He had to reach her.

He palmed the pocket of his combat trousers as he dropped to the street close to her home, feeling the slender tube in it and the weight of what he had to do.

She wasn't safe in London anymore.

He had to take her away to a place where she would be protected.

He hit the pavement and kicked off, launching himself forwards, towards two shadowy figures in the alley next to her apartment building. As they shifted to face him, he caught a glimpse of creamy skin and bright silver eyes beyond them, and snarled through his emerging fangs. He wouldn't let them hurt Aya.

He hurled himself at the two males, tackling them both head on. The left one sidestepped, coming to stand under the single light in the alleyway. He looked like the male from the rooftop, but his eyes were eerily blue. Harbin didn't break his stride. It wouldn't be the first time he had dealt with copies. They were often mistaken for siblings, but Harbin's nose and experience told him that these ones weren't true twins. They were clones created by magic, and that meant the male he had met on the rooftop was pouring his power into the two sacks of flesh before him, weakening himself.

Making it easier for Harbin to kill him.

He snarled and lashed out with his claws, raking them across the chest of the male on the right. The male cried out and staggered backwards, a horrified look crossing his face before it darkened and he launched himself at Harbin.

Harbin ducked, coming beneath the fist the male swung at him and up behind him. He kicked the male in the back, sending him flying across the alleyway, colliding with the other copy. The two went down in a heap. Weak. The male was already withdrawing his power from them, strengthening himself. He was sacrificing the two.

A pale blur shot past him, hitting the wall a few metres above Harbin's head, and then darted across the space between the buildings.

Aya.

She was nimble as she leaped from building to building in an effort to escape. She wouldn't be quick enough though, not unless he did something to buy her time. The red-eyed male was already on the move, heading after her.

Harbin slammed his fist into the first copy, knocking him out with a single blow, and swept his leg around as he turned to face the other one, bringing it high into the air. He drove the heel of his boot into the side of his head, sending him crashing back down on the ground. The male grunted and started to get up again.

Harbin pulled the tube from his pocket, shoved a feathered dart into it, and blew hard. The male slapped a hand over his neck, his eyes rolled back in his head and he slumped onto the tarmac.

Damn.

Harbin checked the pouch in his pocket and grimaced. Gods, he needed to be more careful. The dart he had grabbed in his panic was laced with the deadliest poison in Hell, drawn from the blood of the hydras that lived deep in the Devil's domain. If he had mistakenly used that one on Aya... it didn't bear thinking about.

"What the merry hell do you think you are doing?" The witch's voice echoed around the dimly lit alley.

Harbin glared at him. "This is our fucking job, and I won't tolerate interference. Our guild doesn't take too kindly to people who hire us and then finish the job themselves. Unless you want to deal with one pissed off dark elf, I suggest you back the fuck off and let us do our work."

The witch's red eyes narrowed but Harbin refused to back down. Instead, he shifted to face him, bracing his feet shoulder-width apart, his fingers twitching against the tube in his hand and his thoughts on plucking another dart laced with hydra toxin and shooting the bastard with it. The male glanced down at it and then back up at his face, locking gazes with him.

"Very well… but we expect a result within the time limit, or it will be your head rolling."

Black smoke swirled around the witch and when it dissipated, he was gone.

Wretch. Harbin didn't trust him. It was a long shot, but hopefully he had done enough to cover his tracks and the witch had bought what he had said and had actually left the area and wasn't watching from the shadows.

He raised his head, silver eyes searching for Aya.

He spotted her near the top of the building and nimbly used the same trick to reach it, leaping higher and faster than she had, his body more powerful than hers would ever be. He kicked off hard near the top and sailed over her head, coming to land in front of her.

She stopped dead, her enormous eyes catching the moonlight, glowing with fear and with something else he didn't dare name. That something else grew stronger as she ran a glance over him and he gritted his teeth, willing his body not to respond to the heated look. She was his mate but she would never be his, and the quicker he got that through his thick skull, the better it would be for both of them.

It didn't matter how much he wanted her.

Needed her.

They could never be together.

"I killed one… but they'll be coming back for you," he growled and advanced a step towards her. Her cream satin slip fluttered in the cool breeze, luring his gaze down to her shapely legs. He resisted and kept his gaze locked with hers and his focus on his business with her. "You're not safe here anymore."

Her eyes widened further and he felt the shock that rippled through her. It ran through him too, a warning sign that he couldn't ignore. Their paths were already entwining, their souls pulling together into a union he couldn't allow. He had to act fast, for her sake, because being so close to her was stirring something dangerous inside him.

Awakening a feral need for her.

One he wasn't sure he would be able to resist as it was now, let alone when it grew stronger as he knew it would.

He had to get her to safety, figure out his plan and get it done soon or he was going to lose control, and end up doing something they would both regret.

"I'm sorry," he whispered and she frowned at him.

He chose the tranquiliser dart from the container in his pocket, slid it into the tube and brought it to his lips. He fixed his eyes on her neck and blew, and she flinched as the dart struck.

Her legs buckled.

Harbin couldn't stop himself from catching her, crossing the distance between them with a single leap to cushion her fall with his arms. He froze and stared down at her, breathing hard as the scent of her and her warmth curled around him, seeping into him.

Marking him.

He pulled her closer to his chest and eyed the dart that protruded from her neck. She didn't even twitch as he gently pulled it from her flesh and discarded it. Blood blossomed where it had been and he was lowering his head and pressing his lips to that spot before he could get the better of himself.

Heat bloomed inside him as her blood coated his lips, flowing down into his chest and filling it with light. He shook as he breathed her in and tasted her, and gathered her even closer. It still wasn't enough.

He needed more of her.

Harbin lifted his head and stared down at her. The moon turned her skin white and perfect, and her silvery eyebrows and lashes sparkled in its gentle light.

Gods, she was beautiful.

But she could never be his.

He would only taint her with the darkness living within him.

As his mate, she deserved the best life that he could give to her and that was the life he would give to her.

A life without him in it.

CHAPTER 14

His leather boots were loud on the polished black stone floor that reflected warm torchlight up at him, each step a heavy thud that echoed along the broad arched corridor of the main entrance of the guild. Harbin adjusted his grip on the female in his arms, cradling her closer to his body as he carried her into the heart of the place he now called home.

Her head lolled, falling against his biceps, and he couldn't resist the urge to look down at her that stole through him. Her soft shell-pink lips parted, her warm breath fanning his skin as he held her nestled against him. In his arms. Where she belonged.

He erased that last thought as two assassins approached him, neither of them from the guild. Sometimes the guilds teamed up when a particularly dangerous target with a high enough price on their head came along. What business had these two assassins been doing here?

The blonde females were quick to notice his cargo and even quicker to speak with each other in their native language, one he had never bothered to learn. Succubi made good assassins, but he preferred to keep away from their kind. They had a tendency to kill any male who sampled their wares.

One giggled as he passed them, a snigger that made him want to turn and growl at her in warning. The rules of his guild were known by all in it and even some from other guilds. They knew he was breaking them and he was sure they were just itching to watch the calamity that was about to unfold when he reached the main reception room. He locked his senses on the pair, monitoring them, feeling them swaying between continuing out of the door and turning back to see Hartt rip him a new one.

The bitches turned back.

Harbin huffed and kept trudging onwards, into the impressive black-walled reception room at the end of the corridor.

Four of the guild's longest serving demon members lounged in the horseshoe of black velvet couches that surrounded the monstrosity of a marble fireplace to his left, the satisfied smiles on their faces telling Harbin that the succubi had been here for pleasure, not business. The demons all looked at him the second he entered the room.

One of the male's black horns curled through his thick dark hair, so the points protruded past his cheeks. A sign of aggression.

Harbin had considered he would have trouble with Hartt when he brought Aya to the guild, but he hadn't considered that other members of the guild with have a problem with her presence.

The male pushed onto his feet, coming to stand at least three inches taller than Harbin and twice as broad.

If he fought, the three other demons with him would fight too.

Harbin wasn't sure he would be able to protect Aya from them.

The black door in the far right corner of the room shot open and Hartt strode in, his violet eyes dark with the anger rolling off him in waves so intense that Harbin was sure everyone in the vicinity would sense the elf's fury.

Hartt's black clothing disappeared, replaced in an instant by his armour as it swept outwards from the black and silver bands around his wrist, the scales coming to cover him from toe to neck. They coursed over his hands too, forming deadly jagged talons.

Harbin tucked Aya closer to him and bared his fangs in warning.

He didn't want to fight Hartt, but the male was throwing vibes at him that had his primal instincts firing and demanding he protect his mate.

"What the hell do you think you are doing bringing her here?" Hartt snapped, ignoring his warning, and stormed towards him. His pointed ears flared, poking through the unruly strands of his blue-black hair, and his fangs showed between his lips as he talked. "You were meant to kill her."

Harbin roared at him.

Hartt's eyes widened and he stopped dead.

The entire room dropped into stunned silence.

Fuck, the reaction had shocked even him. It had been feral and powerful, overwhelming him and seizing control, hijacking his body and forcing the response from him when he had felt his mate was threatened.

He breathed hard, fighting for control over his instincts, aware that he had just crossed a line and that if he wasn't careful, Hartt would do more than shout at him.

Hartt would do more than fight him.

This place was his home, his pride, and he couldn't allow anything to jeopardise his place in it. He had already lost one family. He couldn't lose this one too. He needed the guild. It was his life now, and nothing would ever change that.

"You good now?" Hartt whispered softly and Harbin nodded. "Care to explain to me why you brought her here?"

That riled his snow leopard side, making it push for freedom. He needed to shift and show this male that he had no right to question him when it came to his mate. He had no right to look at her in that way, as if she was something to be eliminated or cast out into the dangerous world outside of the guild.

He deepened his breathing, seeking some sliver of calm that he could hold on to while he mastered his animal side and regained control of it. He could feel everyone staring at him, their gazes piercing him. Judging him.

He knew the rules. He knew he wasn't allowed to bring anyone from outside the guild into it with the intention they would stay longer than a few minutes, as long as it took to satisfy whatever urge had struck the assassin in question or take a potential business partner away from the guild to a local bar to talk about a job.

He knew no one had ever dared to break that rule since Hartt had created it centuries ago.

He just had nowhere else he could go.

He looked down at Aya where she slumbered in his arms, unaware of the danger that he had placed her in by bringing her to this dark place. It was danger that he could control though. He hadn't had a choice. This was the safest place he knew. The witch could enter Hell, but he wouldn't dare attack an entire guild of assassins.

"The contract is a trap," Harbin said, his tone flat and controlled despite the emotions that raged out of control inside him, whipped into a frenzy by the memories of what had happened and the thought of Aya being in danger. He lifted his head and locked eyes with Hartt, catching the male's surprise in their violet depths. "It's her... the huntress."

Hartt's eyes widened. "You're sure?"

Harbin nodded. "A male witch made himself known to me when I was tracking Aya. I recognised the huntress's scent on him. They're in league with each other, which means Aya was bait for me."

"Because she's part of your pride?" Hartt's steady gaze challenged him to admit that she was more than that to him but he refused, unwilling to surrender that information when so many of the guild were present.

What Aya was to him was personal and he wasn't in the habit of sharing personal shit with other guild members.

Personal information was another weapon they could use against him if they ever turned on him.

"I couldn't take her to Cavanaugh. I won't place him and the others there in danger." Harbin looked back down at Aya and bit back the sigh that tried to leave his lips as he studied her soft face, losing himself in her beauty all over again.

"You'd put us in danger though," the dark-haired demon muttered.

Hartt whipped around to face the four males. "If you're afraid of a little witch and his lackeys, perhaps you're in the wrong fucking profession? Take your whores and get out of my sight."

The demon snapped his mouth closed and shuffled away, heading for the exit with his friends and the succubi.

"I should set Fuery on them for being whelps," Hartt snarled as he watched them go and then sucked down a deep breath and switched his focus back to Harbin. The darkness in his boss's eyes remained, lingering like dangerous storm clouds. "Cut the crap... she's more than just a former member of your pride. The huntress has been in hiding for two decades. There's no damned way she would risk a showdown with you unless she had an ace up her sleeve and I'm guessing the female here is that ace."

Hartt's eyes narrowed, holding Harbin immobile and unable to escape what he could feel was coming.

"She's your fated one."

Those words seemed to echo around the room forever, each stinging his heart and making him feel the dreaded weight of them. She was his mate, but that wasn't a good thing.

"I've been too close to her. The connection between us is already awakening and that means it's strong." Harbin blew out his breath. "If the huntress harms her, I'll feel it. She'll use Aya to weaken me."

"Fuck," Hartt grunted and dropped his eyes to Aya, and Harbin had to bite his tongue to stop himself from growling and demanding he take his gaze off his mate.

Hell, he had thought that being on the cusp of sexual maturity had been a royal pain in the arse. It was a cakewalk compared with the urges that ran through him every second of every minute that he was close to Aya, a barrage of needs and desires that seemed at odds with each other, tearing him apart from the inside.

Part of him wanted to give her the life she deserved, one without him tainting it, and the rest demanded that he stay with her.

It screamed at him to protect her and claim her as his mate so no other could have her.

"I take it you have a plan?" Hartt said, pulling him back to the room and away from dangerous thoughts of gouging his boss's eyes out so he couldn't look at Aya.

Harbin really wanted to nod and say that he had, because he knew there was going to be a fuck-tonne of disappointment in Hartt's eyes when he told him the truth.

The elf's expression shifted and it seemed Harbin's hesitation was all the answer the male had needed.

Hartt sighed and pinched the bridge of his nose. "We can come up with something. For now, take her to your room and keep her there. I'll send out a mandate to the guild members that will protect her but it's best she isn't left alone."

Harbin couldn't agree more.

He intended to stay by her side for the entire duration of her stay. He wouldn't let her out of his sight. He wouldn't risk her.

He looked down at her again, his heart heavy as he realised that risking her might be his only option, his best shot at drawing out the witch and the huntress.

Harbin turned away from his boss, heading to the back right corner of the room and the door to the east wing, where his quarters were. He stared down at her the entire time, unable to take his eyes off her or shake the creeping sense that he had no choice this time either.

If he wanted to have his vengeance, he would have to risk Aya.

He would have to place his fated female in danger.

It was the only way.

CHAPTER 15

Spice and snow. It wrapped around her, warming her down to her soul and soothing the ache from her tired limbs. Aya rolled onto her side and curled into the thick blankets, pulling them around her and burrowing deep into them. The scent grew stronger, teasing her senses and making her yearn to see the male the pleasing smell belonged to, but she couldn't bring herself to open her eyes, not when she was so warm and comfortable.

Her ears twitched as a distant bang sounded, rattling her from her dream.

She fluttered her eyes open but they were hazy, her vision blurred, blending everything together into one sombre mash of colours with a single golden glow in the centre. When the room around her finally came into focus, she shot up in the bed and her eyes darted over everything from the lamp burning on the side table, to the black walls and to the dark ebony dressing table and drawers opposite her near an equally obsidian door on the right side of the small room.

A room that wasn't hers.

Where was she?

Aya tossed the dark crimson covers aside and leaped from the double bed, heading for the window cut into the thick stone wall to her left.

She stopped dead when she reached it, her eyes widening as she stared at the dark world outside.

She had the sinking feeling that she wasn't in London anymore.

Black mountains rose in the distance, above crooked roofs tiled with dark grey slates. A gloomy sky filled the space above the town and the range of cragged peaks, nearly as black as them.

Where the hell was she?

Aya paused.

Hell.

Gods, it was all coming back to her now. Harbin had been there on the rooftop. He had saved her from the witches. He had drugged her.

He had brought her to Hell.

Her stomach flipped and she shot to face the door when another bang sounded.

Her heart pounded, thundering against her chest, and she threw a panicked glance around her at the room. It smelled of Harbin, but she could scent others too, and she could sense many moving around the building.

Assassins.

She was in their home, and she had a price on her head, a contract that this guild was meant to fulfil.

She was in danger here.

Her every instinct roared at her to run. She shoved at the sash window but it didn't move. Her fingers shook as she fumbled with the lock, managed to get it open, and tried again. The window still refused to open. It was sealed shut.

Her breath came quicker, panic setting deep roots in her as she looked across the room to the door that led outside. She had to risk it.

She bolted for the door and had it open in a heartbeat. Her head swung both ways, eyes landing on a black wall to her left where the corridor ended, and a long hallway that seemed to go on forever to her right, lit by wall lamps at intervals. She shoved off and was sprinting barefoot down the corridor a second later, her cream satin slip whipping around her thighs as she passed several corridors shooting off from the one she was running along. She swiftly bolted down one on her left when she sensed someone ahead of her, and took the next right, which only led to another left and left again. A growl curled from her lips. The place was a damned maze. How the hell was she meant to find her way out of it?

There had to be an exit somewhere.

Another bang sounded behind her, sending a shiver down her spine, and she ran harder, taking a sharp right and then left when she hit the main corridor again. She sprinted at full pelt towards a door at the end of the black-walled corridor and slammed her palm into it as she reached it. It flew open and she stumbled into a large room lit by more lamps on the obsidian walls.

Several pairs of eyes landed on her.

Aya jerked to face them and her legs turned to noodles.

Demons.

The four males rose from the black couches surrounding a rather hideous fireplace directly opposite her, their obsidian horns curling forwards as their eyes darkened. As each one stood, her legs weakened a little more. They were massive. All of them stood well over six-six and all of them were bare-chested and packed with muscle.

She couldn't fight them.

She wasn't strong enough to tackle one demon, let alone four.

But what she lacked in strength she made up for in agility. She could evade them and escape. A foul-smelling breeze was coming from an archway near the far left corner of the room. Freedom laid that way and it would be hers.

She just had to get past the four demons that were moving out from behind the couches now, coming to block her path.

Aya focused on her body and willed the shift, urging it to come quickly this time. She kept her eyes locked on the biggest demon as it swept through her, gritting her teeth against the sharp fierce pain as her bones distorted, cracking and moulding into new shapes. Her ears rounded as thick silver fur rippled over her skin, and rose up the side of her head at the same time as her cheeks puffed outwards and her nose flattened.

The demon muttered something to his friends and grinned.

Her tail sprouted from the base of her spine and she landed on her four large paws, and wrestled free of her slip to give herself the complete freedom to move as she needed. She lowered her head and snarled at the demon through her fangs. The room brightened as her vision sharpened and she quickly took in each demon from head to toe, calculating her odds of escape and the best route to take in order to avoid conflict.

The biggest demon advanced.

Aya roared at him but he didn't even flinch.

He smirked.

The door off to her right bursting open wiped that smirk off his face, capturing his focus and giving her an opportunity she wouldn't waste.

She launched herself at him.

A strong hand grabbed her by the scruff of her neck and jerked her backwards. Her breath left her in a rush as she was slammed into the black stone floor and she immediately began struggling, snarling and growling as she tried to wrestle free.

"Steady," Harbin murmured close to her ear, his warm breath tickling her fur and sending an all too pleasant shiver through her.

He moved back as she did as he instructed, going still and breathing slowly to calm her animal instincts to break free and fight to protect herself, and loosened his grip. When she made no move to attack the demon again, he released her and stood.

Aya looked up at him where he towered over her, a vision of menace and lethal grace in his tight black clothing, his silver hair swept back from his face to reveal his icy eyes. They were locked on the demon and his pupils slowly widened. He was hunting the male, waiting for him to dare to make a move, his focus completely on the demon so he couldn't twitch without Harbin seeing it.

"I thought we made it clear you were to leave her alone?" Harbin said, his tone flat and cold, but holding a note of warning.

He wanted to fight the males.

They wisely backed off, each tossing a black look at Harbin as they went, heading towards the exit to her left. Suddenly, freedom didn't look so appealing. She didn't want to run into them again.

Harbin stepped past her, watching them go. When they were out of sight, he turned towards her and hunkered down in front of her.

"You were meant to stay in my quarters." He huffed and she lowered her gaze, unable to ignore the deeply rooted behaviour that had been branded on her during her upbringing.

Harbin was an elite member of her pride, and she had been taught to never displease any belonging to his bloodline. It was difficult to overcome that instinct, even when she was in Hell, in a guild of assassins, a place he called home and a profession he had chosen.

He had overcome the instincts that had been branded on him, shaking the desire to seek peace over bloodshed. Why couldn't she do the same after everything that had happened to her?

She edged her eyes back up to his face and found him watching her, his silver eyes softer now, giving her the answer to her question.

She had overcome those instincts, she had shaken their hold. It wasn't her upbringing in the pride and the rules she had followed there making her want to avoid his steady but warm gaze.

It was her new instincts, the ones that drummed in her blood and said that the male before her was her mate.

Gods, she wished it had been her old instincts that had made her look away when she had seen the anger in his eyes, because she wasn't sure how to deal with the new ones.

He reached for her and she snarled at him, warning him not to touch her. She couldn't bear it, not right now. Whenever she was near him, he stripped her of her defences and left her weak. She felt too vulnerable, liable to do something reckless and stupid.

Like kissing him.

She had been an idiot back then, believing that she could win the heart of a male of his status, and she had learned her lesson. She wouldn't be that stupid again.

He stared at her a moment longer and then slowly rose to his feet. "Come."

Aya pushed onto her paws and followed him back through the corridors, her mind churning and heart aching as she tried to figure out what she was going to do. It was clear that he expected her to remain in this place, and as much as she wanted to run away from him in order to purge the feelings growing inside her, the hungers that had her eyes lingering on the firm globes of his backside as he prowled the corridor ahead of her, she had no choice but to obey him.

For now.

She couldn't return home, not when the witches knew where she lived.

She wasn't even sure she knew how to return home.

She had heard tales of Hell and legends about gates that could transport people to this realm from the mortal one, but she didn't have a clue whether those stories were real or where to find a gate and how to use it if they were.

She had to bide her time until she had a plan and then she would leave this place.

Harbin held the door to his room for her and she padded past him, her paws silent on the stone floor. She felt his gaze tracking her, lingering and burning into her as he closed the door. The click of the latch sliding into place drove thoughts of running from him and her feelings from her mind and narrowed the world down to the small room.

To him.

He stood there behind her, silent and still, his eyes on her, and the urge that ran through her was dangerous and alluring, and no matter how much she fought it, it was too tempting to deny.

Aya glanced into the small adjoining room to her left. A bathroom. The perfect place for shifting back and finding something to cover herself.

She looked back over her shoulder at Harbin, her breath lodging in her throat as she caught the hunger in his glowing eyes, the same need that coursed through her veins and seized control of her.

She closed her eyes and willed the shift.

The sound of Harbin's breathing turning heavier filled the tense silence as her bones lengthened, her tail shrank and her ears moved back down as her nose narrowed. The fur covering her body was the last thing to change, disappearing into her bare skin and leaving her standing before Harbin.

Naked.

She wrapped one arm across her breasts and covered her mound with her other hand as she turned her head towards him where he stood behind her, his intense gaze drifting over her body. Heat rippled through her in the wake of it and she swallowed hard before slowly shifting to face him and opening her eyes.

The hunger in his sent a stronger thrill through her.

She had never felt sexy, knew she wasn't perfect or had the body the mortal world touted as the one all females should aspire to have. She wasn't thin, but she wasn't ashamed of her figure. This was who she was, but while she was happy, she had never felt beautiful.

But Harbin's silvery gaze, the heat that burned in it, made her feel sexy.

It made her feel confident and desired as he crossed the room to her, those hungry eyes gliding down the length of her body and back up again.

It made her feel beautiful.

Even when she felt certain that she shouldn't fall under his dark spell.

He was an assassin, not the male she had grown up with back at the village, crushing on him from the rear of the classroom.

There was barely a trace of that male in him now.

He was ruthless, dangerous, and always serious, the complete opposite to the wild youth who had always been laughing and seeking out fun.

But gods, that only made him more alluring.

The lethal aura that rolled off him, the air of a powerful male, added to his masculine beauty and spoke to her feminine instincts, weakening her resolve.

Harbin stopped right in front of her, so close she could feel the heat of his body, and stared down into her eyes through ones that held barely leashed desire, before reaching past her. She jumped when he settled a thin blue robe around her shoulders, draping it over her front and covering her.

Aya didn't take her eyes away from his as she slipped her arms into the sleeves and drew it closed, tying the belt around her waist. His spoke to her, telling her how difficult it had been for him to resist touching her, choosing instead to cover her. It seemed she wasn't the only one struggling with her new instincts and her old desires.

She had wanted him forty years ago, and she still wanted him now.

She wanted to believe it was the same for him, even when she felt sure that she was only fooling herself, seeing what she wanted to see in his eyes.

He backed off a step, drew down a deep breath, and looked away from her. His eyes roamed back to her barely a second later, dropping from her face to the robe, darkening with hunger again, need that coursed through her blood too. He flashed his fangs on a snarl and paced away from her, placing as much distance as possible between them in the small room.

Perhaps she had pushed too hard, but she had wanted to see what he would do. She had wanted to make him reveal the feelings he hid from her and had wanted to make him see what he had been missing out on all these years because of his actions back at the pride.

Just the thought of what he had done, and the pain he had caused her, tossed a pail of snow on the fire of her desire, killing the flames and allowing her to regain control of herself. She couldn't let her instincts and the attraction she had always felt towards him rule her now. She had to be strong.

Aya glanced across at Harbin where he had propped himself against the wall, his hands jammed in the pockets of his black jeans and his left leg bent at the knee, the sole of his boot pressing against the black plaster. He stared down at the floor, strands of his wild silver hair caressing his brow, a troubled look on his handsome face.

Gods curse him. He seemed even more handsome now.

"What happened?" She touched the spot on her neck where she recalled feeling the dart sting her.

And his lips caress her.

Had that been real or had she imagined it?

She stared at his mouth, trying to remember whether he really had kissed the spot on her neck. His sensual lips moved in mesmerising ways as he spoke, pulling her firmly back under his spell.

"The night the pride was attacked by Archangel, the charge was led by a single huntress. She got information out of me and used it to locate the pride while it was vulnerable. I discovered last night that she has surfaced and is working with the witch who attacked you."

"Witches," she corrected automatically. "There were three."

He shook his head and finally looked across the room at her, his silver eyes bright and intense. "One witch, but he has the power to make copies of himself. It's a dark art, lost to most witches, but I've come across it before. I'm guessing he's from the same clan as someone I crossed paths with a few years back on a mission."

By 'crossed paths' she presumed he meant 'killed'.

"You think he's working with her because of what you did?" She had to put it out there, because it was the first thought that had crossed her mind and she knew it must have crossed his too.

He sighed and ploughed his right hand through his hair. "Without a doubt. It seems I can't stop pissing people off."

He closed his eyes and tipped his head back, pressing it into the wall behind him.

"The huntress who used you…" Aya started and trailed off when he opened his eyes and fixed them on her, a flicker of hurt in his eyes that he quickly mastered and erased. She cleared her throat and soldiered on, determined to get some answers. "I think I know her. When the research facility where I had been taken closed and Archangel changed hands, a huntress came to me and—"

"She told you I had sold you out," Harbin interjected in a low voice and she nodded. He growled, flashing fangs again. "I didn't. I would never…"

"I know that now. I know a lot of things I heard were lies." She hated Archangel for it too.

It had been bad enough that they had made her feel Harbin had handed her and the others over to them, but the fact that they had convinced her to act as a spy on their behalf, making her believe that she was helping maintain peace between all species, made her feel sick and part of her hated herself too. She had been weak and they had used it against her, playing on it to make her do as they wanted.

Harbin stared across the room at her.

"Why did you avoid me after we kissed?"

That unexpected question hit her with the force of a tidal wave, rocking her and leaving her spinning.

He wasn't talking about the kiss at Archangel. He was talking about that first kiss they had shared close to forty years ago. She wasn't the only one who wanted answers, and the steely look in Harbin's silver eyes said he wasn't going to stop asking that question until she confessed.

"You're the son of our pride's alpha," she whispered to her feet and then lifted her head and looked him in the eye, determined not to let him make her feel that she had done something wrong. She had been muddled, conflicted. "I was afraid… I wasn't sure what was happening, but I knew you were our future alpha."

He snorted. "Now I'm nobody. A ghost. An assassin… a killer."

She didn't need him to remind her of that fact, not when it had played on her mind from the moment he had walked back into her life. It unsettled her that his announcing it didn't change the attraction she felt towards him. He was a killer by his own admission, but all she could see was Harbin standing before her.

He shoved away from the wall.

"I never would have been alpha," he spat out with so much venom that she tensed. "Cav has that title and it would have passed to his kids."

"I thought about approaching you later." She hated the way her voice shook as she confessed that and the way Harbin stilled, his breathing softening, as if her words had soothed him.

But she could feel the dangerous current of anger flowing under his calm surface too, could sense it in the growing connection between them.

Her words had served as both a balm and a poison, soothing yet hurting him.

"Why didn't you?" His voice trembled the slightest amount, revealing the depth of his feelings to her.

Not his feelings now, but those of forty years ago.

Her behaviour had hurt him, and the resulting action he had taken had ended up hurting her.

"Because you had grown up so aggressive... so egotistical... taking whatever female you wanted because they wouldn't deny you due to your position within the pride." She barely stopped herself from adding more, reining in her own anger and reminding herself that it was ancient history now and nothing they did could change it. They had both made mistakes and they had both paid for them.

Were both still paying for them.

"Don't sugar coat it." Harbin growled at her. "Maybe if you hadn't ditched me, I might have grown up differently."

That one cut her deep and she turned her face away from him, whispering, "Maybe."

He huffed and started pacing, his boots loud on the cold stone floor and his agitation flowing through her.

After their kiss, she had avoided him just as he had said, trying to get her head and her heart straight, and find the courage to approach him again. By the time she had realised that she liked him as more than a friend, and that she should have thrown convention out of the window and seized him with both hands, he had already been chasing other females. She had been glad when he had finally started leaving the pride females alone, heading down into the nearest mortal town for days at a time.

It had hurt her, but she'd had no claim to him, and a male of his status was allowed to do whatever he pleased. He hadn't owed her anything.

She lifted her head and watched him pacing, his powerful body flexing with each fierce stride that carried him back and forth along the wall opposite her. He glanced at her from time to time, conflict reigning in his eyes and the feelings she could sense in him.

If she confessed that she had been hurt too, would that please him? Did he want to hear that her fear of crossing the boundary that had separated them had only ended up causing her pain for twenty years, until the night of the attack on their pride?

Gods, who was she fooling? It still hurt her now.

But she couldn't judge him or hold the things he had done against him, because she hadn't exactly been a saint herself. She had slept with many males during her years in London, using them to satisfy her urges, indulging in brief flings that had meant nothing, never allowing her partners to scratch the hardened surface of her heart and see what was beyond it. She had kept them all at a distance, using and losing them. Acting just as Harbin had.

No male had ever affected her in the way he did. Just being in the same room as him made it impossible to breathe, stirred fire in her veins and had her aching inside, yearning for his touch or the soft sweep of his lips across her overheating skin.

Did she affect him like this too?

A voice deep in her heart whispered she hoped so. Why?

Did she still want him as more than a friend?

The fire burning in her chest said that she did, regardless of the things he had done. Things she had no clue about. She felt as if everything she had known the past twenty years had been a lie and her one chance of straightening everything out so she could finally move on with her life was pacing like a caged animal in front of her, radiating tension and something else.

Something alluring that spoke to her instincts and made her want to step into his path so he would walk into her, his hard body pressing against hers and his heat seeping into her skin.

She wanted him to kiss her again, as he had at Archangel—fiercely, hungrily, and as if he would die without her.

She shoved that desire aside and focused instead on him, hearing his words ringing in her mind.

An assassin. A killer.

"What happened to you?" she whispered.

Harbin looked across at her and paused mid-stride. His expression shifted, turning pensive, and he came to rest on his heels. He was quiet for so long that she feared he wouldn't answer, that he would leave her forever wondering about him.

"I never knew what happened to you," he murmured and then sighed as he rubbed the back of his neck, closed his eyes and hung his head. "As soon as I came around and I realised that the pride was in danger, I raced back there. I almost killed myself climbing the mountain… but I died when I reached the village."

His jaw flexed as he gritted his teeth and the pain that flowed into her through their connection stole her breath and had her moving a step towards him, filled with a powerful need to comfort him.

"I saw the carnage… saw my mother and sister dead on the snow… and it was my fault. I cannot imagine what it had been like for you… for everyone… when Archangel had attacked. I only know how I felt then. I only remember the pain and the rage, and the burning need that consumed me."

He opened his eyes and looked at her through his lashes, his irises glowing bright silver.

"I don't remember much of what happened then… it's fragmented. I know I shifted and went after Archangel, and I slaughtered many of them, but others got away. I don't remember how I got back to the village but I think Cavanaugh was there."

Aya's heart went out to him. When cat shifters suffered a great loss, their primal side grew wild and feral, unable to handle the flood of powerful emotions. Harbin's had taken control of him, his grief forcing him into his animal form and filling him with a need to hunt and kill the ones who had murdered his family and his kin. When he had lost track of the people who had attacked the pride, his instincts must have driven him back to his home to rest.

"My father exiled me, Aya."

Hearing her name leaving his lips transported her back forty years and, for a moment, she saw the youthful boy he had been then, smiling and laughing at her. A second later, she saw him drenched in blood, his eyes cold and empty, nothing more than a heartless husk of a male.

She shook away that image of him and focused on the male standing before her now.

He had been through so much, and something told her she had only seen the tip of the iceberg and the path he had travelled after losing his place in the pride had been dark and terrible indeed. She had survived Hell for three years at Archangel's hands, but at least her suffering had ended.

Harbin still suffered now.

It was there in his glowing eyes, his pain and fury still raw and powerful, still controlling his actions to a degree.

He wouldn't stop suffering until he had wiped out every member of Archangel that had been present that night, and now he had the opportunity to do that, and she wanted in on it. She wanted the bitch who had used him and who had shoved her into a nightmare and then lied to her to pay for the things she had done, manipulating them both and changing the course of their lives for the worse.

"After my father made it clear I was no longer welcome at the pride, I did the only thing I could... I drifted from country to country, hunting down the remaining members of the Archangel team that had attacked our kin." Harbin turned and sat down on the end of the double bed, a sigh leaving his lips as his backside hit the mattress and it dipped beneath his weight. "I crossed paths with Hartt when I was tracking a hunter from Archangel and he had been hired to take down the same target. Hartt saw some fucked up potential in me or something, because he convinced me to join the ranks of his guild. I could continue to hunt Archangel while taking care of other targets too and earning some money to support my vendetta."

Aya walked to the wall and leaned against it, standing close to Harbin where he sat on the bed opposite her. He lifted his head and looked up at her. She knew what potential Hartt had seen in Harbin, because she could see it in him too and it hadn't been forged in the fires of his time as an assassin. It had been born that night twenty years ago.

Hartt had known a killer when he had seen one, a male capable of taking lives without regretting his actions or the blood on his hands. Harbin had already killed many, had developed a hunger for tracking and eliminating targets. Hartt's work to turn Harbin into an assassin had probably been minimal. All he'd had to do was tap into the hunger that still burned like ice in Harbin's eyes, the desire for bloodshed and death.

A desire that should have made her want to keep her distance from him, but only made her want to take Harbin into her arms and hold him.

She wanted to take his pain away and show him that it was alright, that he had done the right thing, and his fight was coming to a close now. They would end this and both of them would be free of their pasts at last.

"I didn't take much convincing." Harbin smiled but there was no warmth in it or his silver eyes. "Hartt told me he was short on assassins, the number in the guild diminished by a war between two demon realms, and promised to share all information on Archangel that he received... and any mission that involved them."

He leaned back, bracing his weight on his palms, and his torso tensed beneath his tight black t-shirt. It was a struggle to keep her eyes off his body and on his face, but she somehow managed it.

"I should have kept on with my mission." His expression turned deadly serious again, the feelings flowing through her shifting to match it, becoming cold and calm.

She wished she could lock down her feelings as he could. It would have made standing so close to him easier on her, because she would have been able to shut down the desire that told her to cross the short span of floor to him, lower her hands to capture his cheeks, and kiss him. Something flickered in his eyes, his silvery brows briefly twitching into a frown as he looked up at her, and she quickly pushed away from thoughts of kissing him, aware that the ability to sense emotions ran both ways and he was picking up on the sudden spike in hers.

He shook his head.

"I shouldn't have allowed the jobs that came to me through the guild to distract me from my hunt for the huntress." A soft sigh left his lips, conveying so much regret and guilt that she pushed away from the wall and barely leashed her need to hold him. "I'm sorry, Aya. If I hadn't lost my way… if I had stayed on course and kept my focus… you never would have been dragged into danger again."

She raised her hands and pressed them to her chest as it warmed, heated by his tender words. They touched her, but part of her was glad that he had been side-tracked and had lost his way, because it had brought them to this point.

It had brought her to the start of a new path, a new life where she knew the truth and felt able to finally lay her past to rest and walk forwards into a brighter future.

It had brought them together again.

Aya stepped towards him and his eyes locked with hers, slowly widening as she closed the gap between them.

They were both different now.

She was no longer the meek girl who had been afraid to seize what she wanted with both hands and she was going to show him that. She was going to take what she wanted without any regrets. She was going to have Harbin.

Even when it couldn't be forever.

CHAPTER 16

Harbin tensed the moment Aya cupped his sculpted cheeks and edged backwards, attempting to evade her. She didn't let him get far and his plan backfired, forcing her to move closer to him in order to keep hold of him. She nestled between his spread thighs, their knees touching, and he inhaled hard, his wide eyes speaking to her of the uncertainty she could feel rippling through him.

It reminded her of that day so many years ago when she had grabbed him and kissed him.

She had expected it then, but she hadn't expected it now, when he had years of experience under his belt and had been looking at her as if he wanted to kiss her more times than she could count since their paths had crossed.

He swallowed and shook his head, his voice a mere whisper of warning. "Aya… don't."

She knew his fear, knew that she was pushing him too hard and was walking on thin ice, but she didn't care. She had spent forty years wondering what it would have been like to be with him, and now she had the opportunity to find out. She had to take this chance while she could. In a matter of days, the reason they had come together might be over and then they would have to part ways again.

She might never see him again.

She wasn't going to fool herself into thinking this could be anything other than a brief fling. She knew in her heart that he would never want to mate with her. When he had spoken of Cavanaugh having children, there had been a glimmer in his eyes, one that said he had considered such a future for himself.

That was a future she couldn't give to him.

All she could do was seize this moment.

It was all she could have with him, and although it might end up hurting her, she needed to take it. She needed to know what it felt like to be with him.

She wasn't afraid anymore.

Aya leaned over him, lowered her head and pressed her lips against his.

He responded instantly, his mouth claiming hers in a kiss so fierce that heat blasted through her and she moaned. He pushed forwards, his lips clashing hard with hers and tongue seeking entrance that she granted in a heartbeat, her own tongue tingling as they touched. He groaned and grabbed her hips, his fingertips pressing in, anchoring her in place in a way that thrilled her. This was what she wanted. This passion and intensity, this need. She wanted to feel desired by him.

Needed by him.

He tugged her against him and she went willingly, her hands leaving his cheeks so she could brace herself on the mattress when she ended up on top of him.

The violent shove away from him tore the air from her lungs and it left her in a gasp as she found herself standing before him. His dark silver eyes flashed dangerously as he growled and locked his arms, keeping her at a distance, and her heart stung as the shock of his rejection swept through her.

"I can't," he breathed and shook his head, ice reigning in his eyes, turning them colder than she had ever seen them.

She curled her hands into fists at her sides to stop them from shaking and lowered her head, unable to look at him as she battled the hurt blooming inside her.

She sucked down a deep breath as her feelings settled and bravely lifted her gaze to meet his. "Do you have someone else?"

His eyes widened again, a flicker of confusion crossing his face. "No. It's not that. I just can't do this…"

Aya broke away from him, anger flaring hot in her veins as her mind hurled reasons at her, every one of them striking her heart. "I get it. I do. You'll fuck every female who so much as glances at you but not me. You can't do this with me. What was that pretty speech for earlier? To make me feel better? Are you lying to me now too, Harbin? I don't need people feeding me bullshit to make me feel better. Just say it straight… you never wanted me. That kiss meant nothing."

Harbin's face darkened and he pushed onto his feet, coming to tower over her. She glared up at him, refusing to let him intimidate her.

"I don't fuck every female who glances at me," he growled.

Aya huffed and planted her hands on her hips. "That's all you have to say?"

"No," he snapped and grabbed her shoulders, his grip so tight it hurt. His eyes brightened, molten silver that warned she was pushing him again. "It isn't that I don't want you, Aya… I wanted you all those years ago… I want you now…"

She cursed her heart for doing a ridiculous flip in her chest and knocked his hands off her. "So what is it then?"

He sighed and reached out to touch her face but she stepped back, evading him. He lowered his hand to his side, his jaw clenched as he gritted his teeth and his nostrils flared as he drew in another deep breath.

His silver eyes held her immobile.

"It's too dangerous."

Before she could say a word, he grabbed her arm, pulled her close to him and shoved her right palm against his chest. Gods, he was as solid as a rock beneath her hand, his heart thundering against it.

"You can feel it… can't you?" he whispered, his eyes locked on her face, imploring her to answer that question.

The beat of his heart was too fast, too hard.

Too wild.

He was barely in control and she had only kissed him.

"I'm on the cusp, Aya, and the hungers you bring out in me are too strong. I might not be able to… I don't think I can keep control." He flashed his fangs on a growl and clutched her hand, his short claws pressing in. "What you're asking of me… I can't. It's too dangerous."

Aya stared at his hand, strong and beautiful, holding hers so tightly against his chest. Her heart beat in unison with his, a mad rush that turned her blood to liquid fire and made her burn to feel that hand on her body, satisfying the need that had been slowly consuming her from the moment he had kissed her in Archangel's facility.

"I know it's dangerous," she whispered and slowly lifted her chin, bringing her eyes up to meet his. "I'm not asking you to retain control, Harbin… because I'm not sure either of us can."

He snarled and swooped on her lips, his hands grasping her backside and hauling her up against him as he kissed her hard.

Gods, this was what she needed to feel. This hunger. This need. It poured through him into her, stoking her own need. She clutched his shoulders, moaning as she felt his muscles flex beneath her palms.

His feral growl as he turned and pinned her to the wall sent a cascade of shivers down her spine and had her pulling him closer, needing to feel him against her. She looped her arms around his neck and lifted her legs, locking them around his waist. He groaned and pressed against her, the hard bulge between his thighs rubbing her in just the right spot.

A moan slipped from her lips, she angled her head and kissed him deeper, tangling her tongue with his and seeking to master him. He fought back, his fierce kiss melting her bones and leaving her at his mercy. She needed more.

He gave it to her, using his body to pin her in place as he tore her robe open with one hand. She gasped as his cool hand cupped her right breast, squeezing and palming it, stirring the heat in her veins into an inferno. She rubbed against him, aching to feel him against her.

Naked.

She wanted to be flesh to flesh with him.

Aya released his shoulders, grabbed the hem of his t-shirt and yanked it up. He inched back, keeping his hips pressed hard against hers but giving her a view she would never forget as he helped her, tugging his t-shirt off over his head, revealing delicious compact muscles to her eyes.

Hell, she wanted to run her lips over every powerful inch of his body.

She wanted to kiss every scar, from the thickest ones on his left pectoral and above the ridge of muscle that ran over his right hip, to the tiny silvery ones that were barely noticeable on his creamy skin.

The need to feel his mouth on hers again overshadowed those hungers and she dragged him back against her. He took the hint and kissed her again, so hard that the back of her skull ached where it pressed against the wall. He strummed her nipple with one hand, the other cupping her backside.

Maddening.

She growled into his mouth, earning a low moan as her reward, and raked her nails down his sides, delighting in the firmness of his body beneath her wandering hands. She stroked her thumbs over his hips, the ridges of muscle there sending a hot thrill through her. His body was so hard against hers, the sense of power that ran from him into her cranking up her arousal until she was throbbing with need.

She needed him.

She needed her male.

"Harbin," she uttered, the sound of her voice dripping with that need shocking her.

He growled in response and dropped her to her feet. She could only stare as he pulled his belt open and popped the buttons on his fly, and pushed his black jeans down his lean hips. Her breath hitched, desire pulsing through her as he revealed his cock. Her groin throbbed, wet with her need, and she moaned and bit her lip.

Gods, she needed him.

She reached a shaky hand out, wanting to touch the rigid steel length that rose from a nest of silver curls and stroke the shaft before teasing the soft dark tip.

"Can't take that," he muttered and grabbed her again, grasping her hips and shoving her up the wall. "Next time."

She nodded. Next time.

The tiny sensible part of her mind that remained reminded her that there wasn't meant to be a next time.

Harbin drowned it out by pulling her legs around his waist and entering her in one delicious hard thrust.

Aya cried out and he captured her lips and drove deeper into her, until their bodies were pressed against each other and she couldn't take any more of him. She stilled with him, savouring the feel of him inside her, sensing he was doing the same. His kiss softened, slowing and warming her, filling her with light inside.

Dangerous light.

She couldn't let this become anything other than getting her taste of him, discovering what it was like to be with him. She couldn't. It was too dangerous.

He feared his primal need of her was dangerous.

She feared the same thing about hers. She feared it would make her fall for him all over again and he would break her heart again too.

She deepened the kiss and rocked against him, trying to shatter the softness of the moment and drive him into losing control again, surrendering to his carnal desires. He growled and grasped her hips as he withdrew, his cock almost leaving her before he drove back inside. She moaned in time with him as he thrust into her, each long stroke of his length cranking her need up to startling new heights.

He nipped her lower lip and then pressed his forehead against hers, his breath hot on her face as he pumped her harder, his hips flexing deliciously beneath her hands as she latched onto them.

Heaven.

Heat and tingles swept through her with each meeting of their hips, growing more intense as his thrusts grew fiercer. She moaned and tipped her head back, pressing it into the wall as she clung to him, feeling every intense plunge of his cock into her, feeling him laying claim to her body. She was ruined. She knew it. No male would ever be a match for Harbin. None would ever surpass him.

She had never felt anything like this.

It was mind blowing.

Incredible.

The soul-deep connection between them blossomed as Harbin dipped his head and kissed her neck, devouring it with soft nips of his blunt teeth, licking and teasing her until she quivered with need that only he could sate.

She tightened her legs around him and grabbed his right shoulder with one hand and the back of his head with the other, tunnelling her fingers into his hair.

"Gods," she moaned, white lights dancing in front of her closed eyes as pleasure rolled through her, flowing from the spot where his lips touched her and mingling with the bliss already building in her belly, edging closer to detonation.

Her mind whispered of the danger of allowing him at her neck but she couldn't hear anything above the rush in her ears and her thundering heartbeat.

He snarled and thrust harder, his claws digging into her hips, pinning her at his mercy as he took her.

Claimed her.

She could sense it building within him, her instincts blaring a warning that she didn't have the strength to heed. The hunger building within her, the need for release, was too powerful, consuming her.

She wanted more.

"Harbin," she whispered and he growled against her throat in response and dipped his hips, angling them as he pumped faster, his powerful body flexing hard against hers.

His pelvic bone slammed against her sensitive nub and she cried out as the pleasure bomb that had been building inside her detonated, sending a shockwave through her that stole her breath and left her shaking from head to toe.

She moaned with each delicious aftershock that blasted through her, sweeping upwards in the wake of every hard rough thrust of his cock. He clutched her tighter, might have muttered her name into her throat, and nipped at her flesh again, sending a sharp wave of tingles rushing through her.

Aya started to shift her head to one side, desperate to feel his tongue on the nape of her neck and the sweet press of his fangs.

He inched closer and then snarled and grunted, his actions turning jerky as his cock throbbed and she felt his hot seed shooting into her. He sharply pulled back and pressed his forehead to hers, his hips thrusting slowly as his release swept through him. The feel of his cock pulsing sent more ripples of pleasure through her and she moaned in time with him.

As she slowly came down from her high, realisation dawned on her, cooling the blood rushing through her veins.

Harbin was tense beneath her hands, his feelings in disarray. He pulled free of her, set her down and tugged his jeans back up and buttoned them as he paced away from her, heading towards the bathroom to her left. Without so much as a backward glance at her, he slammed the door closed and she flinched as the loud bang echoed around the silent room.

Aya sank against the wall, her legs trembling, as shaken as he was.

She touched the spot on the back of her neck, the place where she had tried to tempt him into biting.

Into claiming her as his mate.

He had been right.

It had been too dangerous.

CHAPTER 17

Harbin gripped the edge of the black marble counter in front of him and stared at his reflection in the mirror, his face lit by the oil lamps that burned at a low setting on either side of it. Bright silver eyes looked back at him, shining and intense. He breathed hard, trying to quell the buzzing in his veins, the fierce demand that told him to return to Aya and finish what they had started.

His primal instincts commanded him to satisfy the need he had felt go through her with her climax.

The need to feel his fangs in the nape of her neck, marking her as his forever.

He growled and yanked the tap on, not waiting for the murky water to clear before scooping it up and splashing it on his face. The first wave drawn up from the well beneath the guild was warm, but it cooled quickly after that, until it was frigid and helped douse the powerful urge to surrender to that need and bite her.

He shouldn't have let her carry him away like that, stripping down his resolve and his defences until he had given in to the hunger to have her. He should have been stronger.

He should have resisted.

Now he feared the buzzing in his veins would never go away, that he would forever be compelled to find Aya and be close to her, would forever need another taste of her, craving it until he went mad from that unfulfilled yearning.

They didn't belong together. They were separated not only by the worlds they walked in, the realms they called home, but by a million other things, all of which he didn't even want to attempt to overcome because it felt inevitable that there would always be one thing standing between them.

His past.

But gods, she had felt good in his arms, amazing wrapped around him and moaning hotly in his ear, uttering his name in a passion-drenched voice that was his new addiction. Forget the hunger to spill blood and the craving for the quiet calm that came before the kill.

Aya was more potent than that, more addictive, and he wasn't sure he could ever get enough of her.

Harbin shoved his hand through his damp hair, preening it back from his face, and looked up at himself in the mirror. His eyes caught on the red streaks on his bare torso, wrapping around from his back to his stomach just above his hips. He stroked the ones on his right with his fingers, his heart beating harder as he recalled how she had scored him with her nails at the height of passion, a lost and wild thing that had driven him into the same dangerous state, making him let go of the fragile tethers of his control and unleashing his more animalistic side.

A growl rumbled through him.

She had marked him with her claws, and fuck, did he love it.

He loved that she had sought to place a claim on him, marking him as hers.

Too dangerous.

He should have stopped her. He should have been stronger.

He pinned his eyes back on his face in the mirror and then slid them towards the door behind him, feeling the full weight of his situation bearing down on him as he stared at it.

Now she was waiting in the other room, and he was locked in a cramped bathroom, and he would bet his left nut that she was just as confused as he was, searching for answers and not finding any.

The door grew hazy, his focus failing as the buzzing in his veins grew louder, rolling into a deafening roar that had him on the verge of turning around, opening the barrier between them and sweeping her up into his arms for round two.

He clamped his hands over the edges of the counter to anchor himself in place and breathed through it, using every technique he had learned over the past twenty years to master his emotions when they slipped the leash and maintain control.

Calm battled against craving, a fight so fierce he wasn't sure he would win and be able to subdue the urges running rampant through his blood.

Through his soul.

Fuck, he could still sense her, could still feel the need in her. It was there beneath the surface when he went looking for it, easy to detect in her together with confusion, fear and anger. It lingered, as if she couldn't quite dispel it. Need. Hunger. A craving that had his hands shaking against the marble, his fingers gripping it so tightly that his knuckles burned white.

His primal instincts pushed him to return to her, the powerful urge born of the need he felt burning through her and the one it had triggered in him—a need to satisfy his female.

He tensed when he sensed her move, his head twitching to his left, towards the door. It didn't have a lock. He wasn't sure what he would do if she walked in, wasn't sure he would be able to control himself. He needed more time to rein in his desires and master them again, composing himself so he could face her.

Fuck, there wasn't much in this world that scared him, but the beautiful female in the next room was doing a damned good job of rattling him.

A knock sounded.

Not on the bathroom door.

Someone was at the main door of his small apartment. Someone powerful. He whipped around to face the bathroom door and his eyes widened as he heard the quiet creak of the knob on the main door turning.

Aya.

He couldn't hold back the snarl as he yanked the bathroom door open and stormed into the bedroom, driven to place himself between her and the intruder. She stood in the narrow corridor between the bathroom and the bed, barely a metre from the opening door, hastily tying the belt of the blue robe around her waist. He grabbed her arm and shoved her behind him, shielding her with his body just as the door opened.

Fuery pinned cold black eyes on him and then lowered them to his hand where it still gripped Aya's arm, holding her behind him. The elf's eyes narrowed, his nostrils flared, and his ears grew pointier. Aggression. Harbin knew the tells. He had been around elves long enough to have figured out the warning signs he needed to heed in order to keep his head on his shoulders.

He had also been around the mad bastard in front of him long enough to know how to defuse that aggression in most situations.

"What do you want, Fuery?" he said, pulling the elf's attention away from the female behind him and narrowing it down to him.

Fuery raised his gaze back to Harbin and relaxed a notch, but not as much as Harbin had expected. Something about Aya had rattled the elf too. Because she was female? They didn't have a female in the guild, and the times he had asked Hartt why, the elf had always glossed over it, mixing up his reasons between the female body's lack of natural strength compared with a male's, safety reasons, and keeping his male assassins on track at all times.

Harbin was beginning to think it actually had something to do with Fuery.

The dark elf drew in a slow, deep breath, and exhaled. "Hartt."

Fuery never had been a man of many words. In all the years that Harbin had worked for Hartt, he had probably heard Fuery speak around one hundred words in English.

He had heard the elf rant like a crazed son of a bitch in his own language though.

"I'll go to see him." Harbin tugged Aya closer to his back when Fuery glanced down at her hand and she bumped into him, her other hand coming up to rest on his bare skin and sending a thousand volts through him. Heat curled outwards from the place where she touched, slowly sweeping through him and reigniting his desire.

Fuery's black eyes narrowed.

Dark lines traced over him, flickering and broken, and he cast a pained look at Harbin before storming away.

Hartt had also never mentioned why Fuery couldn't teleport.

Harbin had never seen him attempt it before, and he felt sorry for the guy now that he had witnessed how much losing that ability had clearly hurt him. If he had to hazard a guess, he would say it was the price he paid for the hold the darkness had on him. What other abilities would Fuery lose as he sank into the black abyss?

He had the impression that Hartt meant the world to Fuery, and so did this job, just as it meant a lot to him. The thought that he might not be able to fulfil his duties as an assassin didn't sit well with Harbin and he had only been working with Hartt for a couple of decades. Fuery had been with Hartt for centuries.

He couldn't imagine how Fuery felt as he stood on the precipice, in danger of losing the abilities that were vital to his work as an assassin and that were a deeply rooted part of who he was.

Did he feel he was losing himself?

Did he feel he would lose Hartt too?

Aya shifted position, pulling Harbin's focus away from the empty doorway to her where she moved out to stand beside him.

He looked down at her, meeting her steady gold-silver gaze, feeling cold and hollow inside as he considered that he did know how Fuery felt after all.

He knew how afraid the elf was as he stood on the brink of losing everything that was dear to him.

Only Harbin wasn't sure whether he was thinking about losing the guild, his work and Hartt, or whether he was thinking about losing Aya.

Harbin turned away from her and walked to the black chest of drawers against the same wall as the door at the foot of the bed. He pulled the middle drawer open, grabbed one of his clean black t-shirts and tossed it at Aya. She squeaked as she quickly caught it, stopping it from hitting her in the face.

"Put that on," he grumbled and shoved the drawer closed, and opened the one below it. All of his jeans would be too large for her, but there was no damned way he was going to let her wander the corridors of the guild hall in his robe or that godsforsaken little slip of hers.

He groaned. A slip that he had left in the main reception room.

He viciously yanked a pair of dark grey sweats from the drawer and slammed it shut. He would pick up the infernal slip on his way through to Hartt's office. It had better still be there or he would be tracking down whoever had stolen it and teaching them a lesson they would never forget.

When he turned to face Aya with the sweatpants, his breath left him in a rush and his chest suddenly felt too tight.

She stood before him in just his t-shirt, the robe discarded in a pool around her bare feet. Her hands shook as she tugged at the hem of the t-shirt, trying to get it to cover more of her shapely thighs. His mouth dried out. Her eyes darted up to him, a pretty blush staining her cheeks, and he averted his gaze, turning his face away from her, and held the pants out to her.

Heat bloomed on his cheeks as she took them from him, tugging them free of his grip. Fuck, she wasn't the only one with shaking hands now. He kept his eyes pinned on the black stone floor, giving her time to cover herself, and hoped to the gods that she didn't notice that he was blushing like an idiot.

He had been inside her just minutes ago, pinning her to the wall and taking her hard, and now he was blushing because he had seen her bare legs? What the hell was wrong with him?

He blamed his hormones. They were playing with him, messing him up worse than ever now that being on the cusp of maturity had clashed with finding his female in Aya.

She shuffled away from him and he breathed a sigh of relief as the soft click of the bathroom door closing reached his ears.

Harbin twisted and flopped onto his back on the bed, his arms splayed out at his sides. He needed to get his head on straight and kick his heart back into line, but it seemed impossible when she was near him. He couldn't focus on his mission or what he was going to say to Hartt. He could only focus on her where she moved around in his bathroom, making herself at home in his tiny quarters.

He blew out his breath and then chuckled.

He had never brought a woman home. He had never let them get close to him. He was breaking all his rules with Aya and he had a terrible feeling he was going to pay dearly for it. She had torn down his defences and shaken his world all over again, rocking it and leaving him reeling.

His heart was on the line again and this time he felt certain he was going to lose it.

Gods, if he was honest with himself, he had wanted to lose it to her forty years ago, and it had hurt him when he had thought she didn't want it.

Now part of him suspected that she had desired to steal it from him.

She still desired it.

Only now things were different. He wasn't the innocent boy he had been then, wide-eyed and awed by the world. He had seen too much darkness and blood, had spilled too much of it to be a good man. He had no status, no standing, no pride. He had gone against everything he had been taught and in doing so he had destroyed the boy he had once been and built a dangerous man in his place.

One too dark and twisted to be worthy of a female like Aya.

The bathroom door opened and he looked across at her as she stepped out, rolling the waist of his sweatpants over so they fitted snug against her rounded hips.

Gods, she was beautiful.

Damp strands of her black hair hung forwards, her gold-silver eyes intent on her work, making her oblivious to him. Rose still coloured her cheeks and her lips were still swollen and dark from the ferocity of his kiss. He couldn't take his eyes off her.

Not even when she stilled and slowly lifted hers to meet his.

Her blush deepened and he wanted to stand, cross the room to her and gather her into his arms and kiss her again.

He wanted to hold her close and never let her go.

He closed his eyes instead and inhaled deeply, pushing away the tempting thoughts because they were nothing more than torture to him. He wanted what he couldn't have, and no good could come of that.

"Ready," she whispered, her soft voice trembling.

He lifted his feet up and flipped onto them, grabbed his t-shirt from the bed, and pulled it on as he headed for the main door. "Just stay close."

He pulled the black door open and stepped out into the corridor, and was a few strides down it before he realised that Aya hadn't moved. He backtracked and peered into his room at her where she still stood between his bed and the bathroom. Her wide eyes shifted from the corridor to him, her fear hitting him in powerful waves that had him crossing the short strip of floor between them and taking hold of her hand. It shook in his and he sighed.

"You have nothing to fear, Aya," he husked and resisted the temptation to brush his fingers across her cheek when she lifted her chin and looked up at him, her silvery eyebrows furrowing and the fear he spoke of growing stronger in her rather than abating. "I would never let anything happen to you. You know that, don't you?"

She hesitated, her gaze flicking to the hall before returning to him, and then nodded. "I know. It's just…"

"I know. You don't have to say it. I didn't feel comfortable here when I first arrived either." He looked away from her when her eyes widened and wished he hadn't confessed that to her. She did a good enough job of tearing down the barriers around his softer feelings without him helping by opening them up to her. He tugged her towards the door, a little harder than he should have, and she stumbled into him. "Hartt is waiting and he gets pissy if you make him wait."

She nodded and closed the door behind them, and then did something that threatened to completely blast his barriers into smithereens.

She looped her free hand around his arm and huddled close to him, her breasts pressing against his bare skin, jiggling beneath her t-shirt with each step she took.

He gritted his teeth and forced himself to focus on the corridor and his surroundings as he led her through the guild building. It was a struggle until someone came into view, a young new recruit. His senses immediately sharpened, his instinct to protect Aya driving him to go on the defensive. He tightened his grip on her hand and stared the assassin in the eye, locking gazes with him and holding it until the male had passed. He tracked him with his senses then, monitoring him until he was far away enough that he no longer posed an immediate threat to Aya.

He did the same with every male that crossed their paths, gaining a few odd looks from some of them. He didn't care that he was acting territorial.

He wouldn't let anyone frighten Aya.

He would protect her as he had promised.

They reached the main reception room. It was mercifully empty for once. His focus jumped to her cream slip where it lay on the floor where he had left it. He diverted course, bent and scooped it up, and held it out to Aya.

"You lost something."

Her cheeks blazed and she grabbed the satin slip, scrunched it into a ball and shoved it into her pocket.

Harbin smiled, unable to contain it. She was even prettier when she blushed like that and it made him want to say things that would keep that red stain on her cheeks.

She edged her eyes up and he schooled his features, adopting a flat expression that would have hidden his thoughts from anyone but her. Her little smile said she had sensed his amusement and his desire. It was hard to hide anything when she was connected to him already, the depth of it allowing her to sense things in him. Such a powerful bond was vaunted among his kind, most of his species wishing it for themselves when they found their mates and cherished by those who were gifted it by fate. It was rare though.

Many believed it made things easier for fated mates who shared such a connection.

From where he was standing, it made the whole damned thing more difficult.

Because it was making him fall for her.

CHAPTER 18

It had been three days since the meeting in Hartt's office, and while Harbin hadn't come out and told her straight how annoyed he was by the decision she had made and the fact the elf had backed it, he was definitely showing her how much it had angered him.

Harbin's right fist slammed into her cheek, sending her stumbling a few steps before landing hard on the padded floor of the gym. She lay sprawled out on the rubber mat on her front, breathing hard and fighting to quell the pain. Every inch of her ached, but she wasn't going to give up. He wanted to make her throw in the towel and go back on their plan, and she was determined to survive what he had termed 'training' and go through with it.

"You gonna lay there all day?" he bit out and she pressed her palms into the black rubber, drew down a deep breath and pushed up onto her knees.

Aya looked back over her shoulder at him and couldn't miss the anger in his silver eyes. They glowed brightly, shining like liquid metal under sunlight. He paced the mat, radiating tension at a level that had her wary of him. He had grown increasingly aggressive over the past few days and she knew why.

He was worried about her.

This was his way of dealing with it and she had to admit it wasn't a very good one. After the shouting match he'd had with Hartt about the plan the elf had put on the table, and the furious way he had looked at her when she had agreed to play bait, she had tried to talk to him about it.

He only responded in one of two ways each time she attempted to discuss things with him.

He either gruffly stated that he would protect her or he said it was her funeral.

Not entirely the most helpful of responses. His mood had been mercurial, swinging between those two feelings, but one thing had remained constant.

His desire to train her.

Gods, he was pushing her hard and he knew it. The bastard probably savoured it, thinking she would give up if he kept shoving her harder and harder, hitting her with everything he had and holding nothing back.

Well, she had news for him. She couldn't give up, no matter how much she wanted to collapse on the smelly rubber floor and sleep until her aching body healed.

She couldn't give up because she wanted vengeance too, hungered for it now that she knew the truth and knew that the one responsible was within her reach. If she could play her role and lure the Archangel huntress out of hiding, then both of them could turn the page on a chapter of their lives that had been a nightmare.

They could begin a new life.

Aya sat back on her knees and looked up at Harbin as he stopped before her, a towering mountain of muscle and menace, his eyes flashing dangerously. He was angry with her and Hartt, but she could feel other emotions in him. She could sense the underlying tension born of the realisation that he was slowly closing in on the target that had eluded him for two decades, the one responsible for using him and killing so many of his pride. She could feel that he was eager to put the plan into motion, near desperate for her to reach a point in her training where they could set the trap for the huntress, and that waiting was killing him.

He wanted to rush to the final step.

She could understand that.

This moment had been twenty years in the making and she felt the full weight of her part in the plan on her shoulders. He was relying on her to carry it out flawlessly. She would. She wouldn't fail him.

He held his hand out to her and she slipped hers into it. Warmth flowed down her arm from where they touched, heating her blood and making it burn for him. She stifled the need it birthed, a fierce hunger to have him touching her again that had been steadily growing since they had made love. She had hoped the passionate moment they had shared would scratch her itch for him, allowing her to focus again, but it had only made things worse.

The wicked hungry look in his silver eyes said that she wasn't the only one aching for an encore.

The second she was on her feet, he released her and backed off, placing a few metres between them. The room was huge, all of the equipment moved to the edges of the floor, but she still felt as if there wasn't enough space or enough air for her to breathe easily.

Every morning she arrived here ahead of him from her assigned quarters nearby, dressed in the tight-fitting sports tank and sweatpants he had gotten her from the mortal world. Every morning she warmed up alone in the huge room.

And every morning when he stalked into it, a grim look on his handsome face and his eyes instantly locking on hers, he sucked the air from the room and it closed in on her, feeling suddenly cramped and confining.

That sensation only grew worse as they sparred, each blow he landed sending mixed signals through her body, making her angry that he had managed to strike her but thrilled by the feel of his skin on hers.

Gods, she was messed up.

Fighting with him turned her on, and she hadn't failed to notice that it affected him too.

He had stormed away from her enough times, slamming the door and leaving her alone for long minutes before eventually returning and acting as if nothing had happened.

And every time he returned, she ached for him to grab her and pin her to the wall and take her as he had in his bedroom, wild and frantic with need, lost in his passion and desires.

He never did.

She had sworn what they had done would be a one-time thing, but she couldn't stop herself from wanting more from him. She didn't think this yearning for him would end until they went their separate ways.

She wasn't sure it would end even then.

Was she doomed to spend forever aching for Harbin?

Aya exhaled hard.

She had made her mind up about him and she would stick with that decision, no matter how fiercely she desired him.

She readied herself again and he did the same, shifting his feet further apart and adopting a stance that she was familiar with now. She knew which direction he would attack from and she would defend against it, just as he had trained her to do.

He launched his left fist forwards, a lightning-fast strike that had caught her off guard the first few times they had fought. She blocked with her right arm, knocking his aside, and swung her left fist, aiming low. Her blow connected with his side below his ribs, tearing a grunt from his lips that she refused to feel bad about. He wasn't pulling his punches so she refused to go easy on him in return.

Harbin dropped his right hand and went to snare hers. She whipped it back, raised and aimed again, throwing her weight into the blow. He growled as it smashed into his cheek, snapping his head back, and then dropped into a low crouch.

She always hated this bit.

She cried out as his fist struck her in her stomach, sending pain splintering outwards, and recovered a second later, in time to grab his hair and shove his head down as she brought her knee up. It cracked into his face and she released him as he fell backwards from the force of the blow, landing on his backside. He rolled backwards and pressed his hands into the floor above his shoulders.

Every powerful muscle on his torso flexed, distracting her.

She missed her cue as he flipped onto his feet and his fist smashed into her cheek, sending her crashing onto the mats.

"For fuck's sake, Aya!" His bark was startling in the quiet room, the volume of it hurting her buzzing ears as her body swiftly tried to heal the damage he had done, bringing her senses back on line. "I've told you a thousand fucking times… side step, elbow to my face. I'll block it and you can kick out at my ankle to knock me away."

She flinched with each of the first few words but rallied as he went on, her anger mounting as he bore down on her, fury flashing across his face.

"I'm not an idiot," she snapped and found her feet, coming to face him. She planted her hands on her hips and glared at him. "I was distracted."

He huffed and folded his arms across his chest, causing his biceps to flex and distract her all over again. Gods damn him. They could have made her mate ugly in every way, but no, they made him fricking perfect.

"If you're distracted in here, what the hell are you going to be like when you're out there and your life is on the line? They have to buy the bullshit we're peddling, Aya." He stepped closer to her, until she had to tip her head back to keep her glare locked on his face, a face she wanted to smash her fist into right now. Maybe if she messed it up enough, she wouldn't feel so hopelessly attracted to him. "What the hell is there to be distracted by in here anyway? I've removed everything that could possibly make you lose focus."

"Everything except you," she growled before she could consider the impact her words would have and that she was blowing her defences wide open, leaving herself too vulnerable for comfort.

He stilled and stared at her, his anger leaving him in a visible rush.

Aya spun on her heel and paced away from him, unable to bear the way he was looking at her as if she had just confessed that she loved him or some shit like that and he hadn't had a clue she felt something for him. Liar. She might have knocked him with her words, but she wasn't the only one having concentration issues. She had taken him down a few times when he should have been ready for her move, too busy staring at her body to notice her fist flying at his face.

"I'm not alone in this, Harbin." She turned to face him, breathing hard to curb her anger and the pressing need to pretend she hadn't just opened a can of worms she had intended to firmly keep the lid on. She couldn't run away now. She had to keep marching forwards, full steam ahead, even when she wasn't sure what it was that she wanted.

The past three days had thrown her feelings into disarray, leaving her unsure whether she was coming or going, whether she wanted to leave him or convince him that they could make this thing between them work even though she couldn't give him any cubs to continue his bloodline as a good mate could.

He didn't say anything, just stood there breathing hard, his chest heaving beneath his tight black t-shirt. Distracting. Why couldn't he have stayed the skinny rake he had been as a young male? Why had the gods allowed his body to fill out so deliciously?

"I know you feel it too, Harbin," she whispered and his eyes widened further, his heart sounding in her ears as it picked up pace. "We're mates."

He turned on his heel and paced away from her, scrubbing a hand across the back of his neck. When he reached the other end of the room, he stopped and stood still for what felt like forever, remaining with his back to her. It didn't take much effort on her part to feel the turbulent emotions in him. Her animal side was so attuned to his now that she could clearly sense them and the agitation and uncertainty they caused.

The hurt.

"I know." He spun to face her, his eyes cold and devoid of emotion. "But that doesn't mean I'm right for you, Aya. I can't give you what you need... what you deserve."

Gods, it hurt to hear him say that even when she felt the same way deep in her heart. She couldn't give him what he deserved. She couldn't give him a family to soothe the part of him that still hurt from losing his.

"You don't have a clue what I need, and you don't get to decide what I deserve," she said and ventured a step towards him, her animal side prowling just beneath her skin as she stared him down. "It's my choice."

He had made himself a challenge, and heck, her primal nature appreciated that with a rumbling purr. It wanted to defeat him and bring him to his knees. It took all of her will to stop the shift from sweeping through her, carrying her away and making her surrender to that need to fight him and make him submit to her.

Maybe this was a blessing in disguise, giving her the strength to sever ties with him once their mission was done.

She had intended to leave him and not look back after all.

So why did it hurt so much to hear him say he didn't want her as his mate?

Why did the rejection sting like a thousand hot needles piercing her heart?

She had thought she had hardened that heart, but it was as soft and vulnerable as it had been forty years ago, when he had broken it then.

Her primal side stirred in response to her pain, twisting it into anger, and she bared her small fangs as she growled at him. He wanted to see her fight, always goading her into going all out to make their mock-battle as realistic as possible and so he could assess her abilities.

Well, if he wanted a fight, she would damn well give him one.

She would show him that she wasn't a delicate female in need of coddling, one who was too weak to walk in his world at his side. She would show him that she was strong enough to handle him.

Aya kicked off, crossing the span of mat between them in a blur and slamming into him. She knocked him back, sending him off balance, and shoved her hand up, catching him under the jaw with the heel of her palm. His head snapped back, his growl rumbled through her, and then he was on her.

She squeaked as he grabbed her arm and twisted with her, bringing her into a choke hold. The second she found her balance, she stomped on the inside of his ankle and whipped her left arm up, bringing her hand over her shoulder and cracking his nose with it. The metallic tang of blood flooded the thick air, bringing with it a momentary pang of guilt that she quickly suppressed.

Aya brought her right arm down hard and elbowed him in the ribs.

He grunted and lost his grip on her as he staggered backwards.

She turned on him, sweeping her left leg upwards as she did so, aiming for his head. He growled and blocked her with his right hand. His fingers tightened over her ankle and the world whirled past her as he pulled her towards him, bringing her leg under his left arm. He pinned it there, shoved her in the shoulder and sent her crashing onto her back on the rubber mat.

With him on top of her.

Aya struggled, shoving at his chest and trying to move him. He braced his weight on his palms above her shoulders and pinned her legs with his, bringing their bodies into contact. She instantly stilled, her heart lodging in her throat as her body came alive in a hot rush of tingles.

"Where was that fight when we were training?" he murmured, his warm breath washing her face, and canted his head to one side, his silver eyes shimmering with amusement.

Amusement she didn't share. Couldn't.

Not when his weight was pressing down on her in the most intoxicating way, making her think wicked things, filling her head with dangerous thoughts.

His smile faded as he stared down into her eyes, his feelings shifting as if they had caught the current of hers and he was being swept along in the moment with her now.

His steady silver gaze fell to her lips.

Her snow leopard side purred in anticipation, eager for her mate to take his prize for besting her.

Her more human side warned that prize would be her heart and he would crush it.

Aya panicked.

She pushed against his shoulders with all of her strength, shoving him off her, and scrambled onto her feet, her heart hammering painfully against her ribs.

He sat on the floor staring up at her, a lost look on his face.

"I need a break." She ran for the door and bolted down the corridor outside it, not slowing until she had reached the black door of her quarters near Harbin's.

She hesitated and looked back along the hallway towards the gym, her heart steadying as she breathed slowly. The part of her that expected Harbin to be only a few steps behind her was disappointed, and she wasn't sure what to make of that. She wasn't sure of anything anymore. She had survived Hell in the hands of Archangel, had been strong enough to withstand the torture they had inflicted on her for three years, but she wasn't sure she was strong enough to survive this.

The more time she spent with Harbin, the deeper her need of him grew, and the weaker she felt.

She needed him more than air in her lungs or food in her belly.

She still had two more days until her return to the mortal world.

She wasn't sure she could last that long.

She wasn't sure she could last another second without another taste of Harbin.

CHAPTER 19

Harbin slammed his fist into the black punch bag. It swung back violently, the chain rattling, before coming at him. He smashed his other fist into it, knocking it at an angle towards his right, and swiftly shifted around to his left, dropped his torso and brought his right leg up. He growled as his shin connected with the heavy bag and carried through, putting all of his strength into the kick.

The bag lurched, swinging upwards and almost touching the ceiling of the gym before coming back down.

He didn't let up the assault. Whenever the bag came close to him, he attacked again, punching and kicking, each move fast and full of the fury blazing in his blood.

Anger stirred by the way he had handled Aya.

Stoked by the way she had walked away from him with a cold look in her eyes, one he had never seen before and never wanted to see again. She had looked at him as if he was a stranger, and it had left him frozen to his bones, shaken to his soul. He had foolishly opened up to her, allowing her close to him, and now she was distancing herself from him.

Fuck, it was what he wanted.

Wasn't it?

If this distance between them was truly what he desired, why did he feel so wretched?

Why was he yearning for her, aching to feel her in his arms, to have her standing before him with warmth in her beautiful eyes?

He smashed his left fist into the bag, his bones aching from the force of the blow, and snarled through his emerging fangs.

He needed to get away from the guild, needed space so he could clear his head and think straight. That need was strong, but another was stronger. The need to remain near Aya. The thought of leaving her alone in the guild tore another growl from his lips and had his snow leopard side pushing hard, commanding him to go to her and guard her door while she was vulnerable.

Harbin caught the punch bag in both hands and breathed hard, fighting that urge as it grew stronger. Sweat rolled down his spine beneath his t-shirt, soaking the black material. He pushed one hand through the damp strands of his silver hair and exhaled slowly, seeking to steady his heart.

It was impossible when everything in the room smelled like Aya, taunting him with her scent, keeping his need for her at a steady rolling boil.

He wasn't right for her.

No female like Aya deserved a fucked up guy like him, but there was a part of him that just couldn't stay away from her, that only wanted her more because she had turned cold towards him, pushing him away.

He needed to thaw the ice that had been in her eyes.

He needed to thaw the block of it that filled his chest.

He just needed her.

She had snuck into his heart, and he had the feeling that she had already stolen it without him noticing, and now he couldn't function without her. She had become his heart.

She had become his light in the darkness, his reason for moving forward through life.

She had become his everything.

That scared him.

He still wasn't sure whether she could ever accept a male like him as her mate. She hadn't given him any indication that she wanted more from him than a tumble in the hay. Gods, it was a messed up situation. He had spent forty years wanting nothing from females but a quick fuck with no strings attached, discarding them when they tried to get too close to him.

Now he was the one who wanted to get close to someone, and they were the one pushing him away.

Maybe he was getting what he deserved.

Maybe.

But he wouldn't know if he didn't fight for her, if he didn't put his heart on the line and do all he could to convince her that he could be what she needed.

He had to try.

Because the thought of losing her hollowed out his chest and left him dead inside.

Harbin strode across the room, yanked the door open and stormed down the black corridor, heading towards her quarters. He picked up pace as he walked, each stride quicker than the last, until he was jogging and then running through the building, his heart filled with a need to see his female.

He needed to have her in his arms again. He needed her to look at him with that soft light in her eyes, the one that made him feel she could love him.

That he was worthy of someone's affection.

That he wasn't a lost cause, doomed to the darkness.

That he could be saved.

He could redeem himself.

He skidded to a halt outside her room and braced his hands on the doorframe, catching his breath as his thoughts kept running at a million miles per hour, rushing through his head and making him dizzy.

Aya was everything he needed. She was his redemption. Revenge wouldn't grant him the peace he had found with her, the strength to move forward and walk a lighter path with her at his side.

He twisted the knob and pushed the door open, entering quietly and scanning the bedroom. Her clothes lay in a heap on the dark blue bed covers. His ears twitched as the sound of water running reached them and he eased the door closed behind him, his gaze straying to the bathroom door. She was showering.

Fuck, that had his body responding in an instant, mind conjuring an image of her that he couldn't shake. He palmed the growing bulge in his sweatpants, rubbing his hand down the length of it, and tried to stifle the sudden surge of desire. He had come here to talk to her, but his body had other ideas now, and every hard inch of him wanted to go along with them.

He had seen the way she had looked at him, had sensed the depth of her desire back in the gym when she had been pinned beneath him, her soft body cushioning his. She had thought wicked things, and now he wanted to make those things a reality.

His feet carried him towards the bathroom door, a slave to his desire, lost in the thought of having her again and satisfying her needs.

He slipped silently into the room and watched her as she turned beneath the jet of hot water, his heart labouring and cock growing ever harder, until it bordered on painful. She sang as she washed her hair, the damned steam from the water obscuring her body and stealing it from view.

He wanted to see it again.

He kicked off his boots, but didn't bother removing the rest of his clothes, didn't even think about what he was doing as he slowly walked towards her.

She turned back towards the water, raising her head and allowing it to stream over her face.

Harbin's heart beat hard as he slid the double shower cubicle's door open and stepped onto the raised tray.

Aya shrieked and turned to face him, spraying him with hot water. It bounced off her shoulders as she stared at him, wide eyed, her shock rippling through him.

"Harbin—"

He pressed the fingers of his left hand to her lips and claimed her hip with his right one, shaking his head as he drew her closer to him.

"Don't speak. I'm afraid that if you speak, I'll change my mind." He dropped his head and kissed her, and moaned as she responded, instantly opening for him, her tongue seeking his.

He growled into her mouth as he angled his head and kissed her, pulling her up against him and pinning her there, keeping her close to him. She tiptoed and stroked his tongue with hers, tearing another groan from him as he imagined that tongue teasing him elsewhere. His cock throbbed in response, pressing against her belly, and she tensed.

Her hands pressed against his chest and he thought she would push him away and tell him to leave, but she bunched his t-shirt into her fists and kissed him harder instead. The water beat down on her back, spraying over him too, soaking his clothes. A growl rumbled up his throat when she tightened her grip on his t-shirt and the sound of material tearing filled the heavy air. A thrill went through him when he felt her claws pressing into his bare flesh.

Fuck, he needed to be naked with her.

He needed to feel her nails scoring his flesh again as he satisfied her.

He needed her to mark him as hers.

He stepped back, released her and yanked his t-shirt off. It slapped on the floor behind him and Aya's little growl of appreciation almost did him in. He trembled as he forced himself to remain still, to absorb the sight of her standing before him, her hungry eyes tracking over his chest and downwards, lingering on each tensed muscle of his abdomen before drifting onwards to the waist of his sweatpants.

She licked her lips.

He snarled in response, his need stoked to new dizzying heights by the desire rolling off her, hunger that he had stirred in her. He wanted to satisfy that hunger, pleasuring her until she couldn't take any more.

He wanted her to keep looking at him like that, as if she couldn't get enough of him, might die if he didn't touch her or allow her to touch him.

He ran his thumbs around the waist of his sweatpants and her breathing came quicker, her heart pounding in his ears as her eyes followed his hands. Her sweet lips parted, her chest heaving as he slowly inched his pants down over his hips.

Her pupils dilated as he revealed his rigid length, her breath stilling and eyes locking on it. The hunger that poured through him was potent and commanding, telling him to take her. She was ready. He could feel it in her. She wanted what she saw and it was hard to deny her, to take things steady this time.

He needed more from her than a quick dirty fuck in a shower.

She needed more.

He kicked his sweatpants off, shoved them behind him with his foot, and ran his hand down the length of his cock.

She growled, a possessive and hungry rumble that had his balls tightening in response and pushed him to forget about taking things slowly.

He breathed through it, finding his control again, and looked her over.

Gods, she was incredible.

His hungry gaze lingered on the flare of her hips and the roundness of her belly. She turned slightly, her hands coming up to cover her breasts, as if his scrutiny embarrassed her. Her body twisted at an angle, revealing the lush curve of her bottom and hiding the neat thatch of curls at the apex of her thighs.

Hell, she was like Venus in that painting.

All curves. All woman.

A beauty.

Her figure spoke to him on a primal level, one he had never been aware of before setting eyes on her. She was sexy as sin and as alluring as a siren. He had always figured himself to be like so many other males, attracted to model-thin females, but he had never felt as drawn, as deeply attracted, to anyone as he was to her.

She was perfection.

He couldn't keep his eyes off her curves, or his thoughts off placing his hands on them and claiming them as he drew her against him.

The shy edge to her expression pulled words up from his heart, ones he couldn't hold back, because he knew she needed to hear them.

"You're beautiful, Aya… never hide from me… you're beautiful." He stepped towards her and she uncurled slightly, lifting her chin and slowly dropping her hands away from her bare breasts. He exhaled slowly and reached for her, brushed his fingers across her wet cheek and absorbed just how gorgeous she was. "I always thought you were beautiful."

She blushed, the heat of it warming his skin and his chest.

His gaze roamed over her again, taking in that beauty. His primal side whispered to him, the voice coming from a part of him that he never knew existed, telling him that she would be a wonderful mother, a female who could only look more beautiful when she was pregnant with his cub.

He had never considered family before, not in his line of business, and he had no place thinking about it now.

No right to think of her as belonging to him.

Even if they were to mate, he couldn't allow himself to think that she belonged to him, that she was nothing more than a possession or a trophy to do with as he pleased. He wasn't his father, and he would damn well make sure he never turned into that cold son of a bitch. If Aya gave herself to him, she would walk by his side. No, she would walk ahead of him and he would follow her, her loyal male and mate. He would place her on a pedestal, and he would love her forever.

She was his everything.

"You're pretty gorgeous too," she said, a tremble in her voice, and he realised his staring at her in silence, lost in his thoughts, had unsettled her.

He smiled, stepped into her and wrapped his arms around her waist, pinning her against him. She tipped her head back and looked up at him, a rosy hue still staining her cheeks. He wasn't sure he would ever get enough of her blushes.

She rose on her toes, caught him around the back of his head with her right hand and drew him down for a kiss that seared his blood and had him forgetting everything. Even his own name.

He groaned and gathered her closer, losing himself in her and the passion he could feel flowing through her, the hunger and need that called to him. The love and desire that purged the darkness from his soul and filled it with light.

Her belly pressed against his hard length, wedging it between them, and her slick breasts squashed against his chest, warm on his cooler skin. He ran his hands down from the small of her back and over her bottom, and swallowed the gasp that left her as he dug his short claws into her peachy globes. Her kiss grew fiercer, her lips clashing with his and fighting him for dominance. The passionate battle stirred his primal side, rousing it and making him fight harder, eager to subdue her.

She moaned and ran her claws over the back of his neck, and his eyes widened as an electric thrill ran down his back to his balls. He wanted more of that. He wanted to feel her marking him.

He backed her into the black tiles beneath the shower spray, earning a husky groan as his reward as his body pinned hers. He released her backside and pressed his hands to the wet tiles, caging her between him and the wall.

Or so he thought.

Her lips left his and he frowned and went to growl at her, reprimanding her for moving, but it came out as a feeble groan as she dropped to her knees and her breath washed over his rigid shaft. The first sweep of her tongue up the hard length of him had his fingers tensing against the tiles, and the brush of her mouth over the blunt head had his arms trembling as he leaned harder against the wall for support.

He hung his head and couldn't take his eyes off her as she took him into her mouth. Her golden-silver eyes lifting to meet his stole his breath away and heightened everything, until each sweep and press of her tongue was pure torture, and he wasn't sure he could last. His knees weakened and he groaned as she sucked him, hard and long, taking him deep into her mouth. Her tongue pressed into the underside of his cock each time she withdrew, sending a thrill shooting down to his balls as it flicked over the sensitive head.

Harbin grunted and tried to hold back, but couldn't when she cupped his balls and rolled them in her palm. He gave tense shallow thrusts, pumping into her hot mouth, lost in the pleasure flowing through him, bliss that was made all the more intense by the way she kept her eyes on him the entire time, watching him as he watched her sucking his cock.

Gods, it was too much.

He needed to taste her too.

He jerked his hips back, pulling free of her mouth, and grabbed her under her arms. He dropped to his knees and he forced her to stand, and had her right leg over his shoulder and his mouth on her before she could utter a syllable. She cried out as his tongue probed her, her fingers swiftly grasping his hair and tugging on it as desperation rushed through her, a need for release that called to him.

Harbin groaned into her and licked her harder, stroking slowly from her entrance up to her aroused little nub. The tiny bead tensed beneath the touch of his tongue, eager for more that he willingly gave to her. He flicked his tongue around it, teasing and tearing moans from her, driving her wild as she clutched his head and pressed back into the tiles behind her. Her breath shuddered with

Marked by an Assassin

each sweet groan of pleasure he elicited, her body tensing and relaxing, as if she wasn't sure what to do, was lost and unable to find her way.

He was all too happy to direct her.

He took her nub between his teeth and bit gently, and she tensed and cried out, her body rocking hard into his face. She tasted divine. He licked his way down to her entrance, hungry for more of her sweet taste. She moaned and rode his tongue as he swirled it around her core, probing it before withdrawing and teasing her again.

"Harbin." She shook against him, trembling with need.

On the precipice.

He growled and shot to his feet, her right leg caught over his arm as he clutched her backside, and entered her with one swift thrust, right to the hilt.

Aya cried out again, the sound the sweetest thing he had ever heard as her core quivered around his cock, throbbing and milking it as release took her. She breathed hard, little moans leaving her lips in time with each undulation of her body, her hands grasping his head and his shoulder, anchoring herself. Her silver eyebrows remained furrowed, her black hair hanging in slick ribbons against her pink cheeks, her mouth open and eyes screwed shut as she slowly came down from her high.

He withdrew and plunged back into her, tearing a new moan from her lips as he easily slid into her, as deep as she could take him when she was slick with her climax. He rode each quiver of her body, thrusting with long leisurely strokes of his cock, withdrawing right to the point of coming free of her body before pushing back in, making sure she felt every hard inch of him and knew what she did to him.

The calm from her climax slowly faded as he moved inside her, the desire he could sense in her building again towards her next peak. He clutched her backside when she wrapped both of her legs around him and began to join in, rolling her hips and meeting his thrusts. He groaned and kissed her, claiming her mouth as his as he claimed her body, pumping her harder and driving her higher.

Her moans teased his ears, each flex of her body against his making his balls draw up and tighten, pushing him closer to his own release. He ground his teeth and tore himself away from her mouth, burying his face in her neck as he fought for control, mastering his body so she would find another release before his overcame him.

He clutched her tighter and thrust harder, his control slipping as his primal hungers took command again, thundering in his blood and awakening his need to have her as his mate, to sink his teeth into the nape of her neck and mark her as forever his.

Harbin bit down on his own lip to quell those hungers, satisfying them with the taste of his own blood on his tongue as he drove into her, harder now, unable to hold back the ferocity of his need as it overwhelmed him. His balls grew tighter, his shaft thickening as he thrust into her. She moaned hotly in his ear, his name falling from her lips in a chant like a prayer, a plea for more. She was close.

He growled into her throat, grasped her backside and quickened his pace, frantic wild thrusts that had his body slamming against hers. Awareness grew at the back of his mind, a fear that he was hurting her with his roughness, his need to have her and release inside her, spilling his seed and marking her in a most primal way. He couldn't bring himself to heed it, and the way Aya was urging him on, her feet pressing into his backside each time he withdrew and forcing him back inside her, said he had nothing to fear anyway.

She was as wild with need as he was, as lost in their passion.

Her fingers tugged on his hair, yanking his head back, and he groaned into her mouth as it seized his. She moaned back at him, her tongue sweeping over his lips, over the points where his fangs had broken his skin. Her moan turned into a growl and she kissed him harder, gripped him tighter, and did something that catapulted him over the edge.

She bit him.

Her small fangs sinking into his lower lip sent a shockwave through him that stole his breath, made his ears ring and had white spots dancing across his vision. He slammed into her, hard enough to smash her against the tiles and knock the breath from her lungs, and shuddered as his cock throbbed, shooting hot jets of his seed into her.

She quivered around him again, throbbing with her own release, a climax that rolled through him too, their pleasure mingling and heightening, until he couldn't think.

He could only feel.

Pleasure. Bliss. Warmth. Hunger. Desire. Lust.

Love.

It all rolled through him like a wave and crashed over his heart.

Aya stroked his shoulders, her body trembling against his as he held her in place, struggling to bring himself down and find his balance again.

She swept her tongue over his lip and he moaned, shook as the hunger and need that never seemed quite satisfied where Aya was concerned began to bubble up again, simmering in his veins.

He wasn't sure he would ever get enough of her.

The more time he spent with her, the more he wanted her. The more he craved her.

Now, he craved her more than the quiet emotionless calm that had once been the balm for his troubled soul.

He wasn't sure what lay ahead of them, but he knew one thing with startling clarity.

Neither of them could move on with their lives until their pasts had been laid to rest.

If he was going to win Aya as his mate, he had to give her the vengeance they both needed, but to achieve that, he had to place her in danger.

He had to risk losing her in order to win her.

CHAPTER 20

Aya huddled into her thick grey wool coat, wrapping her arms across her chest and tucking her hands under her armpits as she hurried along the quiet street. The lamps were spaced far apart, allowing dark patches between the yellow pools of light. It had never bothered her before, but it set her on edge now.

Truthfully, she had been on edge since Hartt had teleported her back into her apartment, setting their plan in motion, and had announced that Harbin would return to the mortal world and would be tracking her, lying in wait to attack her.

She hadn't slept well that day, or any day after it. She hadn't realised that playing bait would take longer than a day at most, hadn't considered that she would be constantly on alert, waiting for Harbin to launch his attack and trigger the second phase of the plan. It had been over seventy-two hours since Hartt had dropped her off and it was growing increasingly difficult to relax and act normal, going about her usual business.

Harbin had to attack her out of the blue to make it look real.

That really didn't help.

Whenever she left her apartment, she was constantly on high alert, her senses scanning as far and wide around her as they could reach, monitoring everything for a sign of him. Whenever she caught his scent, or felt him near to her, she grew tense, her body coiling in anticipation and her snow leopard side pacing restlessly beneath the surface, itching for her to change and defend herself against the invisible threat.

Now, she was tired, both physically and emotionally exhausted. She had barely caught a few hours' sleep during the past three days and being on alert all the time was draining her. If Harbin didn't attack her soon, she wasn't going to have the strength left to fight him and make it look convincing.

She unfurled her arms and pushed her hood back, sucked down a deep breath of cool night air and blew it out. It had to be soon. She didn't think she could take this uncertainty for much longer. Even with her training, she felt exposed and vulnerable.

Her ears twitched, her senses sharpening when she felt someone watching her.

Not Harbin.

Aya kept walking, heading along the silent street and then banking right at an alley between two brick buildings. The shortcut would bring her out near the entrance of Switch. She had been walking the same route each night, going about her normal routine of heading to the club, chatting with Rocky, and then dancing for a few hours before heading home.

She was glad that Rocky had returned to the club, and that Archangel hadn't had a chance to study him. He had escaped the compound before his scheduled time with the scientists. When she had braved a visit to the club on the first night of her return to the mortal world, he had greeted her with a hug so tight that she had almost cried. She had wanted to tell him that she was sorry, that it was her fault he had been caught, but she had been aware of the other people on the street and that any one of them might have been watching her and listening in on their conversation.

When everything was over, she was going to sit the big guy down and tell him straight what had happened. She valued their friendship too much to lie to him and in her heart she knew that he would forgive her.

Maybe she would tell him tonight that she needed to speak with him in private, because it was eating away at her.

A shadowy figure dropped right in front of her and she staggered back a few steps, heart racing as she gathered her wits and quickly focused.

Not quite quickly enough.

She grunted as a fist connected with her jaw and the male muttered a curse under his breath.

Harbin.

Dressed head to toe in black combat gear, he was a wraith in the darkness. His eyes caught the dim light, flashing silver at her, and her pulse accelerated as he advanced on her. She sucked down a deep breath and tried to quell the trembling in her body, preparing herself for his next move.

The smell of him, spice and snow, awakened her body and mind, and triggered her training. She blocked his next attack and landed her own. He was faster than he had been in the gym and she struggled to keep up with him and his moves, tripped over a few of the ones they had run through, allowing him to land more blows than she should have. She swiftly blocked the kick he aimed at her head, using both of her forearms to stop his shin, and then shoved against his leg. He lost balance and barely recovered, giving her an opportunity she couldn't waste.

Aya spun on her heel and brought her own foot up in an arching kick. It connected hard with the side of his head and he staggered sideways, hit the wall and braced himself against it. He growled and shook his head, tossed her a black look that she could easily read.

She was breaking with the fight they had planned together and it was pissing him off, but he really had caught her off guard and her instincts had seized control, her primal side rising in response to the danger he represented. She couldn't move as swiftly as he could, not when it came to fighting. She hadn't expected him to crank up the speed this much. It was impossible for her to keep up, so she was going to wing it.

He launched at her and she flipped backwards, landed in a crouch and kicked off. She sailed through the air, effortlessly gliding over his head. He skidded, twisted and pushed off again, running right at her. Her feet hit the tarmac and she sprang right, kicked off the wall and landed behind him again. He snarled and turned on her, his frustration rolling off him in warning waves that she chose to ignore.

She was a female shifter, more agile than the males of her kind. It was more realistic that she would use her speed to defend herself rather than attack someone stronger than her.

The second he neared her, she swept her leg up into another fierce kick. Her boot hit him hard on the jaw, snapped his head to his right, and sent him crashing to the ground.

He pushed himself up on his hands and roared at her, his silver eyes flashing dangerously.

Her primal side responded in an instant, rising to the threat he had issued and refusing to back down. Stupid male. If he wanted a fight, he would have one.

She tore her coat off and was out of her boots before he had even found his feet. The shift was quick to come, her bones aching as they stretched or shrank, distorting to new forms beneath her skin. Fur rippled over her body, sweeping up her legs first as they shortened inside her jeans. She landed on all fours and growled as she kicked her trousers off, freeing herself, and then shuddered and mewled as the change reached her arms, the pain of the shift almost blinding her. She hated calling it quickly and was ridiculously out of practice.

Harbin was faster than her, his shift complete well before her tail had finished growing from the base of her spine and her ears had rounded and moved up her head.

Her breath caught in her throat as she looked at him, seeing the majestic male he truly was staring back at her through bright silver eyes. He was larger than her in his cat form, a beautiful big male with thick lustrous silver fur dotted with dark crescents and spots. The sight of him in his animal form sent an unexpected response through her, a powerful urge that she struggled to deny.

She wanted to rub against him, wanted to scent him and get his attention. She wanted him to rub her in response, to show her affection and attention, as a mated male would.

Stupid instincts.

He moved in a blur of silver and she grunted as he landed on her, both huge front paws coming down hard on her shoulders. She growled and rose onto her back feet to dislodge him. He only tightened his hold on her and did something she really hadn't anticipated.

He sank his fangs into the back of her neck, his hold strong but soft enough that he didn't break the skin. She whined and tried to break free, but he refused to release her. He bore down on her instead, using his heavier weight to send her down onto her paws. If she didn't break free, he would have her pinned on her stomach.

She snarled and twisted her body, whimpering as pain tore through the back of her neck and the scent of blood bloomed in the cold air. Harbin released her and backed off, his shock rippling through her, surprise that she had hurt herself in order to escape him. It was what any cat shifter in her position would have done. It shouldn't have come as a shock to him when they were trying to make this fight look real.

Her heart whispered that it hadn't been shock over the fact she had been willing to hurt herself. It had been surprise that she had allowed his fangs to penetrate her neck in the very place he needed to bite to mark her as his mate. She hadn't even considered that in the heat of the moment, but she felt sure that it took more than a little scratch to bind them as mates. Every lesson she'd had about mating, the teacher had said the male had to fully penetrate the female's neck with all four fangs. Harbin had barely scratched her.

She used his momentary distraction against him and leaped at him, splaying her front legs as she sailed through the air. He reacted quickly, rising onto his hind legs to defend against her. His larger paws came at her as she landed just short of him, smashing against her shoulders and the side of her head, but she had won this round.

Aya twisted her head as her front legs wrapped around his chest and bit down on the vulnerable underside of his neck, sinking her fangs into his throat and locking her jaw to stop him from shaking her. His heart pounded wildly in her ears as he went down with her on top of him and struggled against her, kicking his back legs and trying to catch her delicate stomach with his claws.

She held on, refusing to release him.

His movements grew weaker and then suddenly stopped, his body going slack beneath hers. He shifted back and his neck slipped free of her teeth, smaller in his human form. She backed off, her eyes darting over him as she breathed hard, senses locked on him and searching.

Searching.

Her heart hitched, pain pulsing through her as no heartbeat reached her sensitive ears.

No.

Aya shifted back, her t-shirt and deep blue jumper offering her little protection against the frigid night, not as her fur had. She shivered, but not from the cold. The ice in her veins was born of fear.

Had she killed him?

Tears formed in her eyes, hot and stinging, and she shook her head, her short black hair brushing her cheeks as she stared down at Harbin where he lay naked and motionless on the black ground, his throat covered in blood.

No.

She couldn't have killed him.

He couldn't be dead.

Her hands shook and she balled them into fists, trembling all over as she kept searching for a sign of life in him. He couldn't be dead. She couldn't have killed him. Her throat closed, her heart a timid thing in her chest as her ears rang and she tried to comprehend what was happening. She couldn't have lost him.

Her animal side cried out and she bellowed in response, unleashing all of her pain in the call. Her knees gave out but she didn't feel the impact with the tarmac as she fought the need to change and run wild.

The need to kill.

It was too strong.

She clutched at herself, afraid she wouldn't be able to hold her form, would succumb to the raw emotions running through her, rousing her primal instincts. The pain of losing Harbin was too great though, too powerful for her snow leopard side to handle. It fought for control and she wanted to give in to it, wanted the oblivion she knew awaited her if she allowed it to overwhelm her. She wouldn't remember the things she did, would no longer feel as she was now, hurting so deeply she couldn't breathe. Her more human mind would be subdued by her animal one and she would be free.

Fur swept up her bare legs.

A dark-haired male appeared in the alley, morphing out of the shadows, his black robes allowing him to blend into the night and his red eyes cold despite the fire that burned in them as he looked down at Harbin and then at her.

The urge to shift in order to escape her pain became an urge to shift in order to protect herself from this male.

The witch.

The tinny scent of magic was all over him, more potent now, as if he had grown stronger since their last meeting.

She bared her fangs at him and rose onto her feet, quickly taking a few steps back to her clothes. She put her jeans on, not to cover herself from his prying eyes but to restore some control over her animal side, hindering it with the tight clothing. It wanted her to shift and fight, viewed the witch as a threat to her mate, one she had to eliminate in order to protect him.

The male's red eyes edged towards his left.

Aya looked there.

A woman wrapped in a thick black ankle-length coat, the hood up to throw her face into shadow, walked out of thin air, as if she had teleported.

Or perhaps she had been cloaked by the male.

The female pushed the hood back with gloved hands, revealing a spill of golden hair highlighted with silver and a face Aya would never forget.

The huntress.

She might have been there when Aya had last fought the male, the time when Harbin had intervened. They could have ended this back then if only they had been aware that the woman travelled with the witch, shielded from view by magic.

"Aya," the huntress said, a soft smile playing on her lips that didn't fool Aya. She wasn't about to let her guard down and let the woman play her all over again.

Her smile widened, causing crow's feet beside her green eyes. Time hadn't been kind to the huntress, the seventeen years since they had last seen each other taking their toll on the mortal.

"I'm glad to see he didn't hurt you." The huntress looked down at Harbin where he lay on the ground between them, sprawled out and hopefully only unconscious.

Not dead.

Please don't be dead.

Aya looked down at him again, monitoring him with her senses, searching for a sign of life.

The huntress stepped closer to him, triggering a fierce need in Aya, an urge to place herself between him and the woman and protect him. She struggled to tamp down that need and stay where she was, sure that she would only place Harbin in danger if she moved to shield him. She would give away the game they were playing, a trap that had been set and she was ready to spring.

She had to stay where she was and keep her head, no matter what the huntress said or did.

It all came down to this moment.

The woman eyed Harbin, a glimmer of sick satisfaction in her eyes. "Two decades... I've spent two decades living in the shadows... fearing for my life... but now I'm free."

The huntress raised her gaze away from Harbin and pinned it on Aya.

"Can you imagine what that was like?" she whispered, her voice thick with emotion that emanated from her in tangible waves. She looked down at her hands before wrapping her arms around herself, her fingers pressing into her arms through her thick black coat. "Slaughtering my friends... killing everyone I knew. All of us lived in fear, and my own fear grew worse with each letter or phone call I received that told me another was dead. Ten years ago the last call came... I was alone... the sole survivor."

Aya had to bite her tongue to stop herself from saying the woman had brought it all on herself. She might have suffered, but her pain was nothing compared with what Harbin had been through, or what Aya had been through. Aya couldn't find a single shred of sympathy for the bitch who had used him and had killed so many of her kin, and had subjected her and others to torturous experiments.

She schooled her features, hiding her rising anger from the woman and the witch, afraid that the male would sense it in her if she didn't master her emotions and keep her head. She couldn't screw things up now, when they were so close.

"I went into hiding out in the countryside, never leaving my home, afraid he would kill me if I set foot outside it." The woman looked down at Harbin and sneered, her face twisting into darkness. "I couldn't continue living that way… so I looked for assistance in securing my freedom. I wanted to live my life again… and now I can."

The male beside the woman smirked, his red eyes glowing in the low light. There was an air of brimstone about him that was familiar now Aya had been to Hell. He must have come from that dark realm, bringing with him information about Harbin that the woman had used to her advantage. She had taken out a contract on Aya, offering it to Harbin's guild, knowing he would take it and would expose himself, giving her an opportunity to kill him.

The huntress crouched beside Harbin, her green eyes fixed on him, a strange sombre edge to her expression as she studied him.

"I had wanted the kill. I had wanted to deal with him as I should have back then." Her voice turned distant, as if her memories had taken hold of her and she was reliving them. "I had been too soft… charmed by him… a foolish young woman who had allowed her emotions to get the better of her."

She lifted her head and looked over Harbin to Aya.

"You know how that feels though, don't you?" The cold edge to her green eyes chilled Aya and rang warning bells in her head, her heart screaming that the woman was on to her and knew this was a trap, that any moment now the witch would attack her or Harbin when he was vulnerable.

Aya glared down at Harbin. "I was an idiot once… like so many other females. I fell under his spell and he betrayed me."

The huntress smiled and then sighed as she looked back down at Harbin. "We both fell under his spell… and we have both regretted it ever since. I should have remained detached and professional, but I failed. I couldn't bring myself to kill him after drugging him… he had been so handsome… he still is handsome… but I suppose that is a weapon he employs to slay many women."

Aya wanted to growl, not just because the huntress clearly still harboured desire for Harbin even though he wanted to kill her. She wanted to growl because the female clearly intended to finish the mission she had been given twenty years ago by ensuring Harbin was dead.

That fear became a reality as the woman stood and held her hand out to the male beside her. He muttered something in a strange tongue and a blade appeared in the woman's gloved hand.

"It must have felt nice," the huntress said in a soft voice, her eyes locked on Harbin as she lowered the blade to her side and then lifting to fix on Aya. "I want to know… since my victory is a hollow one… how does it feel to have killed the person who brought harm to you and your kin?"

Aya's lips curled into a slow smile.

"I'll tell you when you're drawing your last breath."

CHAPTER 21

"I'll tell you when you're drawing your last breath."

That was Harbin's cue. He flipped onto his feet and whirled to face the witch and the huntress, bringing his leg around in a fast blur at the same time. His bare heel connected with the right forearm of the male as he quickly brought his arm up to defend himself. Fire flashed in the witch's red eyes and his left hand shot towards Harbin's ankle.

Harbin was too fast, shifting his leg beyond the male's reach before he could snag it, and bringing his other leg up as he dipped his upper body downwards to counter his weight as he took another shot at the witch.

This time when the black-haired male blocked, he put a pulse of power into it and Harbin went spinning across the alley, tumbling head over heel until he crashed into the wall and slid down it.

Aya roared and kicked off, and his head snapped towards her. Her gold-silver eyes were locked on the blonde huntress, her emerging fangs bared on a wicked snarl as she ran at her.

His focused leaped to the huntress and the darkness he expected to rise and overwhelm him as it did whenever he crossed paths with a member of Archangel didn't come. Instead, calm rushed through him, clarity that filled him with a sense that he could fight and keep his head throughout the battle, and he knew it was because of Aya. Her presence soothed him, tempering the darkness and his memories, holding them at bay. His eyes darted to her, and every male instinct he possessed said to intervene and protect his mate, but he had a problem.

He slid his silver gaze back to the witch that stood between him and the fighting females.

The male neatened his snug black robe, smoothing the looser tails over his black trousers, and calmly lifted red eyes towards him. The emptiness in them warned Harbin that this wasn't going to be an easy fight, because the witch was already drawing immense power from the well of magic inside him, giving himself over to it and preparing himself for the coming battle. Harbin had watched the bastard fight before and knew some of his moves, but he wasn't going to let his guard down and think they were the only ones the male had in his arsenal.

He wasn't going to take his eyes off the witch until he was down for the count. Only then could he go after the huntress. If he attempted an attack on her now, the witch would use that opening against him and he would be the one down for the count instead.

He had to trust that Aya could keep the huntress occupied until he had dealt with the witch.

They had dealt with the witch.

A familiar ripple of power ran down Harbin's spine and he picked himself up, not taking his eyes off the witch as his backup arrived.

Something soft hit him in the back. "At least have a little modesty."

His lips quirked at the sound of disgust mixed with disappointment in Hartt's voice. It wasn't the first time his boss had come armed with more than weapons, aware that Harbin was going to be naked when he arrived. It wasn't the thousandth time. Hartt had started to sound unimpressed after the tenth, and Harbin was never growing tired of hearing the elf say the same damned thing to him each time he brought him something to wear.

He stepped backwards over the pair of black shorts, kicked them up and caught them, all without taking his eyes off the male witch.

Aya grunted as she tackled the huntress, knocking the female back a few steps, into view beyond the male.

Harbin casually tugged the shorts on, but there was nothing calm about him. He was buzzing with a need to plough through the witch to reach the huntress, and finally have his vengeance.

He couldn't risk it though. He had already placed Aya in enough danger by making her play bait, he wasn't going to turn the witch's focus towards her when she was having enough trouble dealing with the huntress. The bitch had drawn a small compact crossbow and was firing it like the bolts were going out of style. Several zipped past him, and one shot towards the two males at his back.

Fuery's growl was nothing short of vicious as he caught and snapped one of the small metal bolts in half.

The witch's red eyes shifted to the elf and narrowed, a flicker of recognition dawning in them.

Harbin waited, aware that things were about to take a turn for the worse. The male's face twisted into dark lines and his red eyes brightened, and the scent of magic in the air grew stronger, gaining a sickly edge to it that had him wanting to back away and find some clean air to breathe.

Death.

His eyes widened as the air shimmered between him and the witch, shifting like a heat haze at first before shadowy figures grew in the centre of the ripples, taking form and becoming solid as the male muttered beneath his breath.

Clones.

Their milky blue eyes glowed eerily in the low-lit alley.

Three on three didn't sound too bad, although it did give the witch the upper hand.

Harbin's stomach dropped. Fuck.

The two clones stepped aside, breaking apart and revealing another two.

Five on three didn't sound so good.

The huntress shrieked and Harbin looked there, his eyes landing on her retreating back as she sprinted into the shadows, clutching her right arm.

Aya went after her.

Harbin took a step forwards, driven to follow his mate and the female.

All Hell broke loose.

The clone on the left attacked him, swiping his hand through the air, long sharp nails aimed straight for Harbin's throat. Harbin leaped back at the last second, barely dodging the strike, and ignored Hartt's unimpressed muttering.

He held his right hand out to his boss and looked back at him as they edged in unison away from the clones and the witch, gaining some space. Hartt brought his left hand up in front of him and Harbin's twin short curved black blades appeared in them. They were his, but he had left Hartt as their owner, aware that the elf could only teleport items that belonged to him. It was handy at a time like this when they were working together or Harbin had to call on him for assistance, meaning the elf didn't need to leave his side to bring Harbin's blades to him.

Fuery remained in the space between them and the witch. He stared at the clones, his black eyes cold and emotionless, not showing the hunger that Harbin could feel in him. The excitement. The elf's ears grew pointed, flaring back against the tied top half of his overlong blue-black hair. The silver clasp that held it in place flashed under the street lamps as Fuery launched forwards and the golden light chased over the black scales of his skin-tight armour.

His long black katana twitched at his side, skilfully shifted into an attack position, the point facing his enemies and both hands gripping the hilt. He growled and leaped, swung hard and grinned as he came down on top of the clone on the far right. The clone tried to dodge but wasn't quick enough, and Fuery's booted feet hit him hard in the chest, sending him crashing onto the tarmac.

Fuery kicked off, somersaulted in the air and landed in a silent crouch behind the witch.

Harbin huffed.

It was typical of Fuery to place a claim on the most powerful enemy present.

Although, in this case, it did leave two clones for him and two for Hartt, which was more of an even split than Fuery normally managed. Harbin was surprised he hadn't attempted to take on all five at once. It seemed that the mad bastard still had a shred of sense left in his twisted head after all and knew he wouldn't be able to tackle both the witch and his copies alone.

Divide and conquer.

Harbin tossed one blade into his left hand, curled his fingers around the black leather hilts and assessed the two clones on his side. He had to end this quickly. Killing the copies would weaken the witch, and give him the chance to deal the final blow so he could go after Aya.

She was growing distant, still chasing the huntress. He couldn't sense any pain in her, but the connection was becoming hazy as she moved away from him. If she moved much further away, she could be hurt without him sensing it. He might not reach her in time to protect her.

His gaze strayed to the direction she had run.

Every fibre of his being said to forget the witch and go after his mate and the huntress.

"Go," Hartt barked as he lashed out with his black blade at one of the clones, forcing the male to quickly strafe right to avoid the blow, opening a gap in their defensive line.

Harbin glanced at his boss, caught the steely determination flashing in his violet eyes as he clashed with the clone again, and didn't hesitate.

He ran for the opening Hartt had created for him.

Another clone stepped into his path and he growled as he slashed with his twin blades, cutting through the air in vicious arcs. The male raised his arm to block, deflecting Harbin's left blade but leaving himself wide open for his right one. He grinned as it sliced down the male's chest, leaving a gash in his black tunic, revealing a strip of white flesh and crimson. The clone grunted, his pale blue eyes wide and dark with pain as he stumbled backwards and brought his arms up to his chest.

Hartt snarled as he thrust his blade forwards, a violent blur in the low-lit alley, and the copy he had been fighting cried out. Harbin glanced his way as the male staggered into view, the end of Hartt's black sword protruding from his back and his hands clutching the blade in front of him.

Harbin's eyes widened as the clone gritted his teeth and pushed the blade out of him despite Hartt's attempts to drive it deeper, forcing the elf back. They were growing stronger.

He whipped his head around towards Fuery and the male witch where they fought, two wraiths illuminated only by the violent flashes of colourful light as the witch employed spells to weaken Fuery.

But he was weakening too.

Each spell he cast, drained his magic. Each injury they dealt his clones, weakened him too. He was trying to keep them alive, pouring more strength into them. He was desperate.

Harbin thought that only made him more dangerous.

He whirled on his heel, bringing his right blade up at the same time. It connected with the neck of the clone Hartt had been fighting and he drove through the obstruction, growling as his blade sliced deep through bone and flesh. Blood sprayed, slapping onto the tarmac, followed by the dull thud of the clone's head as it dropped and the slam of his body that fell after it.

The male witch barked out a feral roar as he hurled his right hand forwards, unleashing a blast of green light that hit Fuery square in the chest and sent him flying across the alley. The elf smacked into the brick wall with such force that the blocks fractured, fault lines splintering outwards from where he had impacted. He grunted and dropped to the ground.

Motionless.

"Fuery," Hartt breathed and silvery light flashed over him, almost blinding in the darkness.

He reappeared next to his comrade in a crouch, his blade held horizontal in front of him and Fuery, sharp edge facing the enemy. He kept his eyes locked on the witch as he ran his free hand over Fuery's neck. Searching for a pulse.

The brief spark of relief in Hartt's violet eyes before they suddenly darkened was all Harbin needed to tell him that Fuery was fine.

Hartt slowly rose onto his feet, coming to face the male witch.

Harbin ducked beneath a blow one of the remaining clones aimed at him, his heart pounding faster as he tried to keep all three of them with him. They needed to buy some time, giving Fuery a chance to come around, and Harbin couldn't let any of the clones turn their focus on Hartt. The elf couldn't fight the male witch and protect Fuery from the clones at the same time.

Harbin growled as fiery pain shot across his side and turned on his heel, swiftly facing the one who had attacked him. He lashed out with his right blade, forcing the male to block, and drove forwards with his left. The clone snatched his left wrist and twisted it. Harbin gritted his teeth and grunted as pain bolted through his bones and turned his body with his arm, stopping the male from breaking it.

It seemed the less clones there were, the stronger the remaining ones became.

Not a problem.

He just had to move faster, not allowing them to land any attacks or see his moves coming. He flipped his right blade in his hand and slashed at the clone's head. The male's blue eyes shot towards his hand and he tried to dodge it, but he wasn't quick enough to completely evade the strike. Harbin's blade swiped across his cheek and rivulets of red streamed down to his jaw. The clone shoved with the hand that still held Harbin's wrist, sending him staggering backwards.

Giving him the space he needed.

He couldn't shift, because the witch would force him to change back, just as he had Aya, and it would weaken him. He was slower in his human form, but still as agile as and even more dangerous than he was in his snow leopard form.

He flipped his other blade in his left hand, so the black knife ran along the underside of his forearm, his thumbs near the end of the hilts, and sprang at the clone. The male blocked, his forearms and fists knocking against Harbin's with each blow he tried to land. It seemed the witch was on to him, making his clones more agile. Silver short blades that matched Harbin's appeared in the hands of the clones around him. The witch was trying to gain the upper hand, arming his slaves with the abilities and weapons they needed to take him down.

If he had been alone, it might have proven a problem.

But he wasn't.

A black snarl sounded from behind Harbin, words growled in the elf tongue, and a dark wave rolled over him, malevolence in its purest form. It seemed to suck what little light there was from the alley and all the warmth from the air.

The hairs on the back of Harbin's neck prickled and his eyes widened as he spun to face the clone, saw the flash of a silver blade in his hand, and realised he wouldn't be quick enough to block the blow aimed straight at his neck.

His heart lodged in his throat and he swiftly brought his blade up, even when he knew he wouldn't make it.

Black jagged smoke exploded behind the copy and blood sprayed over Harbin, drenching his bare chest.

He stared blankly at the black clawed hand protruding from the clone's chest, dripping with dark liquid, and then beyond the male to the one who towered behind him, a vision of grim death.

Fuery's lips peeled back in a grin, flashing enormous fangs, and the corona of violet shining around his pupils stuttered, beginning to fade. A chill went through Harbin as that ring of dying light changed shape, stretching into points at the top and bottom.

His pupils were turning elliptical.

"Fuery," Harbin barked, dropped one of his blades and dragged the clone away from him, shoving the body to one side so he could reach the elf. "Fuery, listen to my voice. Stay with me, Buddy."

Fuery bared his fangs on a snarl that chilled Harbin's blood.

The remaining violet in his eyes burned crimson.

Hartt muttered a ripe curse and appeared in a flash of silvery light, between Harbin and Fuery. He swung his left hand, his palm striking Fuery's cheek so hard that the crack of flesh-hitting-flesh rang around the alley.

"Pull yourself together," Hartt growled and Fuery blinked, and Harbin could only stare as the red in his eyes faded, the violet shining through again. Hartt grabbed the elf and pulled him into an embrace. "Fucking hell... I thought we'd lost you that time."

Fuery mumbled something in the elf tongue and pushed away from Hartt, an awkward edge to his expression as he called his blade back to his hand and looked down at his boots.

"Pull back," Hartt said but Fuery ignored him, shifting into a warrior's stance as his dark eyes danced between the two remaining clones.

He turned to face the witch.

Grinned.

Disappeared.

Fucking hell. Harbin had never seen Fuery actually complete a teleport, and it had happened twice now. He wasn't sure if that was a good thing or a bad thing, but the concerned look on Hartt's face said it was bad.

"Get him out of here," Harbin barked and lashed out at one of the clones, driving it away from its remaining companion so he could fight it one on one.

"Not going to happen." Hartt's voice was a dark growl as he teleported and appeared behind the other copy, his blade a black blur as he slashed up the male's back. The clone gave an agonised bellow and swung with his silver knife as he turned on his heel to face Hartt. The elf blocked with his sword, following through and knocking the clone back. His violet gaze leaped to Fuery where he battled the witch, a menacing shadow that Harbin couldn't track as he dodged each spell the male cast. "I have to let him finish this or he'll lose control again."

Closure.

Hartt had warned him once not to get between Fuery and an enemy, because Fuery would kill anyone who got in his way once he had locked on to a target. He wouldn't let anyone steal that kill from him. He always finished what he started.

Harbin could understand that.

He looked towards the end of the alley again as he blocked another attack, his senses stretching outwards, scouring the city for Aya. She had gone after the huntress alone, she intended to take the bitch down, but he couldn't let her do it. He needed the closure.

"Go," Hartt barked again and Harbin kicked the clone away from him, sending it slamming into the wall.

He looked back at his boss, saw the determination in his eyes and that it was an order this time. One he would be an idiot to disobey.

"We can handle this." Hartt brought his blade down in a swift arc, slashing down the clone's chest and sending him to his knees.

The witch howled in pain and threw his hand out in the direction of the injured clone. Pouring more magic into it. He was healing them on the fly, trying to keep the remaining two alive, but each time he used a spell on them, he weakened himself and left himself open. Fuery attacked in that moment, raking claws over the witch's extended arm and slicing through his black robe.

Blood spilled, the scent of it rank, tinny and sharp, laced with death.

Fuery grinned.

The witch turned on him, hitting him with another blast of magic, sending him crashing and tumbling across the tarmac. The second he stopped rolling, he was on his feet and springing at the witch, clashing with him again.

"Go," Hartt said and Harbin obeyed, certain that his two comrades could handle the witch and the two remaining clones.

They were powerful elves and he believed in them, knew in his heart that they would win.

Aya needed him more than they did.

He roared, the sound echoing around the dark streets, and kicked off, his blood pounding with a need to reach her.

He focused wholly on her as he ran, aware that she would sense him coming towards her.

"Hold on, Aya," he whispered, praying to whatever gods would listen to him that they would protect his mate until he reached her, watching over her and keeping her safe for him.

He couldn't lose her.

He couldn't lose someone he loved again.

CHAPTER 22

Harbin sprinted through the city streets, following his nose and the buzzing inside him that warned she was nearby. It grew stronger the closer he came to her, running barefoot and bare-chested along quiet residential roads surrounded by elegant townhouses. Something unsettling also grew with it, an echo of her pain in his side, his arm and his thigh. The huntress had injured her. He banked left at a square and then backtracked when a sharp grunt sounded in the leafy area in the centre of it to his right.

Aya.

He growled and ran in that direction. When he reached the wrought iron fence that surrounded the small park, the scent of blood hit him hard. Not just mortal blood. Aya's blood too.

His heart hammered against his chest and he vaulted the fence, landing in a crouch on the leaf litter on the other side. He ran through the barrier of trees and out onto the cool dewy grass.

Aya slammed hard into the blonde huntress, knocking her back before flipping away from her, growling and snarling through her fangs as she fought for space. His heart almost stopped when he saw the blood coating her right thigh, slick on her jeans, and the slash across the left sleeve of her dark jumper over her biceps. Both looked as if they had been done with a blade.

He readied his remaining one, wishing he'd had enough sense to grab the one he had dropped before rushing off to find Aya. He had been consumed by a need to reach her side again though, and that need still rolled through him, commanding him to protect her from the huntress that had brought both of them so much pain.

Moonlight bathed the park in sombre hues, stealing the colour from the world.

It brightened as his animal side rose to the fore, his vision sharpening together with his senses, until he could detect every twitch in the huntress's body, could almost see her moves before she made them.

The blonde female attacked, a frantic and wild thing as she lunged with the knife she tightly clutched in her left hand and fired bolts from the compact crossbow in her right at the same time.

Aya back-flipped and kicked right the moment she landed, hurling herself out of the path of one of the bolts. It exploded on impact, showering earth upwards, filling the air with its rich scent.

The huntress aimed the bow at her again as she recovered from the shockwave from the blast.

Harbin roared and hurled himself at the huntress, catching her attention and distracting her, buying Aya time to find her feet. He brought his right leg up hard, smashing it into the female's arm and sending the crossbow flying from her hand. A pained cry cut through the still night air and the huntress stumbled away from him, readying her blade at the same time as she brought her other arm to her chest.

He flipped his knife in his hand and circled around her, forcing her away from Aya and placing himself between the two females, shielding his mate.

Aya's agitation flowed through him, and he knew it was because he had shown up. She wanted the kill, craved vengeance too, but he couldn't let her have it. He needed it more.

He drew down a deep breath and prepared himself.

The huntress eyed him and then Aya, and then looked beyond them both, doubt surfacing in her green eyes.

"Twenty years," he growled and narrowed his gaze on her, drawing her focus back to him. "Twenty godsdamned years I hunted you… and now I have you. Now you die."

She surprised him by laughing. "No, now *you* die."

He doubted that.

She lunged at him and he strafed left to dodge her wild thrust and swung his fist at her. She ducked back but his blow glanced off her cheek, sending her stumbling to one side and fighting for balance. He pressed his advantage, lashing out with his black blade. The huntress brought hers up, managing to block his attack, and shoved forwards.

Hoping to throw him off balance too?

That attack might have worked on Aya, but it wouldn't work on him, and the huntress knew it. He was stronger than his mate and that was before he had spent two decades training as an assassin and honing his skills.

She didn't stand a chance against him now.

He dropped low as she lunged again, sweeping his leg around at the same time and taking her ankles out with the kick. She hit the ground hard on her back and grunted. He brought his blade down fast, aiming for her chest, and she rolled away from him. His knife struck the grass and he growled as she rolled back, her blade a silver flash through the darkness. It sliced across his left arm, and the strong scent of his blood joined that of Aya's and the huntress's.

He pulled his knife free from the dirt and swung at her, but she was already on her feet. Aya moved closer and he growled over his shoulder at her, sending her a warning to keep back and not intervene.

This was his fight.

The huntress swiftly dodged each attack he made, edging towards the far end of the park. Her gaze darted off in the direction he had come from, the wild edge to her green eyes growing with each glance. Her heart sounded hard in his ears as he advanced on her, stalking towards her, his blade held down at his side. She brandished hers, holding it in front of her, and he smiled as it shook in her grip.

She had realised that the witch wasn't coming to aid her.

She was alone.

His lips curled into a slow smile and he kicked off, his bare feet sinking into the soft ground as he lunged at her. She fumbled her block and cut across his right forearm, slicing deep into the muscle. He snarled as pain rolled through him, the fiery burn only driving him to fight harder, tugging at his primal instincts to defeat his prey and protect his female.

His fangs emerged, canines sharpening into four deadly points that he wanted to sink into her throat.

He slashed at her and she threw herself at him, hitting him hard in the chest and catching him off guard. He lost balance and fell with her, landing with her on top of him. She rammed her blade towards him and he brought his arm up and blocked her.

The silver knife plunged deep into his forearm and he howled in agony, blinded by the pain, his blade falling from his grip.

The huntress pulled her knife free of his flesh and he launched a hand out at her, catching her around the neck. He grimaced as he tightened his hold on her, choking the life out of her as she stared down at him through wide eyes. The second she overcame her shock, she lashed out at him again, slashing across his chest with her blade, a frantic feral thing as she tried to escape his hold. He growled and caught her arm, twisted it and tried to make her drop the knife so he could grab it and end her with it.

She used her free hand to take the blade from the one he grasped and lunged at him with it.

A bark left her lips and she recoiled backwards, her right shoulder jerking hard. A bolt protruded from it.

Harbin didn't hesitate.

He grabbed the short arrow, yanked it free of her flesh and plunged it deep into the centre of her chest. Her cry cut short, her eyes enormous as the tension fled her body and she dropped her head to look down at the crossbow bolt sticking out of her heart.

She raised a hand to touch it, a frown flickering on her brow, and slumped onto the grass beside him.

Harbin tipped his head back and looked at Aya where she stood just a few metres away, upside down in his vision, the crossbow still aimed at the huntress.

Damn, she was a wonderful mate.

He had never had a partner before, but he was glad that he had one now, because she had helped him find the closure he needed. They had found it together.

He pushed the huntress off him and sat up, looked down at her and waited for it to sink in that it was over. He had finished the twenty-year-long mission to avenge his kin.

Warmth spread through him.

He looked back over his shoulder at Aya, and the heat that had been spreading through him, the light that had been chasing back the shadows, turned icy and black.

She rested on her side on the wet grass, her face ashen and eyes closed, clothes stained with dark patches that glinted in the moonlight.

She was hurt worse than he had thought.

His heart pounded as he pushed to his feet and rushed to her. His knees hit the dirt hard beside her and he pulled her onto her back and into his arms.

"Aya," he whispered and jostled her, fear closing his throat and burning through him, destroying the sane part of him that said she would be alright and replacing it with poisonous words about her leaving him.

Dying.

He couldn't lose her now.

He looked her over and his heart plummeted as he saw all of the blood on her right thigh and her side too. Her injuries were deep and she had already lost a lot of blood. Her heart beat slowly, a timid thing that clawed at his sanity, feeding his fears.

Her eyelids fluttered open as he smoothed his palm across her dirty cheek. "Is it over?"

He nodded and cupped her cheek, his hand shaking against it. "It's done."

She smiled faintly.

"That's good." A frown danced on her brow and her smile faded. "You scared me."

Harbin tried to smile for her, but it wobbled on his lips as the whispered words about losing her grew louder and he couldn't combat them.

"I know. I had to pretend I was dead. You can shout at me if you want… tell me how cruel it was to do that to you… be mad at me, Aya." Anything to show him that there was still fight left in her, she was still strong enough to survive her wounds. His blood chilled as she sank deeper into his arms and he jostled her again to keep her awake and with him. "It's a trick Hartt taught me… nothing more than a trick… but… you're scaring me now, Aya."

A smile fluttered on her lips and she opened them, as if she wanted to say something. No words left her lips as she slumped in his arms.

Harbin growled and tried to rouse her again, but nothing he did worked.

"I can't lose you, Aya," he whispered and looked around the park, drawing deep breaths as he tried to clear his head so he could think about what he needed to do to save her.

Cavanaugh.

He had to get her to Underworld.

She would be safe there, able to sleep and heal in peace.

He couldn't move her until he had bound her wounds though.

The air off to his left shimmered and Hartt appeared with Fuery, both of them covered in blood that belonged to them.

"The bastard got away," Hartt growled and looked down at the dead huntress. "He disappeared. It must have been when she died. It broke his contract with her and he fled… I'm not sure we've seen the last of him though."

Hartt's violet eyes swung towards Harbin and widened when they landed on Aya.

"Is she alright?" He immediately crossed the narrowed strip of grass to Harbin and crouched beside her.

Harbin held her closer, the conviction he felt inside him pouring out in his words as he looked down at her. "She will be. I'll see to that. I won't let anything bad happen to her."

Because he would go insane if he lost her.

She was his light, his everything. The sole reason he was alive. Without her, he had no reason to live. Without her, his primal side would consume him and he wasn't sure he would come back from it this time. If the pain of losing her drove him into his snow leopard form, he wouldn't want to come back from it. He would lose himself in that wild oblivion, mourning his mate forever.

Bandages appeared in Hartt's hand and the elf held them out to him. "We must take care of her wounds."

Harbin nodded and pulled down a breath to steady himself and put a leash on his animal side. He hadn't lost her yet. He wouldn't lose her.

He set her down on the grass and focused on binding her wounds, stemming the flow of blood from the lacerations across her stomach and thigh while Hartt dealt with the cuts on her arm. His fingers slowly steadied as her heartbeat grew stronger, a comforting sound in his ears that he focused on as he took care of her.

"I'll take her to Cavanaugh," he said, his voice distant as he worked. "I'll leave her in his hands. She'll be safe there. If the witch wants vengeance, he'll be after us, not her. I'll stay away until we know we're in the clear."

Harbin's fingers paused on the bandage around her thigh. He wasn't sure he could leave her though. He wasn't sure he was strong enough to do it, not when she was hurt. He needed to be by her side, but satisfying that need by remaining with her would only place her in more danger and he had already put her through enough.

Hartt sat back on his heels and then gracefully rose onto his feet. "We shall split up then, but come home soon. You're safest at the guild. We can handle the witch if he shows up there."

Harbin nodded. "I'll return soon."

Hartt was right and the guild could handle the witch. He would be no match for the combined power of the assassins who called it home.

"I don't have the strength left to teleport you both to Underworld… and I'm not sure it would go down well if I did anyway." Hartt's violet eyes shimmered with something like remorse, and Harbin couldn't stop himself from wondering whether it was regret over not being able to help him or regret over the elf female who lived at the club with her jaguar mate. He turned his cheek to Harbin, looking off to his right, and held his hand out. "Fuery."

The darker elf male shuffled closer to his companion, his head bent and lips moving silently as he muttered things in their language.

Hartt eyed him warily, but with an edge of concern, and took hold of his arm. He bent his head to Harbin and silvery light traced over both elves, and then they were gone and he was alone with Aya.

Harbin stroked his fingers through her black hair and studied her pale face for a moment, his senses locked on her and monitoring her. She was stronger already, her body beginning to heal the wounds they had bound. He told himself that she would be fine now, but he couldn't quite bring himself to believe it.

Until she opened her eyes and smiled at him, he wouldn't stop feeling as if he was going to lose her.

Gods, when had she changed him so much?

He scooped her up into his arms, pushed onto his feet and started towards Underworld, cradling her carefully, not feeling the pain of his injuries as the ache in his heart eclipsed it.

Aya.

He had fallen so hard for her, so quickly that the drop had been a dizzying rush and only now that he had landed was he coming to terms with what had happened.

He was in love with her and he wasn't sure he could live without her now, not as he had intended to barely a few days ago, wanting to have a brief moment with her before pushing her away.

Now he wanted to pull her closer and never let her go.

The walk to Underworld was over before he knew it, his feet carrying him towards his brother on autopilot, his keen senses able to track him across the city.

The neon sign above the club was switched off and the heavy dark metal doors were closed, the streets around the huge brick building quiet except for the distant hum of cars on the main roads nearby.

He dragged his eyes away from the door, settling them on Aya, the weight on his chest growing heavier as he saw how pale she still was. This wasn't going to go well, and he was asking a lot from his brother when they had only just got back together, but this was the safest place for her right now.

He had to do what was best for her.

The journey to Hell and his home there would take too long, and traversing the portal between the two realms would drain her strength. She needed to rest and recover, and Cavanaugh and Eloise would make sure she did just that.

He sucked down another sharp breath, quelled his desire to turn away from the door and take Aya with him back to Hell, and knocked instead.

He stared down at her as he waited, losing himself in her, listening to her soft breathing and her steady heartbeat. She would be safe here with Cavanaugh and the others, away from him.

The door creaked open and he lifted his head, instantly shifting his focus to the sandy-haired bare-chested male on the other side.

"Leave," the jaguar shifter snapped, his golden eyes glowing dangerously, and then growled when Harbin shook his head. He jammed his hands into his black sweatpants and stared him down, radiating tension and fury that had Harbin's hackles rising.

Kyter was pissed and Harbin could understand why, because he would be upset too if someone made moves on his mate, but he wasn't going to let the shifter drive him away.

At least not until he had agreed to take Aya inside.

"I'll go... I don't want to cause trouble... but I need to see my brother." Harbin looked down at Aya and felt Kyter's gaze leave him, wanted to growl when he sensed that he was looking at Aya. "I need Cavanaugh to take care of her for me. She's hurt. I need her safe and I need to tell my brother what I've done."

Kyter snarled. "What did you do to her?"

Harbin met his gaze and growled at him, baring his fangs, his animal side pushing at his control when he realised the shifter thought he had been the one to hurt her.

"Nothing. She was injured in a battle. I can't take her with me to Hell... she won't make the journey and she won't be safe there. I need her safe."

Gods, he needed that, more than anything.

His arms shook beneath her slender weight as he looked back down at her, vision blurring as that need pulsed through him, combining with his fears to strip him of his strength.

"Is she your mate?" Kyter whispered softly, all anger gone from his voice.

Harbin sensed his brother nearby, felt the familiar pierce of his gaze, and nodded. "She is my fated female."

He lifted his head and looked past Kyter to Cavanaugh where he stood shrouded in shadow behind him, his loose grey loungewear and silver hair making him stand out in the darkness. He caught the concern mixed with warmth in his bright silver eyes, happiness that Harbin wasn't sure he deserved.

"You can stay," Kyter said, snatching his focus away from his brother and stoking the battle raging inside him, the war between leaving her and staying by her side. "Only until she's recovered, and if that elf shows up, I'll kill you both."

Harbin didn't doubt that, and he couldn't blame Kyter for putting the threat out there either.

Relief flitted across Cavanaugh's face and he moved closer. Harbin looked from his brother to Kyter, and then down at Aya.

Gods, he wanted to stay with her, but in doing so he feared he would bring danger to the doorstep of Underworld. His heart whispered to stay, but it also told him to stick with his plan and go.

He closed his eyes, lowered his head and held Aya closer to him. Her weight in his arms was also the weight of responsibility on his shoulders, something he couldn't ignore.

"I can't," he said and opened his eyes and studied Aya's pale face, aching as he thought about leaving her and knew the time was drawing closer. He vowed that he would come back for her, because they had a lot to talk about and he wasn't sure he could keep away from her for long. He wasn't sure he could live without seeing her face every second of every day. Forever. He pressed a soft kiss to her brow and then lifted his head and looked at the two males. "I won't place everyone here in danger."

Kyter and Cavanaugh looked concerned again.

"I've angered a witch. A very powerful one."

It didn't seem to be explanation enough for his brother, because he stepped forwards and frowned at him, that same look Harbin had seen a thousand times as a boy. He was in for an earful.

"You're staying," Cavanaugh said, deep voice rumbling through the tense silence. "If Aya is your mate, she needs you here. You need to be here."

"I need to be far from here," Harbin countered. "I brought her here so she would be safe. The huntress..."

Cavanaugh paled.

Harbin swallowed hard, and with a dry mouth and pounding heart said, "I've finally killed her... the last of the Archangel team who attacked the pride... but she employed a witch to deal with me. We lost him, and he's dangerous. Aya will only be safe from the witch if I leave her here."

Kyter huffed and folded his arms across his broad bare chest. "There are wards on the building, ones cast by a powerful white witch. They're strong enough to keep anyone out who I don't want entering my club. Now I know of the witch, I'll just decide not to allow any witches in and that will stop him."

"It's true," Cavanaugh said. "Nothing can penetrate the barrier around the building or sense who's inside it if Kyter doesn't want to let them in... so are you going to stay now?"

Harbin was tempted, because he couldn't bring himself to leave Aya's side when she was hurt.

"Listen to your heart, because it's what you seem best at." Cavanaugh moved closer still, coming to stand beside Kyter. "Your love for our family and kin drove you to go on a journey for revenge, and while that journey separated us for two decades, it has finally brought us back together too... and it has brought you to your mate. You need to listen to your heart again now, because I suspect I know what it's telling you to do."

Harbin sighed. It was telling him to stay with her now that he knew the building was protected and that everyone in it would be safe. He could lay low until the witch lost his scent and be with Aya, where he needed to be.

He hadn't won her yet.

If he left her now, he risked losing her.

He looked at his brother and saw in his pale silver eyes that he wanted him to stay for another reason too. He wanted to be a family again, and Harbin found himself wanting that too, even when he wasn't sure how to go about it or how to overcome everything that had happened. It felt as if the past stood between them like a crevasse he couldn't cross to reach the side he wanted to stand on—the side where his brother stood.

But if he did as Cavanaugh asked, maybe there was a chance he would find the right path to take to cross that ravine between them.

Maybe staying would do more than merely reunite him with his brother.

He looked down at Aya.

Maybe it would forge a new family for him, one made up of his brother and Eloise.

And his mate.

CHAPTER 23

Aya slowly became aware of the world around her, the dark veil lifting to bring sounds to her ears and scents to her nose, and sensation to her body. She was in a room, one unfamiliar to her. It wasn't Hell. The air held the familiar sooty smell of London. But she wasn't in her bed in her apartment.

She was warm, cocooned in softness that she didn't want to leave and that made it hard to care where she was, because it was so comfortable here. The soothing warmth wasn't the only reason she didn't want to move. Her body ached, sore in places, and as awareness of her surroundings finished dawning, awareness of what she had been through replaced it.

She recalled the fight between her and the huntress, how desperate she had been to keep the female in her sights so Harbin wouldn't lose her again and both of them could have the closure they needed. She remembered taking blows and dealing them, and remembered passing out after the battle had come to an end.

The moment the huntress's heart had given its final beat, Aya's strength had left her and she had collapsed.

She recalled how afraid Harbin had looked when he had held her, and that drove her to open her eyes, because he was in the unfamiliar room with her, silently prowling around it. His emotions were in turmoil, a turbulent tangled flow from him around her. He was worried about her.

She needed to show him that she was recovering.

The dull light in the room was bright as she lifted her eyelids, bouncing off the cream walls and stinging her eyes and making her flinch away from it.

Harbin instantly swung towards her, the dark shadows leaving his handsome face and striking eyes as he saw she was awake. The relief he felt coursed through her too, but concern quickly overwhelmed it in him. Aya ached with a need to alleviate his fears but she wasn't sure what to say, not when her heart was tearing her in two different directions.

It was over.

The huntress was dead and she wasn't sure what that meant. The part of her that had vowed to leave Harbin once that had happened warred with the part of her that wanted to stay.

"You had me worried there for a while," he whispered hoarsely, and the ache in her chest intensified.

She could finally see the affection in his eyes, love that the deepest part of her soul had wanted to see in them for a long time. All of his feelings were on show for her to see, none of them hidden behind a barrier, because he had let his guard down for her.

Aya wanted to curse him, and she wanted to kiss him at the same time.

The battle between her polar desires grew fiercer, cutting her deeper, right into her heart.

"How long was I out?" She looked around her at the room as Harbin twisted the knob on the lightswitch near the white door, dimming the ceiling lamp and giving her eyes some relief as they slowly adjusted to her using them again.

"It's only been a day." The way he said that made her feel it had felt longer than that short span of time to him. He crossed the room and sat on the edge of the bed, his back to her, and she looked him over. The black t-shirt stretched tight across his muscular back, tempting her eyes, but something else firmly held her attention. Bandages wrapped around his arms. How hurt was he? She wanted to ask, but he spoke again. "We're lying low at Underworld right now. I didn't manage to kill the witch."

He looked away from her and she sensed his shame, wanted to touch his jeans-clad thigh and comfort him. She cursed him for tugging on her heart strings instead and doubly cursed the guilt that welled inside her when she realised why the witch had escaped.

It was because she had run off after the huntress, and he had felt compelled to go after her, his primal instincts driving him to protect her.

"I'm sorry," she whispered.

Harbin just smiled, and it was so strange to see it. He was changing, becoming more like the male she had known in her youth.

Becoming more dangerous, because this male was even more alluring than the one he had been back then, and even more alluring than the one he had become. He was a perfect blend of boyish charm and deadly assassin, intoxicating her and luring her back under his spell.

"How do you feel?" He pressed his right hand into the mattress, twisting his body towards her, and ran a glance over her that had her body heating beneath the covers.

She cursed him again. She was meant to be resting, her body still recovering, but she couldn't stop the flood of desire that swept through her whenever he looked at her like that, as if he would die if he didn't touch her soon.

Gods, she might die too.

She stifled that thought and focused, reminding herself that she was meant to be leaving him.

Heck, just the thought of going through with it tore her to pieces inside, but she had to be strong.

"I'm feeling better. Stronger." She pushed the necessary words out. "I can leave soon."

His face darkened. "Leave?"

She averted her gaze to the pale blue covers, unable to look at him when she could feel hurt flowing through him and she wanted to take it away. She had to be strong. She had to be. He was changing, and that meant he might leave his dangerous life as an assassin behind and what then?

Would he want children?

The thought of building a life with him only for him to shatter it when he discovered she couldn't have children was too painful. She would rather cut her ties with him now.

"I thought we had something." He stood sharply and her gaze automatically leaped to his face.

It wasn't a question. It was a statement.

He towered over her, his fierce silver gaze locked on her, demanding she answer him.

Aya closed her eyes and lowered her face away from him, and thought about what he had said to her back in the assassin's guild in Hell.

She sighed. "I'm the one who isn't right for you. I can't give you what you deserve."

His confusion ran through her, a powerful force that made her want to look at him and explain everything, partly in hope that he would understand and would still want her as his mate.

She pushed her fears away, tamped down her weakness and found the strength to look him in the eye, even when it made her heart pound like crazy and her palms sweat. "I can't have children."

His soft smile threw her and he left her reeling when he spoke, a chuckle in his wicked deep voice. "That's because you're too young."

She was the confused one now. "Too young?"

Harbin sat beside her again, a sigh leaving him as his backside hit the mattress. His weight on it made her roll towards him, so her hip pressed against his back.

"You're only ninety-five." His smile held and she could only stare at him in stunned silence as she realised he knew exactly how old she was. She couldn't believe that he knew such a thing about her. "You obviously weren't listening in class the day that we learned that while males all mature at a century, females vary in age... if you can't have kids, it's because you haven't matured yet. Who the hell told you such bullshit in the first place?"

Aya wasn't sure what to say in response to that.

The smile on his face turned wicked and teasing. "Were you too busy staring at me that day?"

She frowned at him, but he didn't repent.

He only grinned. "You were daydreaming about kissing me, weren't you? Fuck, I was certainly daydreaming about kissing you."

Aya's cheeks burned before she could shut down the flush of heat that swept through her on hearing that. She had never realised that he had liked her that way before she had kissed him.

He sighed and his expression turned sombre, all of the light leaving it. "I wish you hadn't avoided me... I wish that things had been different."

All of the light that had been building in her faded too, replaced by a weight of guilt she had never felt on her shoulders before. The attack on the village was partially her fault. She had rejected him, and he had responded by seeking out other females, landing him in the hands of the huntress. She pushed away from her thoughts, unwilling to let them cloud her heart and mind. There was no way to change what had happened, no matter how much both of them wanted there to be.

"It's ancient history now," she said and he looked across at her, his silvery eyebrows furrowed into a look that made her want to touch his cheek and soothe his troubled soul. "It's over."

"Over," he echoed, and seemed even more troubled, as if he thought she was applying that word to them too.

Was she?

Did she really intend to leave him?

She wasn't sure, but she was certain of one thing. She intended to escape this heavy conversation until she could get her head on straight. She searched for an escape route and found one when raucous laughter came from below. She looked to Harbin for an explanation.

"Cavanaugh and Eloise are celebrating their mating with an official gathering," he said with a smile that warmed the cold parts of her heart, making her wish that smile was all for her.

"You should be there." Aya nudged his right shoulder with her hand, jerking him forwards.

He huffed and scowled at her, and then his face softened and he sighed as he looked at her. "I'd rather be here with you."

Her heart skipped a beat. Damn him. Had he always been this irresistible and charming? She knew the answer to that question in her heart, a heart that was touched by his desire to remain close to her and take care of her.

There was more to his reluctance to go down and join in the celebration than his need to be with her though.

He was nervous.

He couldn't hide that from her, no matter how much he was clearly trying to conceal it with soft smiles and fussing over her.

"Have you spoken to Cavanaugh?" she said.

The look he gave her, a little guilty and shy, such a contrast to the dangerous male she had come to know, told her that he had been in the room with her the past day, hiding from his brother.

She found that a little endearing, but at the same time she wanted to box his ears. This was his chance to heal things with his brother and she wouldn't let him waste it, because she knew he would regret it.

"We could go down together. I'm sure Cavanaugh would like to see you, and will be happy to see I'm well too."

Harbin shot down that suggestion with a dark scowl. "You're not strong enough yet."

Unlike him, she was aware that the connection between them made it impossible for her to fool him, so she didn't bother to deny it.

"Just a little while. It's important." She placed her hand on his knee and he looked down at it, his frown melting away and steely gaze softening. "We can come back when I feel tired, but right now I feel fine."

He frowned again, that single shift in expression telling her that he didn't believe her, but also that he wasn't going to argue with her about it.

He huffed and muttered something under his breath as he pushed onto his feet, trudged across the room and grabbed a stack of clothing off the wooden chest of drawers near the door. He carried them back to the bed and set them down next to her.

Aya gasped as he tugged the covers back, her hands racing to cover herself.

"No need to hide from me." He chuckled softly. "I did get you naked in the first place."

Heat bloomed on her cheeks and he groaned and turned away, muttering more things she couldn't quite hear.

Only this time she didn't need to hear the words to know what the problem was. She could sense his desire skyrocketing, the hunger that swept through him rushing through her too, awakening her need of him.

Aya wrestled it back under control and dressed as quickly as she could. Each time one of her bandaged wounds ached and she hissed through her teeth in response, Harbin looked back at her, concern in his eyes before his cheeks darkened and he swiftly looked away again.

She hadn't realised he could be such a gentleman.

It was another thing to add to the ones she was learning about him, and it made her want to tease him by intentionally drawing his gaze to her just so she could see that boyish blush on his cheeks.

"You done yet?" he growled, disgruntled and snappy, and she stifled her giggle.

She didn't think she would ever grow tired of teasing him.

Her smile faltered.

It hit her hard that she wanted to stay with him, that leaving him really wasn't an option and had never been, not even when she had thought she couldn't give him children.

She closed the button on her pale blue jeans and smoothed the burgundy flowing top over them, her fingers shaking as she looked at Harbin's back and felt as if her future happiness rested on those wide shoulders of his. He was everything she wanted. Everything she needed. She just wasn't sure how to tell him.

"Done." Her voice was a bare whisper, but he heard her and turned around.

The hunger that flooded his eyes, dilating his pupils and brightening his silver irises, made her feel as if she was wearing something sexy and revealing rather than the slightly too tight blue jeans and a little too loose top.

He stared at her for so long that her nerves got the better of her and she looked away from him.

His soft sigh, and his hand appearing in view, drew her gaze back to him. He flexed his fingers, a silent command for her to take his hand, and she swallowed hard, feeling like an idiot as she stared at it. She had slept with him, had been more than a little wicked, but the thought of taking his hand made her nervous.

Made everything seem so much more real.

Because it made her feel that he had feelings for her.

That he might be in love with her too.

She slipped her hand into his, and it was warm, strong as he closed his fingers around hers and held them gently, as if he was afraid of hurting her.

She stared at their joined hands as they left the room and walked down the corridor, her head spinning as she tried to find the words she needed to say to him, the ones that would convey how she felt about him and that she wasn't going to leave him after all.

She was going to stay.

They turned a corner on the metal staircase and she felt eyes on her.

Aya looked at the gathering in front of her, stunned by the number of people crammed into the white-walled space, but moved to tears by the decorations.

A shiver ran through her, unleashing her emotions as she took in the room. Candles glowed, dotted in groups around the space, their golden light warming the white walls that could have easily been the pale perfection of snow. Across the room, swags of colourful prayer flags hung from twisted ropes, adorned with gold scripts and patterns that she hadn't seen in what felt like forever.

It transported her back to the pride village, to a time when she'd had a family and a place where she belonged, and celebrations such as this had been the highlight of her peaceful life.

Harbin's hand tightened around hers, squeezing softly, and she looked up at him. His tender smile stole her breath and she smiled shakily back at him when he brushed a tear from her cheek with the pad of his thumb.

"Something in your eye," he whispered and she nodded, glad he wasn't going to tease her over her reaction to seeing the traditional decorations.

Because it had moved him too.

She could feel it in him as he looked down at her, their joined hands strengthening the connection between them, making it easier for her to sense his emotions and pull them apart to identify each one.

Nerves still ran through him, and they only increased as his brother approached, cutting through the crowd in their direction, handsome in his colourful embroidered tunic.

Cavanaugh beamed at her. "Are you better?"

Harbin huffed. "Of course she isn't better."

His brother's smile dropped and he frowned. "Then what is she doing out of bed?"

Aya stepped forwards, between the two brothers, not wanting them to get into an argument because of her. "It's my fault. I wanted to see the celebration and congratulate you."

Harbin and Cavanaugh huffed at the same time, both wearing the same look on their faces, one that screamed how unimpressed they were. She released Harbin's hand and pressed both of hers to her hips, staring them down. They might have grown up in a world away from this one, a place where females knew to bow to the orders of the males, but they weren't in that world any longer.

In this world, she was equal to them and able to make up her own mind about things.

A soft giggle sounded from behind Cavanaugh and Eloise stepped out, a sight for sore eyes that had Aya welling up again. She looked exactly as Aya remembered her, with her wavy chestnut hair spilling around her shoulders and her golden eyes bright with amusement, and was stunning in her tighter-than-traditional embroidered dress that bore depictions of mountains and snow leopards, and the wild animals of their homeland.

"Ignore them. Boys will be boys." Eloise held her hand out to her. "We should get a drink."

Harbin snagged Aya's arm, holding her back. "I'll go with her."

The way he eyed all of the males in the room made it clear that he wasn't just doing it to support her if she needed his assistance. He viewed the unmated males as a threat to her, his primal instincts telling him that the males would attempt to steal her from him.

She took the steps down to the packed floor, and hadn't made it another inch before Harbin had his arm slung around her, tucking her close to his front. He growled at several males as they slowly crossed the room to the buffet table against the far wall, and played havoc with her at the same time. The feel of his powerful body pressing against her back, shifting deliciously with each step, stirred naughty thoughts, making her feel a little lightheaded.

She breathed a sigh of relief when they reached the other side and he released her, seized her arms and glared at her.

"Wait right here," he muttered, his tone dark and dangerous, warning her not to move an inch.

She caught Eloise's smile as he stalked away from them and couldn't stop her own from coming out.

"They can be a little overbearing," Eloise said, her soft voice light and teasing. "It's so good to see you again. Harbin told us what had happened to you... gods... I'm so sorry, Aya."

Aya shrugged it off, not wanting to think about the past. "It's over now."

Her gaze tracked Harbin as he prowled the buffet table, her smile widening as he kept piling things onto the already full plate. He lingered longest near the sweet things, picking lots of treats that looked delicious. He had come out with her exact age and now he was choosing her favourite foods. Just how well did he know her?

As well as she knew him?

Maybe they really had been made for each other.

He worked his way back towards her, his face a picture of determination, as if he had been issued a mission and refused to fail. He always had been headstrong. She only hoped he would be like it about their bond, telling her straight that he wanted it to happen and not letting her lose her nerve.

Eloise said something and she was so busy smiling at Harbin, thinking about the future they might have together, that she missed it and had to drag her eyes away from him to blankly look at her.

"Sorry?" she said.

The brunette female smiled. "Maybe this is a joint celebration."

Aya frowned, still sure she had missed something. Eloise pointed to her neck.

She touched the back of it and Harbin went pale, the plate of food falling from his hand to smash at his feet, scattering its contents across the floor and drawing everyone's attention to him.

Her eyes widened and her ears rang as silence descended, all thought and feeling fleeing her as she fingered the scabs.

Maybe there had been another reason he hadn't wanted her to leave the room.

The scab marks on the back on her neck were thick, and her fingers trembled as she found four of them. Her mouth turned dry and shivers ran through her, and her eyes sought Harbin's.

The look in them confirmed he was already aware of it.

The bite was deeper than she had thought.

Not a mere scratch at all.

His eyes were as wide as hers and she could feel he was waiting for her to say something. She couldn't find the words, not when her mind was reeling, her heart hammering against her chest as the reality of what she was feeling on her neck slowly crashed over her.

They were already mated.

Harbin walked straight through the fallen food, the scattered pieces of the china plate shattering further under his boots, and didn't stop until he was right in front of her, his heat curling around her and his scent invading her senses.

His eyes darted between hers as she tipped her head back to look up at him.

"I am sorry." Those three words weren't the ones she had needed to hear, the ones she wanted him to say to her as the world came tumbling down around her. It only grew worse when he kept going, rambling on, words she failed to take in until she sensed the growing distress in him and heard him say, "There might be a way to undo it."

That hurled her back into the room, threw her fears and her hurt out of the window as it narrowed her focus down to him and the tremendous pain she could sense in him.

Aya pressed her finger to his lips to silence him, not wanting him to hurt himself further when he was already hurting enough.

"Why would I want to undo it?" she whispered, her eyes locked on his, her feelings steady and constant, there for him to sense if he went looking.

"I'm really not good enough for you. I'm not what you need," he croaked and her finger trembled against his lips, her heart going out to him as he stood before her, stripped of his strength, left bare and vulnerable, waiting for her to hurt him. She didn't want to harm him, or break his heart, or whatever he thought she was going to do. She wanted to hold him close and never let him go.

She knew that he viewed his profession and his past as a barrier between them, but to her it was nothing. The moment she had fallen in love with him, she had accepted everything about him—including his life as an assassin and that his main pride was now a guild in Hell.

"No," she said.

His face went slack and pain rolled through him, shining in his striking eyes.

Aya shifted her hand to his cheek, cupping it as she stared deep into his eyes, and whispered to him, putting every drop of her love into her words so he would hear it.

"You're what I want."

She moved closer, pressing her front against his, and cupped his other cheek, holding his face as he exhaled hard. She tiptoed and brought his head down to her at the same time, and breathed against his lips.

"You're what I've always wanted."

He growled and wrapped his arms around her, gathering her close as he kissed her, a frantic outpouring of love that spoke to her soul and told her the words that he had failed to find too, the ones that seemed so elusive and frightening.

His strong arms crushed her against him, and she knew he would never let her go.

They would never part again.

She jerked when Cavanaugh slapped Harbin on the back, and laughed as everyone closed in, congratulating them. She couldn't take her eyes off Harbin as he smiled, his eyes bright with it, shining with the happiness she could feel in him.

Happiness she had given to him.

They had walked dark paths, had survived terrible times, but fate had made those paths cross again and now they would be together forever.

They had a pride and a family again.

They had each other.

Harbin pulled her back into his arms and kissed her so sweetly that she melted into him, lost in his kiss and his love for her.

She struggled for the words, filled with a need to tell him, even though she was sure he would feel it in her kiss too. He pressed his cheek to hers, his breath warm on her neck, teasing her and making her shiver, and she opened her mouth, the words on the tip of her tongue.

He stole her voice from her as he whispered in the old language of their species, telling her in the most beautiful and traditional way of their kind.

"I love you, Aya."

Tears stung her eyes but she smiled as he kissed her again, her heart filled to bursting as she nestled close to him. She pressed her hands to his chest, broke the kiss and whispered against his lips.

"I love you too, Harbin."

He growled and kissed her again, his love surrounding her and flowing through her, mingling with hers. The love that they shared as fated mates, bonded forever.

A love that would always grow stronger.

A love that was eternal.

The End

ABOUT THE AUTHOR

Felicity Heaton is a New York Times and USA Today best-selling author who writes passionate paranormal romance books. In her books she creates detailed worlds, twisting plots, mind-blowing action, intense emotion and heart-stopping romances with leading men that vary from dark deadly vampires to sexy shape-shifters and wicked werewolves, to sinful angels and hot demons!

If you're a fan of paranormal romance authors Lara Adrian, J R Ward, Sherrilyn Kenyon, Kresley Cole, Gena Showalter, Larissa Ione and Christine Feehan then you will enjoy her books too.

If you love your angels a little dark and wicked, her best-selling Her Angel romance series is for you. If you like strong, powerful, and dark vampires then try the Vampires Realm romance series or any of her stand alone vampire romance books. If you're looking for vampire romances that are sinful, passionate and erotic then try her London Vampires romance series. Or if you like hot-blooded alpha heroes who will let nothing stand in the way of them claiming their destined woman then try her Eternal Mates series. It's packed with sexy heroes in a world populated by elves, vampires, fae, demons, shifters, and more. If sexy Greek gods with incredible powers battling to save our world and their home in the Underworld are more your thing, then be sure to step into the world of Guardians of Hades.

If you have enjoyed this story, please take a moment to contact the author at **author@felicityheaton.com** or to post a review of the book online

Connect with Felicity:
Website – http://www.felicityheaton.com
Blog – http://www.felicityheaton.com/blog/
Twitter – http://twitter.com/felicityheaton
Facebook – http://www.facebook.com/felicityheaton
Goodreads – http://www.goodreads.com/felicityheaton
Mailing List – http://www.felicityheaton.com/newsletter.php

FIND OUT MORE ABOUT HER BOOKS AT:
http://www.felicityheaton.com

Printed in Great Britain
by Amazon